THE ODYSSEY OF A TIME TRAVELER IN FIRST CENTURY PALESTINE

FIFTH GOSPEL:

WILLIAM ROSKEY

iUniverse, Inc.
Bloomington

Fifth Gospel
The Odyssey of a Time Traveler in First-Century Palestine
Copyright © 1983, 2011 by William Roskey

The 20th century characters in this novel are fictitious. Any resemblance to actual
persons living or dead is purely coincidental. The names (with the exception of
historical figures, e.g., President Eisenhower and Albert Einstein) are also inven-
tions of the author. With the exception of historical figures (e.g., Jesus Christ, his
disciples, and others mentioned in the Bible), the 1st century characters are also
fictitious.

iUniverse books may be ordered through booksellers or by contacting:

iUniverse
1663 Liberty Drive
Bloomington, IN 47403
www.iuniverse.com
1-800-Authors (1-800-288-4677)

ISBN: 978-1-4620-2857-3 (sc)
ISBN: 978-1-4620-2859-7 (e)
ISBN: 978-1-4620-2858-0 (dj)

Library of Congress Control Number: 2011910680

Printed in the United States of America

iUniverse rev. date: 7/19/2011

1

The whole thing had a strange dreamlike quality about it from the outset. I'd just landed at Nellis Air Force Base in Nevada after putting my F-100 Super Sabre through its paces in mock dog fights with Grant, Riley, and Janeczek. Darting in and out of the massive canyons of altocumulus clouds, each of us had been piloting what at that time was undisputedly the hottest operational fighter plane in the world. Powered by its mighty Pratt & Whitney J57-P-21 afterburning turbojet, it could clip along at 822 mph at 35,000 feet. Its range was 575 miles, and its service ceiling was over 50,000 feet. The Super Sabre was the first operational fighter to exceed the speed of sound in level flight, and it had the twin distinctions of holding the last subsonic world speed record and the first supersonic world speed record. The normal armament was four 20-mm cannon, and there were six underwing pylons for air-to-surface missiles, bombs, or rockets. But today we had been loaded with nothing more lethal than cameras and film; we'd be viewing the processed films the following afternoon to critique tactics, reaction times, capabilities of the aircraft, and so on. The losers would buy drinks at the Officers Club.

It was 1958, and none of us needed to be reminded that only five years before, too many of our buddies who lost dog fights over

MIG Alley were buried in Korea, or, in some cases, splattered all over it. We were determined not to be caught short again. Lose to a camera today, correct your mistakes, and polish your style so you won't die in a real dog fight tomorrow. It was good common sense and great fun too. I had been a big winner that afternoon, but, as I cut my engine and slid the canopy back, I felt an eerie prickling sensation on the back of my neck. Staring through the shimmering heat waves rising off the baking runway, I saw the blurred images of the ground crew. But there was another figure as well, a civilian in a black woolen suit. Radiating an aura of power and mystery, he stood out among the young, fatigue-clad mechanics. His eyes locked on mine instantly and never left me as I clambered out of the plane, down the side, and onto the ground.

The closer I got to him, the more uneasy I became. He was a big man, not so much tall as he was broad. His gray eyes were intent; he was sizing me up, and those eyes had sized up many men before.

"Captain O'Brien," he said without preamble and without extending his hand, "I'm here to speak with you about your application to become a test pilot. Come with me please." With that crisp announcement, he abruptly wheeled about and headed for the Operations Building. I fell in beside him, matching his brisk pace step for step.

"Where are we going?"

"Debriefing Room B."

He hadn't returned my friendly smile, and I was beginning to get irritated. The air temperature at ground level was nudging 94 degrees, and the desert heat was already starting to hit me. I gave up the idea of having any kind of discussion with my anonymous and taciturn friend; instead, I just concentrated on getting into the air-conditioned building as quickly as possible and wrapping my hand around a bottle of ice-cold Coke. It was then that I realized that, with that black woolen suit on, my friend must have been feeling the same way. A woolen suit? He must have just flown in from the East. It was late November and undoubtedly pretty brisk back there. Could he have come all the way from the Pentagon? The thundering roar of five F-100s revving up just 75 yards away quickened our pace even more.

The debriefing rooms were absolutely soundproof. Rooms A and C were large, always unlocked, and each was furnished with some thirty-odd one-armed school desks, a screen and projection equipment, huge blackboards, a lectern, and coffee and Coke machines. Debriefing Room B sat between them. Its door was always locked and neither I nor anyone I knew had ever been in it. My poker-faced companion pulled a key from his pocket and opened the door. When he flipped on the light switch, I saw that the room was obviously intended for briefing or debriefing a single pilot. It measured about nine by twelve feet, its only furnishings being a gray metal rectangular table, four gray metal chairs, and a water cooler. There were no wall maps, windows, screens, or blackboards. On the table lay a tape recorder and a microphone, a black phone, and a red phone. A paper shredder was next to the table. The lighting was soft and subdued. The room was all business. As if the atmosphere were not already sufficiently discomforting, my escort locked the door behind us, walked over to the table, and sat down without a word or a glance at me.

Things had gone far enough, I thought. There's a world of difference between an interview and an interrogation, and I decided it was time someone taught this guy the difference before things went any further. I followed him to the table in the center of the room, dumped my crash helmet on it in front of him, then casually ambled over to the water cooler. I drank two cups of water, leisurely unzipped my pressure suit at the wrists, ankles, and neck. Then I drew a third cup of water. Still no response. I draped my arm over the top of the five-gallon jug and tried hard to look relaxed. I don't readily cooperate with people who try to intimidate me. I know that stress interviews probably have a legitimate place in personnel selection for certain types of jobs, but I don't have to put up with it. About a minute ticked by before the man sighed and spoke.

"Let's neither of us play games, Captain O'Brien. Please sit down."

"I didn't catch your name."

"Jones."

I stalked over to the table, picked up my helmet, and headed for the door. "I knew it. The word is out that you CIA clowns are looking for another crop of U-2 pilots. Well, wrong number. One of these days, and it's only a matter of time, one of those things is going to be shot down. Mrs. O'Brien didn't raise any fools. See you around 'Jones.'"

"O'Brien, I'm not from the CIA and wouldn't know a U-2 from a Piper Cub. What I do know is this: you'd be a fool to walk out of this room before hearing me out. I've flown more than 2,000 miles just to talk to you, and if I were in your shoes, that fact alone would tend to make me a wee bit curious."

"Come on, *Jones?*"

In response, he pulled out a black leather case and flipped it open. It revealed the badge and I.D. of Clarence David Jones, "a duly appointed Special Agent of the United States Secret Service."

"I think I'll sit down for a bit."

"Thanks, Captain."

Still determined not to give him any psychological advantage by sitting directly opposite him in the classic interrogation pose, I pulled out a chair at the end of the table and sat at his right hand. Jones responded with a wry little smile and nodded as if he had expected me to do that all along. I found out later that he had. I found out over the course of the next several days that Clarence David Jones was no ordinary cop, that he had investigated my entire life with such minute attention to detail that he very literally knew more about me than I did, and most importantly, I found that had I left the room at that point, I would have thrown away an opportunity that millions would have gladly died for.

"All right, Captain. You're cleared for Top Secret already; that, fortunately, saves us some time. But, in addition, I need your signature on this." He withdrew a form from his inside coat pocket, unfolded it, and handed it to me. I scanned it quickly. It was the standard briefing security form, stating that I, the undersigned, understood that if I ever disclosed any of the information about to be imparted to me to any unauthorized person or persons, I would be liable to prosecution under Title XVIII, United States Code, and could be sentenced for up to twenty years in a federal penitentiary. I had signed dozens of them in my six years in the Air Force. Without hesitation, I took a ballpoint pen from the zippered sleeve pocket on my flight suit, signed and dated the form, and handed it back to Jones.

"O.K., what's going on here?"

"I'm head of the White House detail of the Secret Service, but my duties very often include jobs that no one would ever associate with the Secret Service. There are various reasons for that, none of which we need go into. I report directly to the President, and *only* to the President. A certain—"

"You're looking for a new pilot or copilot for Air Force One! Now that's more like it. I—"

"Captain, if you'll just let me do the talking, we'll both arrive at our destination a little faster. As I was saying, a certain very important and very sensitive special project is underway, and, aside from being responsible for project security, I'm doing the recruiting for a key position. What we need is a young man in excellent physical condition, fast reflexes, and proven physical courage—not unlike a fighter pilot with recent wartime experience. You're credited with seven confirmed kills in Korea, all seven MIG-15s. That impresses me, as does your bailout 52 miles behind enemy lines and your subsequent actions: you freed a truckload of American and South Korean POWs and led them back to our lines, going smack dab through the middle of a Chinese division. You were resourceful and inventive. Your war record obviously impressed others as well. In addition to your Purple Hearts, you walked away with the Distinguished Flying Cross and the Silver Star. The Army awarded you an honorary Combat Infantryman's Badge in recognition of all the damage you and your raggedy bunch of POWs did to North Korea's and China's finest on your way back to friendly lines.

"You have a high linguistic aptitude and that is critical. You scored high in the desert survival training course you took last year. So much so that you were asked to stay on as an instructor. You are the only man who ever *gained* weight during the week-long practical field exercise. That says something about you. Your psychological profile indicates that you give your optimum performances under conditions of extreme adversity. You're essentially a loner. Another plus." Jones was ticking the points off on his fingers as he spoke.

"We also would like a man who has a good foundation in the practical or applied sciences, but who doesn't possess the tunnel vision that the professional scientist or technician so often falls prey to. We want a man who has a larger view. One who can look beyond the immediate to see the big picture and be able to recognize the not so obvious consequences of his actions ... or inactions. Say for example, like a serious student of world history.

"I'm truly sorry that I can't tell you much more than that,

Captain. I can only tell you more when and if you pass the interview. The interview, should you decide you want to try out for the job, will be like no other interview you've ever had. It will be just you and me, in this room, for the next three to four days. I'll ask you so many questions and I'll ask them so fast, your head will be in a constant state of spin. Many of the questions will seem strange to you, even bizarre. You'll probably feel that some of the questions I ask are none of my business. At anytime during the interview, you can walk out of here, and that's the end of it. There will be no record made of our talks, written, taped, or otherwise. Whether you go or stay, you must, of course, never discuss this interview with anyone. Your commanding officer has already been told that you'll be assisting me in the conduct of a highly classified investigation for the next several days. You've been temporarily relieved of all duties until further notice. You can tell your buddies at the BOQ the same thing. You guys are all used to keeping your mouths shut. I don't foresee any problem there. No one around here is going to try to pump you about a highly classified Secret Service investigation.

"Well, are you in?"

"It's not the only game in town, but it's by far the most interesting one I've seen in quite awhile. I'm in."

"O.K., then."

Jones stood up, took off his suit jacket, and folded it carefully over one of the empty chairs. Next he took off his tie and unbuttoned his collar. After he drank a couple of cups of water from the cooler, he returned to the table and sat down again. He looked alert and ready to go the distance.

"I'm going to start off with the dirtiest trick in the interviewer's bag: tell me about yourself."

"Any particular areas you're interested in?"

"Everything."

"O.K."

I settled back in my chair collecting my thoughts and concentrating on relaxing my breathing and the tension in my major muscle groups. If he was ready to go the distance, so was I. "I am Aloysius Lightfoot O'Brien, Captain, United States Air Force, serial number 15731429. Date and place of birth: December 18, 1930, Globe, Arizona. Blood type O. No religious preference. I graduated from the University of Arizona in June 1952, at which time I entered into active duty with the Air Force. My major in college was history, my minor, chemistry. I am not now, nor have I ever been married. I—"

Jones had held up his hand. "O'Brien, I asked you to tell me about yourself. The kind of stuff you're coming out with is all either stamped on your dog tags, written in your personnel folder, or both. I already know everything about you that's on paper, and a lot not on paper. I want you to tell me what you think about and dream about. I want your opinions, your likes, your dislikes, your fears. I want you to tell me what you're proud of, what you're ashamed of, how you think about certain books you've read, speeches you've heard, and places you've been. I want to know who you really are and who you want to be. I want to know where you want to be and what you want to be doing five years from today, ten years from today, and thirty years from today. The last thing in the world I need is facts; I've already have more than enough of them. I know what grades you got in each of your school courses, your Air Force test scores . . . I even know who you took to your high school junior prom."

He was laying it on a bit too thick now, I thought. "Who?" I laughed.

"Nancy Josephs."

I stopped laughing. I took a deep breath and exhaled slowly. Whatever this was all about, I was in over my head; I was playing with the big boys. Whatever this was, it was big.

Jones smiled sympathetically. "Look, perhaps it would help if I started out by just asking you specific questions. After a little bit, you'll begin to see what I'm after, and from there it will just evolve into a long conversation."

"Thanks, that would help a lot."

"All right. Your father was killed in a barroom brawl in Globe when you were ten years old. How did you feel about it?"

" Bad," I shrugged, puzzled. "I liked my dad."

"Didn't you feel any anger, resentment, hatred?"

"Why should I have?"

"What started the brawl were certain insulting and obscene remarks about your father being a 'squaw man' and some vulgar remarks about his 'squaw.' Your mother was a full-flooded Chiricahua Apache. He and you and your mother had it tough in Globe. You and your mother especially were the objects of ridicule and bigotry. You were a 'half-breed,' and your mother, well, they called your mother a lot of things. Kids especially can be merciless to anyone who's different. Then your father is killed." Jones had let his voice trail off. I picked up on the cue.

"The fight. Well, my father was an Irishman, and it was Saturday night in a mining town. If the fight hadn't been about my mother, it would have been about something else. It was hardly the only fight Dad had ever been in. It was an accident—the killing that is. He was beaned by a beer bottle, and it just happened to hit at exactly the wrong spot on his skull with just a little too much enthusiasm on the part of the miner swinging it. That's the way my mother looked at it and told me to look at it.

"We moved back onto the San Carlos Reservation soon afterward. Her family was all there, and they took us in. We had a good, happy life on the reservation. I made a lot of friends, and I learned a lot about my heritage from the elders of the tribe. I learned to track, to hunt, and to fight. I even learned to speak Athabascan, the language of the Apaches and the Navajos. You know, the first Apaches arrived in the American Southwest in the 11th century . . . Mr. Jones, can't you even give me a small hint about what kind of aircraft you want me to pilot?"

"First," Jones said, producing a beaten corncob pipe, "let's get a little less formal. Please call me Clarence. I understand your friends don't call you Al; you prefer Lightfoot."

I nodded.

"Second," Jones continued, as he began to pack his pipe bowl slowly with Cherry Blend, "I never said you were going to pilot any type of aircraft." When he saw the look of consternation on my face, he went on, "I don't need to, nor do I want to tell you anymore than that right now. It would be in extremely bad form from a security standpoint; you may not even be picked. Suffice it to say that your status in this project would not be that of a pilot. You'd be more of a . . . passenger."

Now I had it! Now I knew what all this was about! They wanted a loner, someone with a sense of history, but with a scientific bent as well, good physical shape, good reflexes, a good aerial combat record indicating physical courage, and the ability to make quick decisions in a split second. *But* this someone would function more as a passenger than as a pilot. That's what gave it away. The space program. It could be nothing else. The high security classification, the incredible background investigation, the direct involvement of the President himself—it could be nothing else. Ripples of rumors had been running throughout the Air Force for the last year and a half or so. The first step, everyone had pretty much agreed, would be a suborbital downrange flight for equipment checks, followed by putting a man, not a pilot, but an *astronaut*, into orbit around the earth. Heady stuff that, and *I* may, I thought with exhilaration, just be that man. The Charles Lindbergh of the Space Age. The Lone Eagle. From that moment on, Jones couldn't have dragged me from that room with a fleet of bulldozers.

3

When Clarence David Jones had told me that the interview would be unlike any I'd ever had before, he had been understating the case. The next four days and nights merged into a single blur of questions, questions, and more questions. Looking back on it now, I can understand the line of questioning, and the reasons for each one. Looking back, I can see what he'd been looking for. But, at the time, the questions seemed strange, haphazard, whimsical, and unstructured. Did I think that the American Revolutionary War could have been averted? How? If it had been, what would have been the long range impact on world history? Did I read any science fiction? Who were my favorite authors? What were my religious beliefs? Did the "No Preference" entry in my personnel folder mean that I was an agnostic, an atheist, or that I felt that God listened to all, so it really didn't matter which denomination one was? Had I thought about religion lately? How could some of the more negative aspects of the Industrial Revolution been ameliorated? Was there a woman in my life at the present time? How did I feel about her? What did the word "love" mean to me? Did I ever intend to have any children? Why? Why did I spend so much time alone in the desert? Was society becoming too impersonal? What about my tastes in art?

Well, I answered all of his questions in detail, even though they made no sense to me at the time, and even though I felt, as he had in fact predicted, that some were about things that were none of his business. If this was an opportunity to be the first man in space, *I* wasn't going to pass it up. Jones and I lived on black coffee, sandwiches, and six hours of sleep per night for those four days, but I showed it and Clarence didn't. Every couple of hours he'd amble down the hall to the latrine, splash a few handfuls of cold water on his face, and he'd be as good as new. I got the distinct impression that he was used to living like this, and I was right. I also got to know a bit about him. Every now and then, when my eyes started to look like roadmaps and my voice began to get hoarse, he'd give me a break by answering some of my questions about him. Clarence was a fascinating guy. He was 46 years old and had been an associate professor of history until the war had come along. He wound up on Ike's staff just prior to D-Day and had been with him ever since. He spoke of the "Old Man" with frank and open admiration. Ike stood in awe of few things, but as I later learned, one of those things was Clarence's phenomenal photographic memory. (From the beginning I had been wondering how he'd been able to effortlessly summon up specific names, dates, and places from my past without the aid of any notes.) Ike had entrusted Jones with many sensitive extracurricular activities, all of which, Clarence was quick to claim, were "just inconsequential little errands," but which, nonetheless, had sent him into the offices and parlors of such notables as Churchill, Roosevelt, Stalin, and De Gaulle. I got to like him; he was an honest and friendly, straightforward man with a dry sense of humor not unlike Mark Twain's. Once he let you get to know him, that first impression of dour, official frostiness fled. He had a wife named Marge, whom he idolized, and four kids, about whom he felt even more strongly. He also had two Norwegian Elkhounds, a wealth of anecdotes set in and around his hometown near Chattanooga, and, like me, a fascination with the Civil War. There were some times of lighthearted camaraderie, but some dredged-up pain as well. He came, as I knew he inevitably must, to the Accident.

"On December 16, 1952—"

"Yes," I interrupted, wanting to get it over with as quickly as possible, "that's when my mother and my fiancée were killed. My birthday, my 22nd birthday, was on December 18th, and I was due to graduate from flight school on the 22nd. They decided to drive up for a double celebration. I had two weeks of leave coming up after graduation, so we were all going to drive back together and spend the holidays at San Carlos. My mother and Amanda were very, very proud of me, and they wanted to show me off, they said." I grew silent for a moment; the feelings all began to rush back to me. Clarence drew me out of it.

"Amanda Clearwater, she was also a full-blooded Chiricahua Apache, wasn't she?"

I nodded, "Yes. She was very beautiful, very gentle, and she was twenty years old. I loved her. We were to be married in March. I . . . still remember how she looked, *exactly* how she looked at her 'coming out'"

"'Coming out?'"

"Yes, anthropologists call it a puberty rite. Strictly speaking, I suppose it is. Yet to us, it's much more. It's our most important ceremony. It lasts four whole days and nights. The Mountain Spirit Dancers perform the Sunrise Dance and other ancient sacred dances that mark the passage of the maidens from girlhood into womanhood . . . she wore a white deerskin dress . . ." I was beginning to drift again, but quickly brought myself out of it this time. There was a lot at stake here. "Anyway, Amanda and my mother started out on the morning of December 16th in Amanda's car, a '41 Ford. They got as far as Safford before a drunk crossing the center line punched their tickets for them. My mother was killed instantly, but Amanda was pinned in the wreckage and burned to death. The drunk turned out to be a member of the state legislature, so all charges were dropped against him except the one for reckless

13

driving. He had his driver's license suspended for two weeks. No big thing; it was just a couple of Indians killed.

"We had the funeral on the reservation. Both of our families were very traditional, so the funeral was too. All of my mother's and Amanda's belongings were burned. The Apaches have done this for centuries, maybe even longer. It's so no one can ever profit from the death of another. I had taken off my uniform, and clad in nothing more than a breechclout, was given the honor of leading the Death Chant: 'O Ha Le . . . Only the mountains live forever . . . O Ha Le . . . Only the rocks live forever . . . O Ha Le . . . Our shadow bodies come and go . . . O Ha Le . . . But we are together, we have kept the faith . . . O Ha Le . . . O Ha Le.' I spent my leave at San Carlos, but most of it alone in the desert. The first thing I did when I reported back on duty was to volunteer for combat duty in Korea. I was . . . consumed by a white-hot rage, a towering black infernal rage that made me want to lash out, to kill and destroy. My father, my mother, the girl I was to marry . . . all taken from me, not through malice. Malice I can understand. But taken from me through some kind of Cosmic Caprice. Well, you know the rest; I became very good at killing people and destroying things. I even got medals for doing it."

"You christened your F-86, 'The Apache Avenger.' I thought the motto you had painted on the nose interesting too. 'Death Is Our Business and Business is good.' Can't get much more unequivocal than that, although as words to live by, it leaves a lot be desired."

That led into a discussion of Korea, and in some ways, was almost as painful. At any rate, late into the fourth night of the interview, Clarence finally arrived at a decision. We were taking one of our breaks. Our throats were kind of raw, so we'd gone to the Coke machine instead of the coffee machine for our caffeine and had brought the ice-cold bottles back to my home away from home, Debriefing Room B. Clarence leaned back in his chair and propped his feet up on the table. I did the same.

"Lightfoot, the human animal is a curious thing. On the afternoon before D-Day, I was alongside Ike as he reviewed the pathfinders of the 82nd Airborne. These were the very first of the invasion troops to hit French soil. They jumped at fifteen minutes past midnight, and their job was to mark the drop zones for all the other paratroopers. Ike had just finished giving them a little pep talk but it was a pep talk tempered with some straight talking. He told them that his staff estimated that those guys might hit as high as eighty percent casualties. As we were walking through the ranks, Ike stopped in front of a big PFC. 'How do you feel about what I just said,' he asked, 'an eighty percent casualty rate?' The guy looked around him slowly, then replied, 'Sir, I sure am going to miss all these guys.'"

I smiled, and Clarence took a long thoughtful swig from his Coke bottle.

"How do you feel about your own death, Lightfoot? Can you see it? What would you have said to Ike?"

I took a long pull from my own bottle and considered. "I'd be inclined to agree with that paratrooper, I guess. I don't want to die, but you can't let that keep you from doing things that have to be done. . . or," I said with the mind's eye on the stars, "from things that you want to do with all your heart."

"The interview's over, Lightfoot," Clarence said softly. "You passed."

"You mean you're going to . . ." Clarence nodded.

"I'm going to recommend to the Old Man that you be the one. You have only one more hurdle, and that's an interview with the Old Man himself."

"The President himself is going—"

"I told you that this was the big time."

My head was spinning, "Me? With the President? When?"

In reply, Jones picked up the black phone and dialed the number for the Officer of the Day. "This is Clarence Jones. If you'll check the Standing Orders, you'll find that General Forbes has authorized Priority Red One transportation for me. Please have a fast two-seater jet aircraft fueled up, ready to go, and pointed in the direction of Washington. Captain O'Brien will be the pilot, and we'll be taking off at dawn. Right . . . yes . . . that'll be fine. Thank you." Jones picked up the red phone next. It had no dial. "Tango 78, Bravo 4 . . . yes . . . 018836 . . . authentication Papa Alpha 38422 . . . Hotel Sierra Whiskey . . . 490032 . . . Mr. President? It's Jones, sir. Yes sir. Yes he did, with flying colors . . . Yes sir. 1800 hours Eastern Daylight Time. Very well. Thank you, sir." He hung up and turned to me. "Does that answer your question?"

4

We thundered off the runway at 0602 hours in an F-94C Lockheed Starfire, a two-seat, all-weather jet interceptor. If we'd been flying an intercept mission, Clarence, seated directly behind me, would have had his hands full in using the sophisticated radar unit to vector us into a pass at an intruding aircraft, and arming and readying the weapons systems. But it wasn't an intercept mission, and there was nothing for Clarence to do but to catch up on his sleep. By 0620 he was dead to the world. In the coming weeks and months, I'd learn that that was one of Clarence's "tricks of the trade"—the ability to key down quickly when the opportunity presented itself, and so recharge his batteries so he could give it all he had when the old adrenalin hit the bloodstream once more and he had to come through.

I flew low for the first twenty minutes, somehow sadly certain that I'd never see the desert again, and, like a man leaving the woman he loves, reluctant to take his eyes off her for what would be the last time. So many thoughts and images came flooding into my mind. I'd spent my boyhood and adolescence in the desert. As a child at San Carlos, my friends and I were no different from any other American boys; we too played cowboys and Indians. There were only two differences in our play: the Indians were the good guys, and the Indians always won. As we grew into our teens, the desert turned from a playground into a huge recreation area. We hunted, trapped, explored old mineshafts, picnicked with our girlfriends, and found solitude and tranquility in its vastness when we needed to be alone to think. The other guys in desert survival school took it tough because they were too dumb to realize that the desert was not a cruel, implacable enemy; it was a friend. The desert, in addition to the food it fed the soul with its stark beauty, offered a bounty of food for the body as well. The desert teemed with plant and animal life. All one had to do was to look around. During the wars with the United States Army, one advantage that Apache raiders had was that they required no supply wagons or mules to carry provisions. Everywhere they went, provisions surrounded them.

An excellent staple was mesquite: a tree or shrub anywhere from ten to twenty feet high, its pods resemble string beans and have sweet, juicy pulp embedded with hard seeds. The raw beans have a lemony taste, are high in sugar for quick energy, and are nutritious. You can also eat the twigs, seeds, bark, and leaves. Then there's always the fruit from the prickly pear cactus, the saguaro cactus, the barrel cactus, and hedgehogs. Flower buds from the Joshua tree can be eaten hot or cold after roasting and are so sweet they're the next best thing to candy. Yucca produces a short, banana-shaped fruit that is sweet and nutritious. When it's ripe, it can be roasted or baked in the hot ashes of your campfire, and when the rind is removed, it tastes a lot like sweet potato. Then there's the sweet, round, red fleshy fruit of the organ pipe cactus, the berries of the desert hackberry, and of the manzanita. Sagebrush seeds, if cooked, are not bad. Other edible seeds include those of the deer brush and of the desert ironwood (which taste like peanuts). Roasted catclaw seeds are great. Miner's lettuce is a small succulent, the leaves of which form a saucer about halfway up the stem. They can be eaten raw or boiled. If you place the leaves near a red ants' nest, you'll find that the ants give off a formic acid that makes a vinegar-like dressing on them. Mexicans used to make a salad with the leaves of miner's lettuce and peeled prickly pear cactus. And, as for edible roots and flowers, well, they abound.

Meat can also be had without a great deal of effort. Besides birds and rabbits, there are the snakes and the lizards and the insects. Lizards and rattlesnakes have a fibrous flesh, which, when cooked, tastes mighty like chicken. Some say better, but I've had them all and I prefer chicken. Then again, you won't find chicken on the desert, so I developed an early taste for reptiles. Lizards especially are easy to catch. A lot of times they'll freeze instead of run and hope that you haven't noticed them. That's when you bean them with a rock.

Water. That is supposed to be the roughest part. Finding enough water. That's even easier to come by than food to someone who knows the desert. Aside from the water found in natural reservoirs like the barrel cactus, you can watch birds in flight in the morning and evening, because they head for water then. For that matter, all you have to do is to follow any game trail downhill, because the animals know where the water is, and water always flows downhill. You can chew pigweed stems; they contain a lot of water. You can do a lot of things. The desert is a friend.

I sadly watched that old friend zip below me at the rate of 585 mph as we zoomed toward the rising sun. There were a lot of memories, a lot of memories, I thought of that time that a woman tourist/artist came to the reservation to paint "primitives in their natural habitat." My friends and I were around eleven years old. A couple of us had distracted her while Johnny Hawk stole a tube of bright yellow oil paint from her gear. We used it for warpaint in our cowboy and Indian games for months afterward. Geronimo always wore three stripes of yellow on each cheek whenever he was on the warpath.

I thought of the time when, at fourteen, I had tried my hand at prospecting. I had stormed into the cabin howling and yelling like a maniac, only to be subdued by my mother, who had patiently explained the difference between gold and pyrite (also known as fool's gold, although she did not use that term).

I thought of the night, the night that seemed eons ago, when under a bright full moon, with the distant sound of coyotes howling in the background, I had proposed to Amanda Clearwater and she had accepted. Sitting on a large flat rock under a giant saguaro and oblivious of the time, we made plans far into the night. I would return to the reservation to teach history, and she would finish nursing school and work at the clinic. We were very happy.

I thought of the night I had gone out into the desert after the double funeral and climbed a tall rocky hill and howled at the moon and cried and cursed mankind and the universe and even God. I screamed out at the futility of it all, at the cruel, cosmic jest. I raged at the heavens and the earth and the Creator because everything I ever cared about was always destroyed. Not only that, but the destruction was random, meaningless, purposeless. A barroom brawl, a drunk crossing a center line on a highway. It *was* all a tale told by an idiot, full of sound and fury, and it certainly signified nothing.

I took my last look at the desert and pulled the stick back. The climb was swift and steep, and when I leveled off at 45,000 feet, all I could see below me were clouds. Memories of a different sort began to intrude. Clarence had made me go through the Korean experience again. "It's all in the reports," I had objected. "Tell me anyway," was the firm reply. And so I had told him, and briefly hated him for making me live through something again that I'd spent the last five years trying to forget. It wasn't his fault, though. He couldn't have known how it haunted me.

Come warriors like the eagle free.
Come to battle like the eagle.

A Chiricahua Apache War Chant

The last thing in the world I expected on June 23, 1953, was being shot down over North Korea 52 miles behind enemy lines. Although the performance of the MIG-15 was slightly better that that of the F-86 North American Sabre which I was flying, as a general rule, the North Korean and Chinese pilots were not very good. In fact, all but 38 of the 800 MIG-15s destroyed during the Korean War were downed by Sabrejets—a kill ratio of 14 to 1 over the enemy. The six .50 caliber machine guns, three on either side of the nose, gave the F-86 an extremely tight group in air-to-air combat, and our ground crews were the best. Malfunctions of any type were rare.

I was shot down for three reasons: first, we were outnumbered; second, this particular batch of enemy pilots was very good indeed; and third, because I was very stupid. The last was the biggest contributing factor. I had allowed myself to become complacent, lulled into a false sense of security by our terrific track record. I was an ace plus two, having downed seven MIGs. The enemy had never challenged us when we went out in force, and there were 32 planes in the flight that day. The peace talks at Panmunjom seemed to be getting serious at last.

Well, they pulled out all stops that day, proving that General Weyland's dam destruction program was hitting them where it hurt. The month before, on May 13, 1953, 59 F-84 Thunderjets had attacked the great dam at Toksan, twenty miles north of Pyongyang. That night the dam, weakened by the concussions of several hundred bombs, gave way. The sudden flood washed out the main bridges, rail lines, and roads from Pyongyang. General Mark Clark issued a statement saying, "The breaching of the Toksan Dam has been as effective as weeks of rail interdiction." Encouraged by the results, General Weyland ordered missions against the dams at Chasan, Kusong, Kuwongam, and Toksang. All had the same degree of success. It was more than the enemy could take evidently.

So it was that on June 23, 1953, when 32 Sabrejets, each with a thousand-pound bomb under each wing, streaked toward the dam at Tae Gwang Ni, they scrambled everything they could get in the air to intercept us. I was just kind of daydreaming along when what seemed like the whole Chinese Air Force came swooping down straight out of the sun. They hit us hard and fast and with great determination, perhaps desperation. I had no sooner jettisoned my drop tanks and begun to climb when I felt my aircraft start to buck like a crazed wild bronco. Another group was simultaneously hitting us from behind. Almost immediately, I lost some control in the rudder pedals. They were responding with a sluggishness that made my stomach sink sickeningly. I began to lose altitude fast. The cockpit began to fill with thick acrid smoke as I fought to bring her up. The hydraulics had been hit, so I had to brace myself against the firewall, grit my teeth, and strain every muscle for everything I was worth to move the stick back even an inch. Finally something gave, and I came out of the spin at about 2,000 feet in something approximating level flight but not close enough for comfort.

The MIG-15s had two Nudelmann-Suranov 23-mm nose-mounted cannon on the left side and one 37-mm cannon nose-mounted on the right. Hits by those monsters were not to be taken lightly, and I had been hit hard. As smoke continued to fill the cockpit, I saw to my astonishment that the MIG was still on my tail. It wasn't enough for him that I was flaming and smoking like a Pittsburgh steel mill on Monday, or that the after part of my fuselage was totally engulfed in a raging fire, or that a major portion of my control surfaces had been shot away. This guy was staying on my tail, continuing to fire, wanting to make sure. Dedication. There's nothing like it.

My options were nonexistent. I couldn't climb. I couldn't evade. I couldn't engage. I was too low to eject. There was nothing for it but to ride the old Apache Avenger down if she held together long enough. But where? I was over typical North Korean terrain, which is to say mountainous. The mountains are Archean rock, and while few of the peaks are very high, the ranges are steep, abrupt, and stony. I was sliding down toward a small valley ringed by those inhospitable mountains.

The little valley was a quiltwork of rice paddies and dikes. A river wound through the valley, and there was the inevitable farming village consisting of no more than forty thatched huts. Its name, I later learned, was Pang A Da Ri. No level terrain. No level terrain. My final course of action was one I decided on very quickly when my friend behind me began to open up again. I'd just have to use the narrow dirt road that more or less paralleled the river. Like it or not, that would have to be my landing strip. I kept losing altitude, and now the smoke was so dense that it fairly filled the cockpit. I couldn't see the instruments clearly, and only snatches of the valley were visible through the smoke. I slid back the canopy to get rid of it. That worked, but now the wind was howling about me like a thousand banshees. Using every last drop of adrenalin in my entire body, I somehow managed a wobbly landing approach to the road. Fortunately, there were no vehicles or people on the road. I was going in for a belly landing and was at 400 feet when the tenacious Chinese pilot behind me tagged me yet again. That was point, game, and match.

Now all power and virtually all control were gone. It was not only a belly landing on a narrow dirt road that wound around a mountain pass, but also a dead-stick landing. I hit that road hard, bouncing three times, and losing major fragments of my aircraft on each bounce, before it settled into a rapid slide that assaulted the ears—the tortured airframe screeching as ten tons of steel grated and ground its way along the road. Struts caved in, rivets popped, and the whole craft was rapidly being rendered into junk by the incredible shrieking stress that seemed like it would never end.

I rode that road for a good half mile but was still doing about 80 mph and using up my "runway" much too fast. The road took a sharp curve around an outcropping of rock dead ahead, and I, of course, couldn't steer. Regardless of where the road went, I was condemned by the laws of physics to go in a straight line. I could only sit there as a spectator. I wasn't going to make it. I remembered the centuries-old farewell of the Apache warrior going into a battle from which he knew he would not return: It is a good day for dying.

I was about to begin my Death Chant, when suddenly deliverance came in the form of a North Korean Army two-and-a-half-ton truck rounding the bend and coming head on. I'm quite certain that the very last thing in the world that the driver and officer in the cab of that truck expected to see, as they rounded the bend in that quiet little valley 52 miles behind the front, was an American jet fighter coming straight for them on the road. If it is possible for men to die of fright, they did for a certainty. At least, that's what it looked like. Their eyes bulged like frogs' and the driver probably didn't recover in time enough to make the futile gesture of putting his foot on the brake. An F-86 weighed 20,610 pounds, and the contest wasn't even close. It was like a Greyhound bus colliding with an MG midget. I plowed into the truck head on, collapsing the cab, and sending both the truck and my Sabrejet sliding back down the road in the direction from which the truck had come. The truck had been doing about 50 mph when we'd collided, so its forward momentum slowed me sufficiently. Both truck and plane come to a shuddering stop only ten yards from the outcropping of rock at the bend in the road. That's what you call close. In fact, that's what you call a miracle.

The occupants of the cab posed no immediate threat; it looked like they'd never again pose a threat to anyone. But I still didn't know how many, if any, men were in the back of that truck. A two-and-a-half-ton truck could hold the better part of a platoon. I popped out of that cockpit like a rabbit and ran around the back of that truck as fast as I could, hoping to be there before any possible passengers could recover. Pilots were unofficially given some latitude in their choice of sidearms, and I was carrying my father's Colt .45 Peacemaker. It was in my hand with the hammer on full cock when I reached the rear of the truck. Five men had been catapulted out of the back onto the ground. One was a North Korean soldier, whom I promptly shot as he scrambled to retrieve his burp gun, a scant yard away from his outstretched hand. The others were American POWs. Inside the truck, a dozen other Americans and four KATUSAs (Koreans Attached to United States Army) had already subdued and were enthusiastically beating the brains out of the other North Korean guard with his own rifle butt. In fact, before I could open my mouth, I saw that they *had* beaten his brains out. One of the South Koreans let out a vicious stream of words that I didn't understand, kicked the body, and then spat on it as if to punctuate his last sentence. I gathered that the prisoners hadn't been treated well.

Things had happened so fast. Twelve minutes before, I hadn't a care in the world. Now I owned two hunks of junk—one had been an advanced jet aircraft, the other, a truck. I was also, at least for the foreseeable future, in the infantry.

"You guys O.K.?"

"I think my arm is busted," a voice issued from the bottom of the pile of tangled arms and legs on the floor.

"I cracked some ribs," said another. "I heard 'em crack."

"Who's ranking man?" I asked.

"I am, sir," replied a thirtyish Marine staff sergeant.

"O.K., listen up. My name's O'Brien, second lieutenant, Air Force. I'm assuming command. Everybody out of the truck! Move! We can't afford to hang around here too long." They were a game lot and quickly complied. What's more, they appeared to be in good health, indicating that they hadn't been POWs for very long.

"You KATUSAs," I said, "strip the bodies of the guys in the cab and the two guards. Get into their uniforms and grab their weapons." There was some hesitation. "Sir," one said, "we fear that we will be treated as spies in the event we are recaptured. We would be tortured in the dire extreme, and thenceforth be executed."

I was all too painfully aware of the rapidity with which the second and minutes hands on my watch were moving. I had no time for debates about the Geneva Conventions or similar twaddle. No time.

"What is the duty of a soldier?" I asked rhetorically. "It is this: to obey orders. I order you men to put on those uniforms, and in so doing, I accept full responsibility. In the event we are captured, I will make a sworn written statement for the record to the effect that you wore enemy uniforms under protest and that you were only following orders. Refusal to obey orders in the face of the enemy is, in both the United States and South Korean armies, punishable by death. I will point out that you had no choice and that you consequently bear no responsibility."

This seemed to satisfy them, whether because of my implicit threat to shoot them for disobeying orders or because they had never heard of Nuremberg and really believed that line, I'll never know. All that really mattered was that they moved quickly and began to strip the bodies.

"Sergeant," I said, going down on one knee in the dusty road, "draw me a map and tell me what's behind you and where. Don't take any longer than five minutes."

The Marine was a career man, a World War II vet who really

knew his business. I was to learn in the following days that he'd been through some of the toughest—Iwo Jima, Guadalcanal, and Tarawa, among others. He expertly sketched in what lay behind them. They'd been POWs for only three days. For the most part, the last thirty of the fifty-odd miles they'd traversed presented no real obstacles. There seemed to be no minefields, and they'd seen only two major installations, both of which we could skirt. There were, however, eight checkpoints they'd gone through. Avoiding those would mean leaving the road and adding days to our journey. The men carried no food. These things all meant that hijacking another truck was essential. We had to get as far away as quickly as possible. The only vehicular traffic they'd seen going in either direction, aside from the occasional, lone jeep or truck, had been at about 0100 hours, when what appeared to be an entire Chinese infantry division, had passed them, headed south. (All large-scale movements in the latter stages of the war, especially on roads, were performed at night, due to American air superiority.) The sergeant, Duncan was his name, was good; he was very good. He had finished briefing me at almost precisely the same moment that four of the KATUSAs appeared at my side, dressed and armed as North Korean soldiers.

"O.K.," I said, getting to my feet, "there's nothing for it but to get ourselves another truck. Meanwhile, let's do some marching. Every minute counts."

I strung us out in two columns, one on each side of the road. The KATUSAs kept their weapons at the ready, "guarding" us POWs. I took up my place at the very end of the right column, and I had Duncan directly across in the left file; there were seventeen of us. I carried my Colt .45 tucked into my belt inside my flight suit, and Duncan had one of the North Koreans' bayonets concealed under his unbuttoned fatigue shirt. I'd given the KATUSAs their instructions by the time we'd covered the first mile on our way south. Our lives were in their hands. Their sense of timing was all important.

We'd gone about eight and a half miles before we finally saw what we were looking for—a dust cloud on the horizon rapidly heading our way. The orders that I'd given stipulated that we were to hit only single vehicles; two or more were to be let by, and, if they stopped to ask any questions, we'd just have to try to bluff our way through. I had prepped the KATUSAs for that eventuality, although they really didn't need it. Armies are alike the world over, and confounding officers comes second nature to enlisted men. It's not only a sport. It's an art. Where are we going, sir? Why, down this road. He said not very far. Who, sir? The captain. The captain that was with the major. We don't know why, sir. He didn't tell us. The major. The major that was back there. The one with the captain. The major that told us to take these prisoners with us. No sir, we didn't catch his name. No sir, but maybe he was with the engineers. Something about using the prisoners on a work detail. To repair a bridge or build one, something like that. He said he'll rejoin us shortly. He had to go somewhere first. No sir, he didn't say. Is there anything else we can do for you, sir?

The dust cloud was getting closer and closer, and the butterflies in my stomach were having a field day. We all strained our eyes to see the type and number of vehicles. Now it was only a mile off. A North Korean Army three-quarter-ton truck. Nothing else.

"This is it, guys. Remember what I told you."

Holding up a hand MP-style, one of the KATUSAs stood in the middle of the road to halt the vehicle. It didn't reduce its speed; it just kept on a-comin'. The driver just put his hand on the horn and kept it there. The truck did not show any intention of stopping, but our stalwart KATUSA stood his ground. The other three that were also in NKA uniform joined him in the road and took aim with their burp guns at the windshield. The driver hit the brakes so fast and hard that he almost threw himself and his passenger through it. He screeched to a shuddering, dead stop and began to yell and curse. Afterward, one of the KATUSAs told me it went like this:

"What do you idiots think you're doing?" the driver had demanded. As we'd planned it, the two KATUSAs he'd driven by at the head of the column checked the back of the truck. The one who'd halted him approached the driver, while the last KATUSA casually approached the passenger side.

"Trying to help you, sir," he saluted the passenger, an NKA captain. "There's trouble back there, a helicopter commando raid. That's where we captured this scum. We even got one of the pilots," he said, gesturing to me. "But there's still some mopping up going on. We suggest you turn around and take a detour, sir."

The KATUSA at the rear right hand side of the truck shook his head at the KATUSA doing the talking, indicating that the back of the vehicle was empty. He, in turn, gave an almost imperceptible nod to the KATUSA opposite him on the driver's side.

The NKA officer puffed out his chest and blustered, "I am Major Lee Soon Mi, chief of battalion intelligence. I am under orders to proceed directly to division intelligence without delay." He held up a battered leather briefcase that was handcuffed to his left wrist. There were two additional locks on the briefcase itself. "This material is of the highest priority, and I am to deliver it immediately. I order you to let us pass." Since both North Koreans were looking at the KATUSA on the major's side of the truck, neither saw the burp gun of the KATUSA on the driver's side come up to shoulder height. When his partner on the other side suddenly hit the dirt, he opened up. The North Koreans never knew what had hit them.

Things were improving. We now had a serviceable truck, two more weapons, and a briefcase full of what could be interesting reading for our intelligence boys. We dumped the bodies in a roadside drainage ditch, turned the truck around, and resumed our trip south. Luck was with us. The stenciled markings on the bumpers indicated that the vehicle was assigned to an intelligence unit, and a narrow sign at the bottom of the windshield read in Korean, "URGENT—COURIER—DO NOT DELAY." That, along with one of our stern-faced KATUSAs now in the major's uniform, carried us through checkpoint after checkpoint. We got to within five miles of our lines before we had to do any more fighting, but from then on, it was pure hell. The kick-off to that last five miles was a raid I led against a Chinese supply depot, where we captured some much needed food and enough arms to give our little band considerable firepower—firepower far out of proportion to our numbers. We walked away from there festooned with Chinese potato-masher-type grenades, bandoleers, and magazine pouches. Each of us had a submachine gun and a pistol. In addition, I had three of the guys carry light machine guns and assigned a feeder to each of them. I assigned a mortar to the KATUSAs, and I grabbed a rucksack and stuck in about thirty sticks of TNT, some primers, and a few yards of fuse. We were a pretty potent force to tangle with after that.

What went on after that as we fought that last five miles could (and does) fill a book. Duncan subsequently wrote, *Behind Enemy Lines: O'Brien's Raiders*. It's a good book and absolutely accurate. At first, I was put off by the title, but needlessly so, as it turned out. The book didn't sell very well anyway. It created hardly a ripple the few short months it was on the stands. That's too bad, not because I care about any recognition for myself, but for quite the opposite reason. What Duncan brought out so eloquently was the fact that none of us were heroes. Someone once said that a hero is nothing more than a man who has become so tired and hungry and scared that he no longer cares; he just gets so mad, becomes so outraged, that anything or anybody who gets in his way is in for big trouble. Duncan tried to tell that to the world, but throughout history, it's always been a message that the world doesn't want to hear.

They gave me the Silver Star for leading nine other men out, and three of us were wounded. One subsequently died of his wounds. In all, we lost eight men, or, I should say *I* lost eight men. Some hero. They had started the paperwork for awarding me the Medal of Honor, but stopped when I told them that if it were awarded to me, I would refuse to accept it. No one had ever turned down a Medal of Honor, and no one knew what the protocol would be in such an event. On the other hand, they had to give me something; the commanding general told personnel that public relations wanted a hero to bolster morale at home. There wasn't much good press coming out of Korea since the war had gone into a bone-wearying, grinding stalemate. The war was sapping more than national resources; it was sapping national spirit. Then too, there were the other men. Those eight guys had gone through more than most can even imagine, and I didn't want to demean their achievement. I insisted that they all get Silver Stars too. Personnel said how about Bronze Stars, and a deal was struck. Months later, at a surprise ceremony, I was also awarded the Distinguished Flying Cross. It was such a surprise, that before I could figure out whether or not I should accept it, the general had pinned it on me and had already moved on.

Seven men were lost, eight if you count Stack, the guy who had died of wounds after we got back (and you'd better count him). I was also awarded two Purple Hearts for wounds I picked up when I was crawling that last mile, setting TNT charges. We literally blew a path through that last mile of mines and concertina wire and bunkers and pillboxes. Using fire and movement, we covered each other as we ran that bloody gauntlet to safety. Eight men lost. Sure, I could have done worse. But I could have done better too. You see, the cease-fire agreement was signed at Panmunjom on July 27, 1953, only a little over three weeks later. If I had just left well enough alone, instead of trying a grandstand play like that, those eight guys would have probably done a month as POWS, and all of them would still be alive today.

Sure, the Air Force psychiatrist told me that there was no way I could have known that. And he's right, of course. But that doesn't seem to help too much. The story of that last five miles is a long one and has little to do with this book. It's also a tragic and terrifying story, and I decided in 1953 that I would never talk about it or even think about it again. Then along comes a Secret Service agent, and I have to reopen that door and live through it again. Every last detail. And for what? As we raced toward the rising sun in the Lockheed Starfire, I realized that I still knew little more than I did four days before.

6

We refueled in Ohio, where we also grabbed a couple of American cheese sandwiches and a couple of cartons of milk out of a machine in the Ops building. The guys there were cordial, but when we finally landed at Andrews Air Force Base outside of Washington, I saw what it was really like to be treated like a VIP. I taxied off the runway behind a fast blue FOLLOW ME pickup, which led me to a remote corner of the installation. As I killed the powerful Pratt & Whitney J48-P-5 turbojet, I noticed that the aircraft on our immediate left was none other than Air Force One. In front of us were three immaculate passenger helicopters, each painted a deep rich blue-green, and emblazoned with the Great Seal of the United States. A bird colonel met me and Clarence on the ground. He looked like he was going to salute Clarence and click his heels.

"Mr. Jones, it's good to see you again. The President wants to see you and Captain O'Brien immediately. We have chopper number three standing by."

Clarence, apparently used to being treated with such deference, simply grinned and headed for the chopper. "Thanks, Colonel," he said over his shoulder, "appreciate it." I hefted by B-4 bag and followed him. "Appreciate it," I yelled inanely to the colonel over the now increasing roar of the idling helicopter.

We were airborne the instant, or actually an instant before, the door was slammed behind me by a crewman. The lurch almost threw me off my feet as I overbalanced with the B-4 bag. Clarence, after all the sound sack time on the cross-country flight in the Starfire, now looked disgustingly fresh, bright-eyed, and bushy-tailed. He motioned me to one of the plush upholstered seats and took one himself. After I sat down, I looked around. This was one of the helicopters used for formal occasions to ferry heads of state, cabinet members, and the President himself hither and yon, and it looked it with its ankle-deep royal-blue rug, massive reclining chairs, and incredible soundproofing. I couldn't believe it.

We landed on the White House lawn, where we were met by two youthful and athletic Secret Service agents. "Chief," the taller of the two said to Jones in an all-business fashion, "he wants to see you and the captain here immediately. The chopper's to stand by. I'll take care of it." Clarence's eyes twinkled.

"Nobody stole the silverware while I was gone?"

"No sir," the junior agent replied, then reddened.

Clarence snapped him a mock serious salute. "Then carry on, mister. As you were. Avast on the poopdeck and shiver me timbers. Fire one, and take her down to 500 feet. Rig for silent running and belay that!" The guy got even redder. "Aw, relax, Charlie. I'm just funnin' with you."

"Yes sir. I understand."

We set out across the beautifully manicured grounds for the White House, and the two agents stayed with the chopper. "He's O.K." Clarence said by way of explanation. "We recruited him out of Annapolis not too long ago. Family is fourth generation navy. Has money too. With his brains and connections, he'd have been an Admiral in fifteen years, no sweat. God knows why he signed up with our lot. Glad he did though; he's first rate." Jones's pace was brisk and assured, and before I knew it, we were inside, and our footfalls were echoing hollowly on the dark parquet floor. "Do you know I'm the only guy who's ever called him Charlie? Even his family has always called him Charles . . ." Clarence shook his head wonderingly, "Charles." At the end of the quiet corridor, we turned into a handsomely appointed office tastefully done in Early American. Its three occupants smiled and nodded at us.

"Go right in, Mr. Jones and Captain O'Brien. He's waiting," said an elegant and elderly woman, whom I later learned was the President's personal secretary.

"Thank you, Miss Hotchkiss," Clarence replied without breaking stride. Things were happening so fast that I was having real trouble adapting. Another door opened; we took a few more steps, and suddenly, me, humble little Lightfoot O'Brien from the San Carlos Reservation, found himself in the august presence of the President of the United States. The Oval Office.

Holding his hands open to warm them, Ike stood staring thoughtfully into the roaring fire in the huge and ornate fireplace. He rubbed his hands briskly, then turned to face us. He looked exactly like his photographs, but he was shorter than I'd expected. I've since come to the not very original and not very brilliant conclusion that we all seem to expect world leaders, movie stars, war heroes, great writers and artists, and similar luminaries to be larger than life. They're not.

Nevertheless, he was an imposing figure. He had what professional military people call "command presence," and he had it in abundance. He was a man who had commanded millions in the greatest war in history, and he was now President of the United States of America. He smiled.

"Clarence," he said, while his eyes frankly appraised me, "have you got us the right man?"

"Yes sir."

The President extended his hand. I dropped my B-4 bag and shook. His grip was firm.

"Captain, I hope all your worldly possessions are in that bag. You won't be getting a chance to go back for them. At least, I hope you won't."

I managed a lopsided grin. "I travel light, sir."

"Good," Ike said, turning to Clarence, "you ready for a little trip to the farm?"

"Mr. President," Clarence smiled, holding up his battered brown leather attaché case, "you know me. I travel even lighter." That attaché case, the only luggage he'd carried out to Nevada with him, the only luggage I later learned, he ever carried anywhere with him, contained a razor, tooth brush, tooth paste, extra ammo for the .357 Magnum in his shoulder holster, a few sets of underwear, two shirts (white), three pairs of socks (black), an extra bag of Cherry blend for his pipe, and a bottle of aspirin. Travel light? I guess you could say that.

"Good. Captain, you're not finished traveling yet, but you will be soon. Then you'll be getting a breathing spell. We're going to Gettysburg."

"Yes sir."

He turned to Jones. "Mamie's already there. She left this morning, and my valise went with her. I've just been waiting for you two. O.K., let's go." With that, he took his hat and overcoat from a walnut clothes tree and headed for the door.

On the flight out, Ike chatted amicably about inconsequential things. A combination of his clearing his mind for a few days' vacation and trying to put me at ease, I suspect. At ease. He needn't have bothered. I was flat out exhausted and running on nothing more than nervous energy anyway. Everything was catching up with me—the grueling four-day interview with Clarence, with all the attendant dredging up of memories I'd spent years trying to free myself from, the transcontinental flight in the F-94, meeting and being whisked off to rural Pennsylvania by the President of the United States, the sheer mystery of it all. I was running on that nervous energy plus two American cheese sandwiches washed down with a small carton of milk. The fuel finally ran out somewhere over the Maryland countryside. One moment I was politely listening to the President tell me about the trout fishing in Adams County in the spring, and the next moment Jones was shaking me awake.

"O.K., Ace, we're here. You can wake up now."

"Huh?" I replied from my stupor.

"End of the line, Lightfoot." I managed a kind of fuzzy semiconsciousness. It wasn't much, but it was the best I could do at the time. There were no longer any vibrations or engine noises. We were on the ground. My mouth tasted horrible and my eyeballs felt raw. I was long overdue for a shower, and my uniform was wrinkled in a thousand places. I needed a shave. As my eyes began to focus, I saw the President standing over me right behind Clarence. His expression was firm, but his eyes were twinkling. He'd just finished saying something about the conduct of junior officers who show disrespect for their superiors by falling asleep right in the middle of an exciting tale about the size of the fish that got away.

"I'm sorry, Mr. President. I—"

"No excuses, Captain. The penalty is confinement to the guest cottage and the grounds for 24 hours." We were exiting the chopper, and as we hit the ground, he indicated a small red brick cottage no more than fifty yards from the main house. "You'll find it comfortable. If it's good enough for Churchill, it should be good enough for you. You strike me as a much easier man to please," Ike smiled. "I'll send Cook over with a hot and hearty meal within the hour. While you're waiting, you might want to wash up. Have you any civilian clothes in that bag?"

"Yes sir."

"Good, wear them. From now on, I don't want to see you in uniform. If anyone on the spread asks, and they shouldn't because they're used to being very discreet, you can tell them your name. Period." I nodded and he continued. "The Secret Service detachment here at the farm has been notified of your presence. All the agents have been given copies of your photograph, so you can stroll around all you want without fear of being shot. Just don't leave the farm, and although there's a telephone in the cottage, I ask that you don't use it to let anyone know where you are. There's no need for that anyway, is there?" I shook my head. "Good. This is really big, O'Brien. The classification of this project is Top Secret Cosmic Eyes Only. In this particular instance, that means that there are only 36 people in the world who know about it. Let's keep it that way, shall we?" I nodded grimly, the set of my jaw, I hoped, a clear indication of how serious and trustworthy I was. Suddenly he laughed, the kindly old man once again. "O.K., son. Now take tonight and tomorrow off. Let's talk tomorrow night. I'm warning you in advance to be well rested. You'll need to do some heavy and clear thinking."

With that, he gave me a hearty clap on the back, which propelled my weary body toward the steps of the cottage. With a Herculean effort, I mustered up the last of my reserve strength and made it up the five steps to the small porch. My B-4 bag dropped from my nerveless fingers with a thud, and my hands automatically began a clumsy search of my pockets. "Key," I mumbled absently to myself, "no key."

"Don't need a key here, cousin," Jones said from behind me. "Not even a jackrabbit gets onto the grounds without us knowing about it, what with our electronic sensors, roving patrols, and so forth. No need to lock anything here on the farm." He came around in front of me, opened the door, and preceded me in. "All the comforts of home," he said as he flicked on the lights. He was right. It wasn't fancy, but it was cheerful, clean, and cozy. It was furnished in Pennsylvania Dutch style, even to the point of a few gaily colored hex signs on the walls. The stone fireplace was already set up with logs and kindling. All it needed was the touch of a match and I was in business. The late November weather in Pennsylvania was something my desert acclimated body wasn't yet ready for.

Walking into the small kitchen, Clarence opened a couple of cupboards and the refrigerator door, gesturing to me as he did so. "You've got utensils, plates, fresh milk, eggs, coffee, bread, and some canned goods if you feel like cooking or having a snack. If you don't feel like cooking tomorrow morning, just mosey over to the Secret

Service bunkhouse, visit a spell and we'll have breakfast together. They made up the bed and put in fresh towels while we were on our way up here. Got any questions?" I shook my head. "Hit the sack right after you eat, Lightfoot. You look like something the cat dragged in."

I awoke at about three o'clock in the morning, but not in bed. I had fallen asleep right where I had stretched out the night before. On the hearth before a lively hickory fire. Except for the busy little sounds of the flickering fire, all was silent. I was still in my uniform. The fire was so soothing. I looked into the mesmerizing flames, remembering all the fires that I had shared on the desert with Tom Pinole, Johnny Straight Blade, and Bill (Loco) Coyote when we were teenagers. Oftentimes, the revered Dark Cloud, a reclusive shaman of great repute, would join us. He was as imposing as the mighty Superstition Mountains, twice as old, and ten times more mysterious. He would tell us of the old days, the days of Victorio, of Mangas Coloradas, of Cochise, and of Geronimo. He would tell tales long into the night, tales of perfidy and treachery that would make us want to howl for justice, to fight for it without considering the cost, tales of courage that told of men of honor who faced overwhelming odds but fought and often died rather than betray a trust, tales of great and wise chiefs and shamans, of cold sparkling water from crystal lakes, of the animals of the desert, and of beautiful maidens. He spoke of the history of our people, of the coming together of the Bedonkohes, the Nednis, and the Chokonens, all uniting to fight as Chiricahuas. He was never seen on the reservation, and he shunned the company of adults. He was seen only at the campfires of young people. Then one day, he came no more. But, as I only realized much later in my life, it didn't matter. He had completed his task; he had passed on to a new generation their heritage. That was the gift he gave our people, as shamans of old had. He had told us who we were and made us feel the pride of it. Few men can accomplish more.

As I continued to stare into the fire, I thought I heard a coyote howl nearly a continent away. Then I drifted off to sleep again.

7

I awoke totally refreshed, every last cobweb banished from my mind. The fire had gone out, and it was a bit chilly. I got up and rolled up the blanket I always slept in—the blanket my mother had woven for me, the blanket that she had intended to give me as a graduation present when I graduated from Air Force flight school. It had been salvaged from the wreck, and I had slept in it every night since. Few, almost no, Apaches weave. That is a specialty of the Navajos, just as jewelry making is primarily done by the Zunis, and basket making by the Papagos. That made the blanket all the more precious to me. It was a one-of-a-kind, done slowly and painstakingly, by unaccustomed and loving hands, for me.

Next, I climbed out of my uniform of a thousand wrinkles and hit the shower. That was followed by a cup of hot coffee. I felt human once more, so, after dressing in civilian clothes, I headed over to the Secret Service bunkhouse, a long, low, white washed cinderblock building only about sixty yards from the cottage. Clarence wasn't around just then, but the other guys were friendly enough, if a bit reserved. Aside from my name and the fact that I was a VIP, they knew nothing about me and knew they weren't supposed to ask. Nevertheless, we chatted amicably about sports, the weather, the surrounding countryside, and how they liked working for Ike. They had been told that I had been given the highest security clearance possible, so they were more than ready to talk about work. They proudly showed me the electronic monitoring room, a place that looked like something out of Buck Rogers, only more sophisticated. The farm was enmeshed in invisible waves of antipersonnel radar for a start. There were also pressure sensors just below the surface of the ground along the perimeter as well as at critical locations in approaches to the house. There were numerous photoelectric beams set up and infrared sensors set to pick up the body heat of would be intruders. The main house itself was hardwired with your good old fashioned contact and magnetic switch burglar alarms. The agents carried out roving patrols at random places and random time intervals, and they had two German Shepherds, either of which, the agents claimed, could track a man through Manhattan at lunch hour without losing the scent. I believed them.

There were thirty-some agents assigned to the farm at any one time, with about eight sleeping, seven on patrol, one managing the sensor console, eight on ready reserve, and about eight off duty in town or back home. I was astounded at the weaponry they had. In addition to the .357 Magnum pistols they all carried, there were high power rifles with telescopic sights for counter-sniper work, BARs, Thompson submachine guns as well as the M3A1 grease guns so popular in Korea, riot guns, hand grenades, a bazooka, and even a flame thrower. They joked about the last item, saying that they used it only once each year—at the annual bull and oyster roast that the President threw for the Secret Service agents and their families at the farm. They claimed that it was the only way to roast a bull. I do believe that they were pulling my leg.

When I saw all this exotic stuff, my first reaction was that they were nuts. And, being Aloysius Lightfoot O'Brien, I told them so. Hand grenades, machine guns, and bazookas in the tranquil, pastoral setting of rural Pennsylvania? This was Norman Rockwell country, I told them. What could they possibly be thinking of? Well, they didn't throw me out, just kind of casually mentioned the storming of Blair House by Puerto Rican nationalists intent on killing President Truman. That had happened only eight years before, in November 1950. And, although the assassination attempt was unsuccessful, it had left one White House policeman dead and two wounded. Furthermore, it could have been worse if one of the terrorists' guns had not jammed. Four years later, in 1954, three members of the Puerto Rican National Party entered the visitors' gallery in the Capitol and began shooting. Shot were Representatives Kenneth Allison Roberts of Alabama, Benton Franklin Jensen of Iowa, George Hyde Fallon of Maryland, Alvin Morell Bentley of Michigan, and Clifford Davis of Tennessee. The world was getting to be a pretty tough place, the agents remarked. Properly chastened, I retreated to the cottage.

I'd no sooner pulled a Louis L'Amour Western off the bookshelf and settled into a comfortable recliner, when there was a knock on the door and Clarence entered. He was in casual dress—old beat-up corduroy pants, a red-checkered flannel shirt, and a blue parka.

"Hey, how do you feel today?"

"Great, Clarence. What's up?"

"Well, since our meeting with the Old Man isn't until 7:30 tonight, I figured that you might want to take in the sights. This being Gettysburg and you being a history buff. High Water Mark of the Confederacy and all that. Grab your coat and get your hat, leave your worries on the doorstep."

"Sounds good to me," I said, putting the novel down. "Let's go." I pulled on my denim sheepskin-lined coat, put on my beat-up Stetson, and we were off. Clarence had a white '54 Buick with Maryland tags waiting outside.

"Yours?"

"All mine."

We drove down the tree-lined drive in silence, but it was not an uncomfortable silence. It was December 1, 1958. A light snow was falling, and Christmas carols were issuing forth from the radio in the dash. Clarence began to hum along, and I sat back in the plush (they really *don't* make them like that anymore) seat and luxuriated in the blast of hot air coming from the car's powerful heater. We were a long way from the desert. The radio announcer broke into the last chorus of "Good King Wenceslas" to remind everyone that there were only 21 shopping days left until Christmas. Clarence glanced at me.

"I take it you don't have any plans for Christmas."

"You tell me. Where am I going to be at Christmas?" Clarence laughed. "Well, what's so funny?"

"Nothing, just that you're right. We haven't been too informative, that's true. Just hang on until 7:30. Trust me; it's worth the wait."

"I had planned to take a nurse to the Christmas Party at the Officers Club at Nellis, but I hadn't even gotten around to asking her. No big deal," I shrugged. When we came to the main road, Jones turned right.

"You've never been to Gettysburg, have you?"

"No, I've done quite a bit of reading about the battle, though."

"A good place to start is the Electric Map."

"Electric Map?"

"Yeah. Some buff spent years in research into the battle, in designing the circuits, in constructing the contour map of the area, and in wiring the console. Very impressive. It's a huge topographic map of the entire surrounding countryside, inlaid with hundreds and hundreds of tiny multicolored light bulbs. A lecturer sits at a console and the lights are dimmed. As he narrates the three days of the battle, he uses the controls to illustrate. For example, the sequential lighting of a row of lights denotes the movement of a column. Flickering lights indicate skirmishes and battles . . . well, you've got to see it to appreciate it. It gives you a great overview of the whole battle. You cover the whole three days in forty minutes."

It was a short drive, and we were inside the Visitors Center in just fifteen minutes but had to wait another half hour for the next show to start. We spent the time wandering about the halls, looking at the exhibit cases. Most of the display items were weapons, but there were also uniforms, battle flags, eating and cooking utensils, faded tintypes and daguerreotypes, pages from diaries, even a Civil War surgical kit.

"Hey, Clarence," I said, indicating the last, "you can see why one of the nicknames for doctors used to be 'sawbones.'" The kit consisted, for the most part, of a variety of saws.

"Yeah," Clarence answered, "that was pretty much SOP. You got a bad wound in the arm or leg, and because they didn't know the meaning of sterile procedures, you invariably developed sepsis, which in turn meant that the arm or leg had to be sawed off." He shivered. "How'd you like being treated by a doctor whose idea of sterilization was washing off his instruments in a bucket of creek water? Or being in a field hospital where no one has ever heard of penicillin? The docs in the field hospitals in World War II and in Korea thought they were doing meatball surgery, but compared to these guys, they were operating under Mayo Clinic conditions."

The electric map presentation was fascinating. Since it was December, I wasn't too surprised to see that there were only eight people besides us in the auditorium. It made the room seem colder, but it also made for no distractions. I folded my arms on the iron railing in the first row, laid my chin on my forearms, and was transported back 95 years in time. I almost felt like some sort of supernatural being, floating ethereally above a battle raging hundreds of feet below on the physical plane. I watched in a most detached fashion while tens of thousands of men strutted and fretted their allotted times on the stage and then were heard no more. I saw, on July 1st, 2nd, and 3rd of 1863, the battle lines ebb and flow as men made desperate charges and flanking movements. I heard the crash of musketry, the yells, the screams, the clanging of metal against metal. The flashes below were not tiny lights flickering on and off, but muzzle flashes; the dull red glows did not emanate from bulbs, but from campfires. I was rapt.

We rode around a bit after that, taking in the sights as we followed the battle in chronological order. From the Marsh Creek bridge to McPherson's Ridge to Little Round Top to Devils Den to the Wheatfield, we were taking it all in, oblivious of time. It was turning into a pleasant day. The snow had tapered off to flurries, and the temperature had risen to a tolerable 38 degrees.

"Lightfoot, why don't you join me and my family for Christmas? We'd like to have you," Clarence said as we were getting back into the car after looking at Spangler's Spring.

"Thanks, but no, Clarence. Christmas is a day for family. Anyway, over the years I've kind of gotten used to spending it . . . without family." A thought suddenly struck me. I don't know why I'd been too blind to see it before. "Clarence, the fact that I don't have any family . . . or anybody else . . . would that have anything to do with why I was selected for this job?" He didn't answer me immediately. First, he started up the car and fiddled with the rear view mirror for a moment.

"Matter of fact, it does. That was one of the factors, among many others, that was taken into consideration."

"It's that dangerous?"

"It's that dangerous, but there's more to it than that. Just hang on until 7:30 tonight, Lightfoot. All of your questions will be answered."

"O.K., I'll lay off. You're a mighty mysterious man, Clarence Jones. You and your 'special and very sensitive project.' How did you come to be involved in cloak and dagger stuff? I thought you Secret Service types were primarily bodyguards. I thought the CIA or the FBI ran around doing the stuff you're doing."

Clarence continued to drive sedately through the winter countryside. "I guess I've been involved in what you're calling 'cloak and dagger stuff' ever since I've been with the Old Man. As I told you back in Nevada, until June of 1942, I was a harmless associate professor of history at Notre Dame. I marched straight from grading my students' final exams to the recruiting office. A quotation kept running through my mind, something Oliver Wendell Holmes once said, 'It is required of a man that he share the passion and action of his time—at peril of being judged not to have lived.' An incurable romantic, perhaps that's what I am. I had visions of being a latter day Stephen Crane or Joyce Kilmer. I don't know.

"Anyway, to make a very long story short, somebody decided that SHAEF needed a historian because history was being made. I wound up on Ike's staff before I knew what hit me. I became somewhat of a curiosity there because of my photographic memory. People were flabbergasted when they saw a historian who took no notes, just leafed through reports, maps, charts, and orders of battle. The day when Ike found out that he had a man on his staff who could flip through a three-foot stack of intelligence reports, tables of organization and equipment, and so forth, then read them back in his mind's eye verbatim, was the day Ike made me a major and made sure that I went everywhere with him. We grew especially close to each other during all the planning for D-Day. There were a million things that had to be taken into account— meteorology, times of high and low tides along the coastal areas of Europe, topography, organizational charts, tables of personnel and distribution of equipment, radio codes, intelligence estimates on the strength and locations of all enemy units in Europe, technical specifications and capabilities of all the weapons that would be used on each side, times of sunrise and sunset, strengths and locations of the Resistance units . . . Well, Ike just had me look at every scrap of paper that came into his office; then he carted me around with him instead of a briefcase. In all modesty, it would have taken more than a briefcase anyway to carry around all the stuff I carried in my head. Around fall of 1944, the Old Man thought of yet another use for my freakish talent—as the ultimate courier, a courier who needed to carry no papers or microfilms or anything. I had my share of adventures, and, as I told you in Nevada, my errands brought me into direct contact with a lot of high-level people—Stalin, Churchill, Montgomery, De Gaulle, Bradley—the lot. I collected a veritable treasure trove of anecdotes that I'll never be able to tell, used my mind to 'photograph' more documents in English, French, German, Russian, Italian, and code than I care to remember, and logged so many miles I swore that after the war I was going to never wander any more than ten blocks from my house for a long, long time."

"So how come you wound up in the Secret Service?"

"The Old Man," Clarence shrugged. "After the election, he called me to ask me to come back to work for him in my old capacity. 'As a historian?' I asked. 'No,' he said, 'historians I don't need. Washington is full of them. I want you to be at my side, ready with all the facts I need, just like during the war. I also need a man I can trust implicitly to take care of highly confidential and sensitive projects and missions. Someone with a low profile who can come and go as he wishes from the White House at all hours without arousing any attention.' I objected, thanking him for the offer, but said that I was quite content to be back at Notre Dame teaching history. Then he hit me in my weak spot, 'Jones,' he said, 'would you rather be teaching history, or helping to make it?' And, my friend, that's how Clarence David Jones, mild-mannered history professor, became a G-man." Jones pull the car over to the side of the narrow road.

"This is my favorite place. I think you'll like it too." We had parked next to an imposing statue of Robert E. Lee astride Traveller. We gazed at the statue in silence for a moment; then Clarence turned around and gestured across the open field to the top of Cemetery Ridge. "You see that small clump of trees at the top of the ridge?" I nodded. "That was their objective. It's just a little more than a mile away. At about one o'clock on July 3, Confederate artillery opened up from these woods to the right and left of us, 140 guns in what was the biggest artillery bombardment in history. No one had ever seen anything like it. The firing went on for two hours in an attempt to soften up the center of the Union line. The Union guns were responding, and, to many, it seemed like the end of the world. Finally, a little after three o'clock, when the guns on both sides fell silent and the ground stopped shaking, the silence was eerie. What happened next only added to the haunting, otherworldly atmosphere. In the hush that followed, 15,000 gray-and butternut-clad men emerged from these woods, 15,000 men in a line a mile wide. Up ahead on Cemetery Ridge, the Union troops were awestruck. Because what they saw, as Bruce Catton describes it, 'was an army with banners, moving out from the woods into the open field . . . moving out of shadow into eternal legend, rank upon endless rank drawn up with parade-ground precision, battle flags tipped forward, sunlight glinting from musket barrels—General George Picket's Virginians, and ten thousand men from other commands, men doomed to try the impossible and to fail.' In another of his works, Catton suggests that Pickett's Charge was the Civil War in microcosm—doomed from the very beginning to failure, it was a gallant effort to storm the very stars themselves. And still, through sheer raw courage and will, it almost succeeded.

"Lee stood here and watched them go, three divisions of his incomparable Army of Northern Virginia. He watched Union artillery blow huge gaps in their ranks, then saw the ranks close up as his men continued marching across that bloody mile. When they reached Emmitsburg Road up there, about the halfway mark, the line narrowed, as they all prepared to converge on that clump of trees. Once across the road, they began to double time as the Union troops poured increasingly withering fire into their ranks. The Union artillery began to use canister, then as the Confederates got closer, double canister, mowing down whole companies like ripened wheat. The lines began to ripple as they got within musket range of the Union troops. They were outnumbered, outgunned, and the enemy held the high ground. Nevertheless, through sheer iron nerve and guts, they breached the Union line. You see that low stone wall to the left of the trees? That's where they broke through. General Armistead led two hundred men through the line, and, for a brief time, silenced the Union guns at that point. But it was too late. The Unions troops quickly rallied, and, in any event, there were by that time simply no Confederate troops left to exploit the situation. There was bitter hand-to-hand fighting, and the gap was closed. Armistead and most of his men were killed. And that, my friend, marks the High Water Mark of the Confederacy. The Charge of the Light Brigade was a fair fight compared to this.

"Lee began to ride forward to meet the dazed and bloody survivors," Clarence said as we walked forward, and I got a vivid picture of it in my mind's eye. The grand, gray, beloved old man with his regal bearing, for whom his men would have gladly marched into hell. And just had. "No one had ever seen him like this," Clarence continued. "'It's all my fault,' he kept repeating to them. 'It's all my fault.' Neither the Army of Northern Virginia, nor, I suspect, General Lee, was ever able to recover from what happened on this field that day." Clarence ended softly. The wind picked up and screamed through the barren trees in the wintry landscape. The sky darkened suddenly and, for some inexplicable reason, I could see that gallant old man looking down upon me from that majestic horse, ineffable pain in his eyes, saying softly, "It's all my fault." Just for a moment, that man was Eisenhower. I shivered and pulled my collar tighter around my neck.

At precisely 7:30 p.m., we were ushered into Ike's study. Except for the comfortable leather-upholstered couch and two matching armchairs, it was spartan by anyone's standards. The President's Texan origins were reflected in the two Frederic Remingtons on the wall and a well-used Winchester 1873 carbine that hung on two wooden pegs over the stone fireplace. Otherwise, the walls were lined with bulging bookshelves. A small rollback desk occupied one corner, and a large and sturdy mahogany conference table was set squarely in the middle of the room, with six straight-backed chairs around it. A globe sat on the table. Ike rose from one of the armchairs as we entered, setting aside the book he'd been reading

"Clarence, Captain O'Brien, welcome. Come on," he said, taking off his reading glasses, "let's go over to the table." He sat at the head and Jones and I sat on either side of him. We sat quietly; he seemed to be lost in thought. My pulse must have been hitting 120 before he finally spoke. It seemed that the beating of my heart must have been audible in the stillness.

"Captain, I've had my share, more than my share of moments which made history, of difficult decisions, and of directing that . . . remarkable courses of action be taken. Moments totally without precedent in human history." He stopped and gave a faint smile. "And if that opening doesn't scare you, I want you to know that it sure scares me.

"Quite seriously, I must confess that even in my wildest dreams I have never envisaged a meeting like this. Frankly, I find myself at a loss for words, although I've spent long hours trying to find them . . ." He took out his reading glasses again, and absently began to polish them, seeming to sink into a strange reverie. A moment went by like this, then he shook himself and spoke briskly. "As a general rule, the best place to begin is usually at the beginning. Clarence, would you please begin the briefing by sketching in some of the technical background for the captain?"

"Yes, Mr. President." Jones leaned across the table toward me. "Lightfoot, there are three ages of modern physics, although the general public, for security reasons, is as yet aware of only two. First, we had classical or Newtonian physics. Isaac Newton's *Principia* was published in 1687. His physical theories described a beautiful clockwork universe and were accepted as inviolate for two centuries. His three basic building blocks were the law of inertia, the law stating that the acceleration of an object is equal to the force acting on it divided by its mass, and third, the venerable law of action and reaction. Every school kid still learns Newtonian physics because in any fixed inertial frame of reference, Newton's laws hold true.

"However, once you get into the late 1880's and into the 1890's, you run into some phenomena that just don't square with Newtonian physics. The real kickoff was the Michelson-Morley experiment in 1887. It was designed to detect the motion of the earth through the ether by measuring the difference in velocity of two perpendicular beams of light. Results of experiment: the ether that Newton had insisted permeated the universe did not exist. Newtonian physics was at a complete loss. Neither could it explain some of the questions raised by the discovery of other phenomena in the 1890s—Henri Becquerel's discovery of radioactivity in uranium, William Roentgen's discovery of x-rays, or J. J. Thomson's proof of the existence of the electron.

"Well, Albert Einstein, who had incorporated Planck's quantum mechanics into his own unique and brilliant special theory of relativity, could and did explain these things in 1905, thus ushering in the second age of modern physics—the Einsteinian Age. As was the case with Newtonian physics before it, the practical applications of Einsteinian physics explained and predicted many heretofore inexplicable and unpredictable events. Many new discoveries were made; many doors were opened. We learned to think in a new way. While Newton had held that time and space were separate, Einstein proved that they are not. Something can't exist at some place without existing at some time and neither can it exist at some time without existing at some place. He said that there is no such thing as space *and* time; there is only space-time. While Newton had us living in a three-dimensional universe, Einstein showed us that, in fact, we live in a four-dimensional universe—or, to be more precise, a four dimensional space-time continuum. It was a whole new ball game. Solid geometry was thrown out the window. It was now fourth-dimensional, or space-time, geometry that the universe had to be described in terms of. Traditional mathematics couldn't cope with the Einsteinian model; a whole new calculus, called tensor calculus, had to be invented.

"Well, things went swimmingly for a while. Then, just like Newtonian physics before it, Einsteinian physics met its Waterloo; something happened which it said could never happen. But first, some background: you see, according to this equation ...," Clarence scribbled on a legal pad. He then slid it to the middle of the table and pointed to it:

$$L' = L \sqrt{1 - \frac{v^2}{c^2}}$$

"According to this equation," he repeated, "which governs

the contraction of an object with velocity, you can see that the faster an object travels, the shorter it becomes. As *v* approaches the velocity of light, *c*, the length of the object approaches zero. When *v* equals *c*, the length *is* zero. The object no longer has length; it disappears. O.K., suppose *v* exceeds *c*. Let's say the object is traveling at twice the speed of light, or 2*c*. That gives you minus three under the radical. This means that the length of the object is now its original length times the square root of minus three. *But*, any mathematician will tell you that you cannot take the square root of a negative number—such a number is imaginary. Therefore, in this case, the length of the object will be imaginary, and the object will no longer exist.

"Now let's take a look at another of Einstein's equations." Clarence scribbled again and showed me the results:

$$m' = \frac{m}{\sqrt{1 - \frac{v^2}{c^2}}}$$

"The *m* here is for mass. You can see that as *v* increases, the radical in the denominator decreases, and, since the value of a fraction increases as the denominator decreases, the mass of the object will increase. If *v* increases to the point where it is equal to *c*, the velocity of light, the denominator becomes zero, which means that the mass becomes infinite.

"Einsteinian physics, then, obviously shows us that nothing can travel faster than light. Clearly, the velocity of light is the maximum possible velocity. There it is, engraved in stone. Just like Newton's ether. Enter tachyons.

"Up until the mid '30's, there was universal agreement among physicists that the only subatomic particles were electrons, protons, positrons, and neutrons. Period. Then, in 1935, the Japanese physicist Hideki Yukawa theorized the existence of a particle of mass intermediate between that of the electron and the proton. In 1936, Anderson and Neddermeyer discovered such a particle.

It's called a μ meson, or muon. There are two muons, one positive and one negative, each with equal mass and a charge equal to the electron's. They're highly unstable, each decays into an electron of the same sign, plus two neutrinos, with a half-life of about 2.3×10^{-6} second. That's 0.0000023 of a second to us laymen. In 1947, another family of mesons was discovered: π mesons, or pions. Then things just took off.

"In the eleven years since, a whole new branch of physics, high-energy physics, has emerged. Scientists have discovered, accelerated, employed in interactions, and otherwise tinkered around with mesons, or kaons, nucleons, Λ, Σ, $\equiv$, and Ω hyperons, and a whole host of other hadrons and leptons. And one of these years, word of quarks is going to leak out. Scientists have been discovering more and more particles all the time. A case of the more you learn, the more you realize you don't know. Every new discovery raises fifty new questions." Ike cleared his throat. "To get to the point," Clarence continued quickly, "a subatomic particle called a tachyon was discovered just this past January. Its name comes from the Greek word 'tachys,' which means swift. An appropriate name, really. It travels faster than the speed of light." For what seemed an eternity, the only sound in the room was the stately measured ticking of the antique clock on the mantel. Then Clarence resumed.

"So, in turn, Einsteinian physics was revealed to fall short of the mark just as Newtonian physics before it. It's a mistake to think that either of them is wrong; they're not. They're just incomplete. They're both models which hold true up to a point—that point being fixed inertial frames of reference with Newtonian physics and velocities greater than the speed of light with Einsteinian physics. Once you attain speeds faster than the speed of light, all bets are off. Or perhaps I should say were off, because now we move into the third age of modern physics, Jankorian physics. Erbil Jankor . . ."

"I never heard of him," I said. Ike smiled tightly. "Almost no one has or possibly ever will. The lid on Jankorian research makes the Manhattan Project look like show and tell time."

"The President's hit the nail on the head. Jankor is a genius, quite eccentric, and lives for his work itself; he neither wants nor needs any recognition. There are only four other scientists in the entire country who can understand what he's talking about, and even they're not too sure sometimes. All four readily agreed to work under his direction at Oak Ridge, and they'd do it even if we didn't pay them. That's how excited they are about this. They swear it's the biggest thing since the discovery of electricity."

Already my thoughts began to race wildly. So that was it! I was going to pilot a spacecraft that could travel faster than the speed of light! They were talking about a starship!

"Clarence," the President said gently, "get to the point. Can't you see that you've got our young friend here worked up to a fever pitch?"

"Yes sir. O.K., Lightfoot, let's back up a moment to Einsteinian physics, specifically to the time dilation equation. One of Einstein's equations which is sometimes used to 'prove' that nothing can travel faster than the speed of light is this one." He scribbled once again on the pad of legal paper and slid it toward me:

$$ t' = t \sqrt{1 - \frac{v^2}{c^2}} $$

"In other words, as velocity increases, time slows. If v is equal to c, the speed of light, time is totally suspended, and, if v exceeds c, you run into the same situation we did a few minutes ago in discussing the Fitzgerald-Lorentz contraction, which is that the number you get will be an imaginary number. What we're talking about is imaginary time. The equation was and still is perfectly acceptable as long as you don't look at anything that goes faster than the speed of light. That's the limitation, the boundary if you will, of Einsteinian physics—the speed of light. Once you enter the realm of hyperlight speed, you need a new model."

Jones stopped and took a deep breath. "Now here's where you better hang onto your hat, Lightfoot. This is what you've come all this way to hear: Jankorian physics coincides with Einsteinian physics up to c, but proves beyond any shadow of a doubt that, at speeds in excess of light, there is a time reversal effect."

I stared at Clarence, and he looked inquiringly at Ike. This was easily the greatest breakthrough and the greatest secret in the history of civilization, and he was, even at this point, reluctant to go ahead and say the next couple of sentences. Ike nodded.

"What it is is this, Lightfoot if you can accelerate an object beyond the speed of light, you can send it backward into time, the fourth dimension." I looked at Jones and then at the President, then back to Jones, then back to the President. My mouth opened, but no sound came out. Clarence continued. "That's why it took so long for scientists to discover the existence of those crazy tachyons. They're so ephemeral because they're traveling through *time* as well as through space. They're only in our space-time window for about one ten-millionth of a second. We catch them 'on the run' so to speak."

I'd regained my voice, if not my composure. "I must be misunderstanding you. This is straight out of H. G. Wells."

"Precisely," answered Ike. "Wells also accurately forecast a lot of other things that were quite incredible at the time."

"You're telling me that it's actually possible to . . ." Ike and Clarence nodded. "But that's . . ."

"Yes," said Clarence, "it does appear to be quite impossible. A perfectly natural first reaction. We all had the same initial reaction. But that just proves how limited, how small, our own minds and imaginations are. 'It can't be so because we can't conceive of it.' Rubbish. Rubbish that we haven't managed to jettison even in the middle of the twentieth century. I forget who said it, but someone once remarked, 'Not only is the universe stranger than we imagine, it's stranger than we are *able* to imagine.'"

"But how can it be done?"

"As you may suspect, we're talking here about an enormous amount of power," Clarence replied, "an amount of energy that we can't even comprehend, energy far beyond what can be approached even through known techniques of atomic fission and fusion."

"So what's the answer? How do you produce, let alone harness, such power?" Clarence looked at Ike once more and received the nod.

"Antimatter."

"Antimatter?"

"Yes, the analogue of matter. As far back as 1932, some scientists speculated that there might be antiprotons, bearing the same relation to the proton as the positron does to the electron, that is, particles with the same mass as the proton but negatively charged. In 1955, proton-antiproton pairs were created by impact on a stationary target of a beam of protons with a kinetic energy of 6 GeV (6×10^9 eV) at the Bevatron at the University of California at Berkeley.

"But to go one step beyond that—to construct whole atoms of antimatter—took some doing. Nevertheless, seven months ago, under highly controlled experimental conditions at the L-2 Facility at Oak Ridge, Dr. Jankor created a carbon atom of antimatter, or anticarbon. History will, we believe, mark that day as the beginning of a whole new era."

"But why?"

"As I said, the power. You see, antimatter is quite inert, quite safe, as long as it doesn't make contact with its counterpart in matter. However, once an amount of antimatter, say for example, an ounce of anticopper, is combined with an ounce of copper . . . well, the energy released would be enough to put North America into orbit. It makes atomic fission and fusion look like very primitive techniques by comparison. And indeed they are. In the pre-Jankorian world, there was simply no known way to convert matter completely into energy. For example, when you burn wood or oil or coal or gasoline or whatever, sure, you've converted matter into heat energy, but the energy output is not very impressive when you look at all the matter which has *not* been converted into energy, but into other substances: ashes, exhaust, soot, residue, charcoal, smoke, and so forth. Byproducts. Waste. Even in atomic fission, although there is a vast increase in efficiency, there is still matter residue. However, in matter-antimatter reactions, *all* matter is converted into energy, and the speed and totality of the conversion . . . provide for incredible, hitherto undreamed of, power." Clarence reached into his pocket and brought out the inevitable corn cob and pouch of tobacco. Ike shook his head and smiled at me.

"Capitan, this man's mind never fails to amaze me. May I offer you a drink?"

"No sir. Thanks, but now that I'm on the edge of my seat, I'd just as soon continue with the briefing. I have the feeling that we're just about to get to the bottom line."

"And so we are, Captain," Ike said without preamble. "We intend to send you back into time."

9

"**B**ack . . . into time," I echoed woodenly.

"Yes."

"But surely that's impossible."

"Son, when you get to be my age, you'll no longer have that word in your vocabulary."

"But . . ."

"Clarence, you've been doing an excellent job so far, please continue."

"Yes sir. It's like this, Lightfoot. First, all particles—electrons, photons, tachyons, whatever—share a dual wave-particle nature. Like a beam of light, a stream of particles can be focused, amplified, and directed toward any target you wish. Second, unstable particles *decay*. Pions decay into muons, which in turn decay into electrons; lambda particles decay into protons, and so forth. Tachyons are unstable. Third, Jankorian physics is able to tell us at exactly what rate particles decay. Fourth, as tachyons decay, their speed slows. They ultimately reach a point where they cease to exist because all their mass has been converted into energy.

"Therefore, we can control how far a beam of tachyons will travel by controlling its speed at release. Obviously, the faster the speed, the further it will travel back into time before ceasing to exist.

At the L-2 Facility in Oak Ridge, we've built a super accelerator according to Dr. Jankor's specifications. Using the power generated by a controlled interaction between a grain of zinc and a grain of antizinc, we can get tachyons up to about any speed we want.

"That beam, along with anything 'riding' on that beam, such as you and your equipment, for example, can be sent back into anytime and anyplace with an accuracy of up to plus or minus one month per 500 years and plus or minus two kilometers in distance."

"How do I 'ride' the beam?"

"Nobody except Jankor seems to really understand it. But the general idea is that the atoms of your body and equipment, and, more importantly, the spaces *between* the atoms of your body and equipment will be stretched out, the gaps widened. The sizes of the atoms and molecules and the distances between them will be terrifically increased, but their relative positions to each other will not change. This expansion will be effected in a chamber set into the L-2 cyclotron. The Jankor Cyclotron, a circular accelerator capable of generating particle energies between a few million and several hundreds of billions of electron volts, is where the tachyons are generated at a central source, the core, and are accelerated spirally outward in a plane at right angles to a fixed magnetic field by an alternating electric field. When the tachyons reach the speed we want, your particles are polarized and inserted into the stream, where they are magnetically attracted to the tachyons. The tachyons are then focused and beamed out to their space-time destination. You 'ride' the beam. As the velocity of the tachyons decreases, the atoms and molecules of your body and equipment begin to contract, to spring back to their original distances between each other; remember, their *relative* positions with respect to each other have never changed. When the velocity hits zero and the tachyons cease to exist, you are you once again, and your trip through space-time will have lasted, in your relative time, two ten-millionths of a second."

Next Ike spoke. "O'Brien, we'd be less than candid if we didn't tell you that although every last equation checks out, it may not work. Jankor and the other physicists will tell you that it's no more dangerous than crossing a street or riding in an elevator, but remember that this is their lives' work. Quite understandably, they may play down the risk involved. They don't want to spook you."

"I understand, sir. But where are you sending me?"

Ike leaned back in his chair, and, putting his index finger alongside his nose, suddenly looked remarkably like Kris Kringle, twinkle in the eye and all. "Ah, now that's an interesting question, is it not? One that we wrestled with for weeks—especially because of the cost in terms of money and resources. Aside from the magnitude of the scientific breakthrough and the secrecy, that's something else that this operation has in common with the Manhattan Project—tremendous cost. We needn't go into the specifics here. I'm sure that columns of figures bore you at least as much as they bore me. Let it suffice to say that for the foreseeable future, we can afford only one trip. This made an already difficult decision a thousand times more so.

"I convened a very small and very special task force to consider the question." The President shook his head sadly in reminiscence. "The Director of the CIA wanted to send you back to 1917 Russia so that you could somehow prevent the Bolsheviks from coming into power. He also expressed a great deal of interest in the possibility of your assassinating, in order of preference, Marx, Lenin, Trotsky, Stalin, and Engels." Ike had been ticking off the names on the fingers of his left hand, "and a host of others. The Chairman of the Joint Chiefs of Staff wanted to send you back to December 6, 1941, so that you have a whole day to warn of the Japanese attack on Pearl Harbor. Had our Pacific fleet not been so thoroughly crippled at the very outset of the war, he argues, the war would have been considerably shortened, not to speak of saving the lives of the more than 2400 people killed. The Director of the Smithsonian, a man whom I greatly admire, was certain that the only thing to do was to send you back to prevent the assassination of Lincoln. The Secretary of State, on the other hand, insisted that you be sent back to kill Hitler when he was nothing more than a two-bit paper hanger . . . pretty heady stuff, isn't it?" I could only nod in agreement. Ike had stopped smiling that tired smile, and he now leaned forward. "It surely hasn't escaped you that there's a common thread running through all these scenarios?"

"Revolution, assassinations, violence . . ."

"Precisely . . . you know, this is a great, I might even say a miraculous, opportunity for the human race. It would be a shame; it would be criminal to use it to kill people. I refuse to use it to send out an assassin, even an assassin who would assassinate evil people. By the same token, it would be a waste or could even be a mistake to use it to alter a single isolated event—*if* history can be altered at all, but we'll get to that later. What if, for example, you prevented the sinking of the *Titanic?* On the surface, you've saved more than 1500 lives. Good. But good enough to justify the terrific national effort to carry out this project? Then too, what if one or more of the 1500 you saved turned out to be an evil person? What if you saved a potential American or British Hitler? Or a Jack the Ripper? You begin to get the idea.

"Panic reigned over western Europe in 1348 and 1349. Over one-third of the entire population died from the Black Plague. What if we shipped you and some crates of vaccine back to exactly the right time and the right place to prevent the epidemic before it even got started? A good idea? I don't really know. Perhaps the only thing we'd achieve would be to hasten all the problems brought on by an overcrowded planet.

"No, I'm afraid that whole line of thinking is barking up the wrong tree. No one on that task force could see the forest for the trees. So I'll put it to you as I finally put it to them. What was the single greatest event in human history?"

Inside my head swirled a kaleidoscope of views at fantastic speed. Images appeared, dissolved, and were replaced with others in a totally haphazard fashion. Some cavemen crouched around a fire. The Gutenberg press, the Wright brothers at Kitty Hawk. Christopher Columbus . . . the snow outside, Christmas carols over the car radio, the birth of . . . "Jesus Christ?" I asked. The President nodded vigorously, beaming from ear to ear.

"Clarence, I think you may have found us the right boy." My mind reeled.

"Sir, Mr. President, do you mean that you want me to go back to . . ."

10

★ ★ ★ ★ ★

"**M**eet Jesus Christ," Ike finished for me. "Yes, that's precisely what I mean."

"But what do you want me to do?"

"Listen to Him, observe Him, speak to Him, follow Him. Then report to us. If at all possible, I want you to approach Him in private, to tell Him who you are and where you come from. And then ask Him . . . I scarcely know how to put this . . . ask Him if we, the United States, if we are on the right track. Write down everything about Him that you see and hear, put it in your report, and when your report is finished, seal it in the vacuum canister that we've provided and bury it. We'll show you the exact place on a map."

"Bury it?" A gigantic apprehension was beginning to loom over me.

"Of course," the President replied nonplused, "unless you can think of a better way to protect your documents."

"Oh, you mean you're afraid that the documents may not survive the trip back with me, so . . ." I stopped dead when I saw the look Ike and Clarence exchanged. Clarence looked at me with distress.

"I'm sorry, Lightfoot. It's all my fault. I thought it would have been evident from my explanation of the process. The fact is you're not coming back." I sat frozen while he continued. "You see, in order to send you back, there'd have to be an installation on that end, which would have to be a sister of Oak Ridge's L-2 Facility, super cyclotron and all, so that another tachyon beam could be generated, amplified, and focused, and expansion and polarization of your constituent particles effected . . ." He spread his hands eloquently.

"So," the President picked up, "we're providing you with a very special canister. When your records are complete, you put them in the canister, lock it, and throw away the key. Actually, come to think of it, destroying the key by melting it down would be better. At any rate, after locking the canister, you flip a red toggle switch on the lid. That automatically evacuates the interior. Next, you flip a yellow toggle switch. That releases pure nitrogen gas inside to further protect the documents. Bury the canister at a spot we've predesignated. Just to cover our bet, in case of a little navigational error on your part, a quantity of several radioactive isotopes with extremely long half-lives will be embedded in the outer cover of the canister, so we'll be able to use a Geiger counter to locate it. The isotopes will also aid in dating the canister. We'll be running a lot of tests besides the old Carbon 14 to determine and to prove how long the canister's been buried.

"After you've completed your report, sealed it in the canister, and buried the canister, your mission is completed. Go anywhere in the world, pursue any occupation. The only thing we ask is that you don't attempt to alter history, whether by violence, the introduction of advanced technology, becoming politically active, becoming a prophet or seer, or anything else that might affect history." I sat in mounting horror as I listened to the President's calm, reasonable, and well-modulated voice. I was simply unable to respond. After a long silence, Clarence spoke.

"Another very important point, Lightfoot. When you delve this deeply into theoretical physics, you reach the point where philosophy and science seem to converge. There are, as you know, a number of classic time-travel paradoxes. What happens if you go back and through design or accident, cause the death of your great grandfather before your grandfather was conceived? Or, is that, by virtue of the fact that you *have* traveled back, impossible? What if . . . well, there are a lot of what ifs. One of the most important, and this is why, during your training phase, we want you to bone up, not only on the history of the world during the first half of the first century, but on world history in general," he stopped to tap the ashes from his pipe into the large glass ash tray. "Time is an invention of man." He extracted a pipe tool from his pocket and began to methodically ream out the bowl, seemingly with great concentration.

"Time is an invention of man. There is a school of thought that compares time to a river. We are on a boat traveling down that river. As we pass certain landmarks, or activities, and they fade from our view, well, that doesn't mean they cease to exist. A time traveler is a man who leaves the boat, swims to shore, and walks back upstream. Everything is still there, just as it was when he passed it in the boat. And he can go to any chosen point and see it again. It's not a bad analogy, as far as analogies go, and can serve to illustrate a few points: first, can you, from the bank of the river, so to speak, influence anything, or are you merely an observer? You're no longer in the boat. The great-greatgrandfather paradox again. If you go back, will you be able to physically interact, or will you be nothing more than a ghostly shadow viewing things from a nether world? Or, perhaps time travelers, perhaps even you, have *already* changed some historical events and we just don't know about it.

"Second, some highly respected people postulate that, just as there are whirlpools and eddies in the current of a river, so there are in the river of time. Events which are so powerful and have such monumental importance that they act as vortexes. You could be drawn to and sucked into a vortex. A vortex could be viewed as a navigational hazard on the river or as a stupendous opportunity to change history at some crucial pivotal point. In short, in spite of our best efforts to send you back to the time of Christ, you could be diverted along the way and find yourself in Ford's Theater moments before John Wilkes Booth pulled the trigger. You could find yourself at Philadelphia in 1776, at Hastings in 1066, on board the Lusitania in 1915, sailing with Christopher Columbus in 1492, or, as we profoundly hope, and pray, at the side of Jesus Christ at the height of His ministry. But the plain fact, Lightfoot, is that just about anything could happen," he said, quietly laying his pipe in the ashtray.

"Including me not getting reassembled at all. Including . . ."

Jones shrugged. "It's very easy indeed to get yourself killed as a test pilot or as an astronaut, and you were more than ready to sign on the dotted line for those jobs. You flew twice as many combat missions as you had to in Korea."

"That was different," I turned to Ike, "With all due respect, sir, you've got the wrong man. What you want is a man who's . . . more . . . religious than I am."

"That's exactly what I don't want, Captain. I want the closest thing to a totally objective man that I can possibly find. I do *not* want to send a man dedicated to proving that Christ was God. I do not want an apologist; I want a witness. I want a man who'll report exactly what he sees and hears. No more and no less. We did our homework; long before Clarence interviewed you, we had reviewed everything that had ever been committed to paper about you—school records, military records, a special psychiatric profile prepared by a panel of the three best psychiatrists in the CIA. We know you're not a Christian. It doesn't matter; if anything, for the purposes of this exercise, it's a plus.

"No doubt a lot of questions that seemed strange to you at the time of your interview with Clarence are now beginning to fall into place. Nevertheless, let me spell some of it out for you. We went after a fighter pilot with combat experience because such a man is trained and accustomed to assess a situation quickly and act decisively. When you're in a fighter and moving at several hundred miles an hour, the ground below you a blur, you don't waver and hesitate. You make judgments and you act instantly and instinctively. That attribute can turn out to be critical in this mission, especially if there's anything to this vortex business. You may arrive at a totally unexpected but pivotal point in history and find that you have only a moment to act or not to act, as the case may be. We can't possibly brief you on every contingency. Which, as I've said, is why we also wanted a man with a passion for, and a sense of history.

"We wanted a man with an excellent aptitude for languages because you'll have to learn first century Aramaic in a very short time. You'll also need to brush up on the classical Greek you took in college, as well as learn as much Hebrew as you can, given the little time you have to prepare for the mission.

"We wanted a young man in excellent physical condition, and with no dependents, for obvious reasons.

"Your combat record and your legendary performance at survival school interested us greatly because—above all else—our man must be a *survivor*. He must have the will to survive, the stamina, the intelligence to improvise, and the ability to think and analyze when his subconscious is telling him to panic. He must be a man who is cool under pressure. He must also be the quintessential loner because he's going on the mission alone, he can confide in no one, and he can never come back.

"Above all, I say, above all, he must be an honest man. It may interest you to know that the code name for the selection and recruitment phase of the operation was 'Project Diogenes.' Deep down you must have been wondering why we would be so eager to recruit an obscure captain in the Nevada desert for a mission of such magnitude that it's being run out of the Oval Office. A man with your record and your abilities should be a major, going on lieutenant colonel. But you're on a shelf.

"Let's speak frankly, O'Brien. You've made a lot of enemies and precious few friends. You're not academy, and you have no influential connections. You're in a dead-end job in a dead-end squadron on a dead-end air base in the desert. You'll stay there until you're passed over for the third time for major, at which point you'll be forced into involuntary retirement. Men like you are very important in wartime. You're given medals and promotions and you belong. In peacetime, no one seems to know quite what to do with you. At best, you're not needed; at worst, you're an embarrassment. So they stick you in some out-of-the-way place just like they put a ship in mothballs, and let you gather crud, hoping they'll never need you again."

I felt the hot flush in my face as the President's words hit home. The truth hurt; it hurt a lot. I struggled to control my voice. "You certainly do know how to be frank, sir. If I may be permitted to be equally frank, as a student of human history, I have every confidence that another war is just around the corner. Then 'men like me' will be in demand once more."

"Cynicism," the President nodded in apparent satisfaction, "that's one of the other qualities we wanted as well." That only made me madder.

"Then may I ask why you did pick me, sir?"

"Of course, I was just coming to that. You see, we know *why* you've been shelved, and that makes all the difference. We know about your refusal to confirm a kill supposedly made by General Parkinson's son, Lt. Paul Parkinson. A great deal of pressure was brought to bear on you since it would have meant that Lieutenant Parkinson would have finished the Korean War as an 'ace.' It meant a lot to him, and it meant even more to his father. So General Parkinson leaned on your wing commander, your squadron commander, your flight commander, and all creatures great and small in your chain of command. 'Look, O'Brien,' they all said, 'what's the big deal? The kid's probably telling the truth anyway. It's no skin off your nose. Just say you saw him shoot down a plane. You were the only other pilot in the area at the time; otherwise; we'd get someone else to do it. Just confirm the kill and everybody'll be happy.' But you didn't."

"I didn't see the plane go down." Ike nodded and continued.

"Then there was that matter at Kadena Air Force Base on Okinawa. You had a minor accident with a jeep and insisted that you pay for the fender bending out of your own pocket because you said it was your fault. The motor pool OIC kept trying to dissuade you from that. He said to forget about it; they'd repair it. He didn't want to fill out all those forms. You insisted, you paid for it, and you also got the reputation as a screwball and a troublemaker.

"At Clark Air Force Base in the Philippines, you refused to accept 'gifts' from suppliers to the Officers Club when you were a junior member on the club's board of directors. One of the consequences of your action was the discovery of improper conduct on the part of some of the other board members; there was subsequent disciplinary action, and one of those affected was your squadron commander.

"We know of other incidents as well. 'This above all, to thine own self be true,' Captain?"

"Honor, sir. Without that, a man is nothing."

"Well put. 'Duty, honor, country' is the way MacArthur likes to put it. And as vexatious as that man has been to presidents past, I for one like him. No, Captain, you're the man for the job. And now, to business. H-hour is set for 2019 hours Eastern Daylight Time on July 8. The unusual timing is set by technical constraints. If we miss that time window, we'd have to wait for two more years, and, in July of 1961, someone else is going to be in the White House. Whoever it turns out to be may not give the green light for the mission. Even if he does, I wouldn't be here to see it. I want to shoot for this coming July. I know it's a big decision, but may I have it by 2000 hours on the day after tomorrow? If it's yes, we've got to get moving. If it's no, there are two other candidates for the job I want Clarence to interview."

"Yes sir. I'll make my decision no later than then." Ike stood up, and Clarence and I rose too. The President extended his hand. "Good luck, son. I'll pray that you make the right decision."

"Thank you, Mr. President," I said, shaking his hand. "If I go, I won't let you down. I'll give it all I've got." A faint smile played about his lips.

"I know that. I didn't get to be where I am by misjudging men, Lightfoot."

11

★ ★ ★ ★ ★

I longed to go out into the desert to think. To be out in the middle of the desert living off the food that the desert supplies. To sit in perfect solitude watching the sunrise and sunset. To lie out under the clear chill canopy of a myriad of bright stars, the only sounds those of the creatures of the desert. In such an atmosphere a man can think. A man cannot think in a building, especially in a city. Although the Eisenhower farm was not in a built-up area, it was still a man-made habitat; it was still civilization. It would have to do though. As least I was not in a city, where even in "the still of the night" a man's mind is continuously assailed by trucks and buses thundering by outside like crazed leviathans, their horns trumpeting for others to stand clear, the wail of police sirens, the blaring of a neighbor's stereo set, the flushing of a toilet, the hysterical shriek of fire engines racing through the night, the angry and suspicious barking of a guard dog, the distant sound of factory whistles greeting the midnight shift, the mournful wailing of an ambulance, the ponderous hourly bonging of huge clocks in steeples and towers, automobile engines coughing and sputtering into life, brakes squealing, the minute settling of the foundation, the creaking of the beams in the house, the kicking on of the furnace or air conditioner, the ticking of a watch.

Can a man think in such a cacophony? The insane asylums are full of people who have tried. Only when a man is away from, apart from other men and the works of man can he see visions and dream great dreams. Only then can he put his spirit in order and see where he has been and where he is going, and where he must go. I did the best I could under the circumstances. I turned off the furnace and everything else that could be turned off, including the refrigerator. I took the phone off the hook. I unplugged everything that was plugged in, including the clock. I sat cross-legged on the hearth and stared into the roaring fire, blocking out all else around me. Years before I had chosen the way of the warrior. I had become skilled in my life's work and, with one exception, could look back to my accomplishments with pride. Now I was being asked to become a reporter, a scribe. They were asking me, Aloysius Lightfoot O'Brien, to become an observer rather than a doer. Unthinkable. And yet . . .

And yet, I was being presented with the opportunity to undertake what was undeniably the greatest adventure in history.

But never to return. Never.

The hours wore on, and, as if it were planned, the very last ember in the fire went out just as the sun announced its appearance on the horizon with false dawn. What of the thoughts that went through my mind that long night? I cannot tell. They were many, varied, and, for some of them, there are no human words—only symbols that the spirit alone can understand, not the conscious mind. I had lost track of time. Standing, I took my mother's blanket from around my shoulders and folded it. I had arrived at a decision.

12

At breakfast in the Secret Service bunkhouse, I learned that the President had set aside a small area on a remote part of the farm as a sort of informal range for target practice. He used it himself to zero in his guns for hunting season and to plink with .22s, and encouraged the Secret Service boys to use it too. I grabbed some empty tin cans from the kitchen and headed there with my Colt. 45 Peacemaker. Shooting has always helped to relax me. The concentration required for good shooting blots everything else from your mind. There is just your eye, the front and rear sights, and the target, all four points falling on a perfectly straight line. Nothing else exists until a gentle squeeze from your finger sends the bullet speeding toward its target. Ten years later, in the late '60s, hundreds of thousands of upper middle-class and upper-class adolescents would "discover" that thought technique when they'd explore Eastern religions and philosophies, either never learning or conveniently overlooking the fact that this Zen exercise was developed, and reached its highest state of perfection at the hands of Buddhist warrior monks as they sharpened their archery, knife-throwing, and stick-fighting skills for combat. Like peace, man.

I was enjoying being under the open sky, drinking in the fresh air, and reveling in the comparative solitude when the President came up behind me. A Secret Service agent was about fifty yards behind him, and there was another about a hundred yards to the right, but he appeared not even to notice them. Maybe he didn't. I guess it's something you get used to. His smile was the smile of a man enjoying a private moment.

"You're pretty good with that thing, Captain. A Peacemaker, isn't it?"

"Yes sir."

"May I see it?" I handed it over, and he hefted it, appreciating the legendary balance. It had a five-and-a-half-inch barrel and weighed thirty-seven ounces. I had recently had it reblued, and the finish was almost lustrous. Although mine was only forty years old, it in no way differed from the model that Colt was turning out in 1873, nor, for that matter, from the Peacemakers that Colt is turning out today. There is a certain mystique about the Colt .45 Peacemaker, at least as far as we Westerners are concerned. Also known as the Single Action Army and the Frontier Six-Shooter, it *is* the Old West. It was used by Wild Bill Hickok, Wyatt Earp, Billy the Kid, Calamity Jane, and, when Custer went down at the Little Big Horn, it was a Colt .45 Peacemaker he was blazing away with.

Ike cocked it and squeezed off a round at a tomato can. He missed but not by much.

"You're no stranger to the Peacemaker, sir."

"No, remember I'm a Texas boy—Abilene. Not only that, but I was using a Colt .45 a good twenty years before you were born." He held it in both hands, and, as he looked down at it, his eyes took on a faraway cast. "You're an Apache, so you can appreciate this more than most. Geronimo finally surrendered the year I was born; he died when I was a nineteen-year-old cadet at West Point. In fact, some of my instructors at the Point had fought against him. Against him and Cochise. Isn't that amazing? I can clearly remember when automobiles were something you read about, a curiosity, rather than something you saw every day.

I can remember when there were no radios or aircraft. Funny, isn't it? That all in one lifetime, we've gone from that world to a world of nuclear weapons, intercontinental ballistic missiles, computers, and God knows what else." He stood frozen for a long moment looking at the Peacemaker with an expression of deep sorrow in his eyes. "And we haven't gotten any smarter." Abruptly, he shook himself and handed the gun back to me. "It's got to stop, Lightfoot. It's got to stop. We're all going down a road that can only end in a nightmare. Perhaps an eternal nightmare . . . We have only one hope, and that is God. We've taken, somewhere along the line, we've taken the wrong turn. If we don't get back on the right path and soon, our future holds nothing but horror." I stood there speechless for a long moment.

"Sir, I've decided to go."

"Good," he smiled without surprise. "You'll do a first-rate job. I'm certain of it. Clarence and I had a long talk earlier this morning. He's arranged for Aramaic lessons to be given for you in Washington by one of the foremost scholars in the country, and for some other training as well. You and he will work as a very close team in the preparation phase. While you're undergoing language and physical training, Clarence will be poring through hundreds of books in the Library of Congress gathering information on customs of the time, the geography, the literature, songs, poetry, food, prices, laws, and a hundred and one other things you'll need to know. He's suggested that you stay at his house, so you can make the best possible use of what little time we have to prepare. During the day, language, and physical training, then, when you return home in the evenings, Clarence will spend a few hours briefing you on what materials he's gleaned that day in his research."

"Oh no, sir. I couldn't inconvenience . . ."

"It's settled, O'Brien," Ike said in a tone that assured me it was. "Say," he said with a sudden smile, "that Peacemaker, it just dawned on me that must be the Peacemaker you carried when you fought your way back through enemy lines in Korea."

"Yes sir. It was my father's. He left it behind, and this," I said taking out the old railroad watch. Ike examined the watch with open admiration.

"It's a beauty. So is that Santa Fe fob. You don't see things like this around much anymore."

"No sir, you don't. I remember the night the other miners carried his body home from the bar. My mother handed me his gun and watch and said, 'You're the man of the family now.' Ever since, wherever I've gone, they've gone. I carry them with me and my mother's blanket. They are my only real possessions, the only things that mean anything to me."

"Son, do you mean that you pack that .45 wherever you go?" Ike asked incredulously.

"No sir. I only carry it on my person in a combat situation or when I'm in the desert. But it goes with my personal effects, wherever they go."

"I hope you realize that you're not taking your watch or Colt back to the first century with you."

"No sir," I said, sticking the gun back into my belt and slipping the watch back into my jeans pocket. "I hadn't really thought about it. As you know, this pistol saved my life in Korea. It also saved my life in the desert once when I used it on a rattler. I've hunted with it, done target shooting with it, and have never imagined going into any potentially dangerous situation without it. It's been a part of me since I was ten years old."

"I'm sorry, son. I can appreciate how you feel about those things. I don't see any problem with your blanket, but the gun and watch have got to stay behind. Is there anyone you'd like to have them? We'll make the arrangements."

"No sir, there's no one. That's why they mean so much to me."

"I'm sorry." He turned and began to walk away. He stopped after just a few steps and turned back.

"Lightfoot, did you really wear warpaint during your ground action in Korea?"

"Yes sir. I kept a small tube of yellow oil paint with me whenever

I flew in the event that I was shot down. I put it on the first chance I got, which was right after I sprung the POWs." Ike shook his head in wonder.

"And just where in the world did you learn guerrilla warfare and commando tactics? Surely not in Air Force flight school?"

"From the old men on the reservation, sir."

"Of course," Ike smiled and said softly, "where else?" He turned once more and walked away.

We left for Clarence's home two days later. He was going to be taking a couple of weeks of annual leave, and he needed to tie up some loose ends with the Secret Service detail before shoving off—duty rosters, training schedules, standing orders, and the like. During those two days, I just walked the frozen and deserted Gettysburg battlefield, a solitary figure lost in space and time, suspended between two worlds, wandering over the ghostly snow blown landscape.

Finally we were off, I had been longing to get moving but, at the same time, was a little afraid about the prospect of being integrated into a normal middle-class American family. I had seen "Father Knows Best" as well as "Ozzie and Harriet" on television, and I had read "Dagwood and Blondie" in the comics, and I knew I was never going to fit in. Four children. Two dogs. House in suburbia.

Well, there was nothing for it but to take one day at a time. We began the trip at about 10:00 a.m., and the snow was coming down in huge moist flakes, which, overnight, had already added an additional two inches to the snow on the ground. Jones was an expert driver and a fast one. I later learned that all Secret Service agents are. They are, after all, the people who must be able to coolly maneuver the Presidential limousine through snow and ice and a hail of gunfire all at the same time if need be. The Buick flew southward on Route 15 through the Catoctin Mountains, its powerful heater keeping its Apache occupant comfortable, despite the alien environment beyond its frosted windows. Mrs. Eisenhower, a very nice lady, had sent us off with a large thermos of steaming hot chocolate, and that too was welcome. We found a radio station that was broadcasting a dramatization of Dickens' *Christmas Carol*, and we both began to unwind.

Clarence and I took turns telling each other about our respective boyhoods. We had a tacit understanding that we'd both enjoy a few days of genuine vacation, without any intruding word or thought about the forthcoming incredible mission. We were determined to think of and speak of only happy things and innocent times. Clarence spoke of his growing up in Tennessee. He had a thousand anecdotes illustrating exactly what life in a sleepy southern hamlet in the 1920's was like. It was all there, the fishing for catfish in the river, the slingshots that had shattered the wrong windows at the wrong times, the maiden aunt with the mustache, and the slobbery kisses that invariably accompanied her exclamations of "My, how you've grown! I remember when . . . ," marble-shooting, rabbit-hunting, the school bully, the banker getting the first automobile in town, the town drunk, the one-room schoolhouse, the raiding of the watermelon patch (and how good stolen watermelon tastes), the village idiot, the first harvest hayride and the first kiss from the wholesome country gal he later married . . . it was all there and more. Clarence Jones was the nearest thing to Tom Sawyer or Huckleberry Finn that I'd ever seen. Perhaps that anyone has ever seen.

By comparison, my boyhood world was, well, just that— another world. I spoke of a one-room schoolhouse too, but one on an Indian reservation. My rabbit hunts were not through verdant pine forests, but across barren and near trackless desert. While Clarence spoke of times when he and his pals sat around the courthouse steps listening to the old men spin yarns of their fighting at Manassas, Shiloh, Antietam, Vicksburg, and Cold

Harbor, I spoke of me and my friends sitting rapt listening to the old men on the reservation tell of fighting alongside Victorio, Loco, Mangas Coloradas, Cochise, Juh, and the legend himself, Geronimo. Another difference was that everything the old men said on the reservation was true. There was no embroidery or exaggeration. For the most part, Indians do not spin yarns. Why this is so I cannot say. I supposed that it all goes back to the Apache concept of honor. In my briefing, the President had spoken of honesty and asked me for an explanation of some of my actions in years past. In response, I had simply blurted out that without honor, a man is nothing. An answer that was both good and bad at the same time. Good because it sums up all Apache metaphysics, and bad because, to an outsider, it is a woefully inadequate way to express an entire way of life.

The Japanese are usually credited with the tradition of, and adherence to the code of the warrior, and with the sanctity of a man's honor and the steadfastness of his loyalty. People think of Bushido and the Samurai when they think of death before dishonor, and of courage that springs up from a well deep within a man's spirit, making him better than he really is. We Apache have lived that code for a thousand years that we know about, and almost certainly long before. It is we who are the Samurai of the Western Hemisphere, not only in the philosophical context, but also in terms of skill, endurance, and effectiveness. In the latter part of the nineteenth century, American and European professional military men were able to lay aside their bigotry long enough to admit that mounted Apache braves were the finest light cavalry in the world.

Honor. That's what the fighting was really all about. Apache leaders weren't stupid. From 1850 on, none of the chiefs ever believed for a moment that they could win. The fighting didn't go on because of culture shock or greed or hatred, although these all played their parts in the misery recorded in human blood on the shifting desert sands. Geronimo, the last and the greatest of the war shamans, fought until 1890 because he was sickened by the loss of honor that the Chiricahua Apache had suffered at the hands of the white man. Once a proud and totally self-reliant people, free to go where they willed, they had allowed themselves to be enslaved to the point where they had become nothing more than cattle. They were herded onto a reservation, where the white man controlled them in the most elementary way—by the use of food as a weapon. The sites that were chosen for reservations were chosen because, quite simply, no one else wanted them. They were locations deemed unsuitable for farming, ranching, or mining. Neither was there much game available. No one could leave the reservation, and Indians had no money. Even if one could have left the reservation, he could never have obtained a job. No one hired Indians except the U.S. Calvary, who used them as scouts to hunt their own people. That meant that the only way to survive was to allow oneself and one's family to be fed by the white man, and to obtain food from the white man. A man and his family (all his family, including sick infants and old people who were dying) had to march to the fort to present themselves to the Indian agent once a month. All Apaches, including babies, wore metal tags around their necks, and the numbers on the tags were duly recorded by the soldiers when the rations were given out. The rations were meager and most often wormy, rotten, rancid, or full of weevils, and this was because the system was so corrupt that money, supplies, and food were siphoned off at virtually all levels. The Indian, once proud and independent, had become a scrawny, ragclad, parasitic-ridden beggar. He had allowed himself, and more importantly, his family to become kept dumb beasts. People wonder why Apaches followed Geronimo, why they fought fiercely against all odds, without any hope of winning, until 1890. That is why. They saw what they had become and had decided that death as free men was preferable to living like that.

Many different people have expressed it in many different ways. "Give me liberty or give me death," "It is better to die on one's feet then to live on one's knees," "Cowards die many times before their deaths; the valiant never taste of death but once," "Live free or die." The way the Apache says it is simply, "A man without honor is nothing."

I've digressed a bit here, but it is part of what I am, and it is one of the things I must say in this book. The world may never recognize Aloysius Lightfoot O'Brien, and it will promptly forget him as soon as he is buried, but it must never lose sight of this code. Many great men and women have lived by it and died by it, too many for us to let their struggles have been in vain.

As I said, that was a digression. During the ride, Clarence and I spoke only of happy things. We had just finished a good laugh when Clarence suddenly grew serious. When he opened his mouth to speak, I interrupted before he could begin.

"Remember, we're taking a couple of days off. No talk about business."

"It's not about the project, Lightfoot. It's about the business at hand—meeting my family."

"I know. I look like a wino, but with me being half-Indian, my beard is just not coming in too fast. Stubble is all you're going to see for a while. You're the one who said I'd be less conspicuous in first century Palestine with a beard. I'm just following orders."

"No, it's not that."

"O.K., jeans and flannel and denim and sheepskin is pretty casual attire. I know I look a little seedy, but you guys told me not to wear my uniform anymore, and that's what I've always worn when I needed to dress up."

"Lightfoot, just be quiet a minute and let me talk. It's Cindy, my daughter. She's thirteen years old. I just want to prepare you. She's dying." My heart sank. I felt like reaching out to put a hand on his shoulder but didn't. I tried to think of something wise and right to say to ease his pain, but I couldn't.

"That's one reason why the Old Man is letting me have some time off," he continued. "This will be her last Christmas."

I felt stupid. Just plain stupid. Here I had been babbling on about my beard and my clothes as if the world revolved around me. My tongue felt like a log. I switched off the radio. "I'm . . ." I started to say, but stopped just in time. Too many people had said that to me when I'd faced personal tragedy, and it doesn't do any good. I know. Sometimes it can even make things worse. "How long does she have?" I finally asked.

"Anywhere from two to nine months, depending on whether she responds to the drugs they're giving her. Nine months tops. She has acute myeloblastic leukemia." Keeping his eyes on the road, he blinked rapidly a couple of times and went on. "It came on very quickly. At first we thought it was some kind of flu. She had a high fever and some infection of her throat. Then she started to complain of joint pains. We called in a doctor, and he diagnosed it as acute rheumatic fever. Then . . ." he took a deep breath, "there was some bleeding from her mouth and nose. Then . . ." his voice broke, "God help us all, she's dying, Lightfoot." For a long time, the only sounds were the rhythmic two-stroke movements of the windshield wipers as the heavy snow continued unabated. "You see, I just wanted to prepare you. She's very weak already. She's in a wheel chair, and her skin is the color of this snow."

"Does she know?"

"Yes."

"How's she taking it?" He gave me a proud smile as he turned and looked me straight in the eye.

"Like an Apache, Lightfoot. You'll like her. She's prepared. She's not afraid. She's more than ready to meet her Creator."

"Ready to meet Usen," I said softly. "I am twenty-seven years old, and a Chiricahua warrior, and I, Aloysius Lightfoot O'Brien, am not yet ready. Yes, I think I'll like Cindy."

"They why don't you find some music on that radio and pour me another cup of Mrs. Eisenhower's famous hot chocolate while I tell you about the time Fatty Rutherford got a harmonica wedged in his mouth?"

14

hat with the snow and the leisurely stop for lunch, it was getting on toward 4:30 p.m. before we finally pulled into Clarence's driveway in College Park, Maryland. College Park was then as it is today—a combination of a typical university town and a nice, quiet middle-class suburb, whose inhabitants consisted mostly of federal employees who commuted into Washington. U.S. Route 1 bisects it and also serves as its main street. Downtown College Park in December of 1958 consisted of two bookstores, two pizza parlors, a record store, two bars, a gas station, a drug store, a grocery, and a motel. I understand it hasn't changed too much since then except for the addition of some fast food outlets, a "head" store, and a few more bars.

Marge met us at the door, along with the four kids and two dogs. I think the dogs made more noise than Marge and the kids, but it was too close to tell. Clarence had more spontaneous love bubbling up all around him than he knew what to do with. The pandemonium gradually diminished as we got the door closed behind us and began to take off our snowdusted coats and stepped out of our cold wet shoes onto the colder linoleum kitchen floor. I couldn't believe it. Clarence's kids were right there, handing him his slippers, and me a pair of his loafers. They didn't fit, but appreciative of the thought, I grinned and beared it. I really felt out of place, as must any man who steps into a Norman Rockwell painting.

"So," Marge beamed, "You're the new agent Clarence told us about! Unmarried too! I'll have to take care of that." Clarence let out a mock groan.

"I should have warned you, Lightfoot. Marge is an inveterate matchmaker. I've lost more single friends because of her than I care to count." He turned back to her. "Now leave him alone, do you hear? He's got a lot of very important work to do." She smiled and nodded but I didn't like the looks of that smile. I could hear the whir of little cogwheels. As she went to hang up our coats, I was formally introduced to the children, something that made me even more uncomfortable. Since the time I had left the reservation to go to school at the University of Arizona in 1948, I hadn't been around any children, nor did I care to. Now I must admit that this aversion was due to fear, and the fear came through ignorance. Children were a completely unknown quantity to me. I couldn't tell any two kids apart. They're all short, and most have no distinguishing scars or tattoos or other similar characteristics. Younger children all have high-pitched voices regardless of sex. The worst thing is that you can never tell what's going through a kid's mind.

"Lightfoot," Clarence beamed proudly, "this is Clarence Junior; he'll be fifteen next month. The twins, Mark and Ann; they're eleven. And," he said, kneeling to embrace the little figure in the wheelchair, "this is Cindy." All the young eyes turned to me.

"Good afternoon," I said in a somewhat stilted fashion. "I am Aloysius Lightfoot O'Brien."

"Are you a real Indian?" Mark asked breathlessly.

"I am real," I acknowledged. "I mean, yes. I am a Chiricahua Apache." Great, I thought, now a thousand questions . . .

"Hey, you guys, Mr. O'Brien is pretty tired, and he's going to be around for quite a while. Let's let him rest." I smiled at Clarence in gratitude. But he had turned back to Cindy. The poor kid looked like she had one foot in the grave and the other on a banana peel.

"How's my good girl?" The love and warmth in his voice were indescribable.

"Daddy, I'm so glad you're home. Can you stay awhile this time?"

"You bet, baby, I'll be here. How's the pain?"

"Worse, but I feel better now that you're here."

"Well, I won't be going on any more out-of-town trips, Cindy. Mr. Eisenhower gave me a couple of weeks off, and when I start back to work, I'll be coming home every night." Her smile broke my heart, so I can imagine what it did to Clarence.

"Daddy, the pain is getting real bad. Will it be much longer?" Boy, did I want to leave that room. I was an intruder on a very private moment and a very painful one. At least for me it was. But I couldn't think of a graceful way to exit.

"No, honey. The doctor says not much longer." There was a catch in his husky voice. "Not much longer." He kissed her forehead.

Suddenly Clarence's wife was kneeling beside him, her face and voice bright, almost radiant. "Just think Cindy! You and Jesus will be waiting for the rest of us, but the wait with Him will seem just like a minute! Then, before you know it, we'll all be together again. You and me and Daddy and Mark and Ann and Clarence. And we'll all have perfect bodies. You'll be able to run and jump and play. Your friends will be there too." I began to run my right index finger around the inside of my shirt collar. I felt like bolting from the room.

"I know, Mommy. It's just that sometimes the pain is so bad, I can't think of heaven or Jesus or you or Daddy or anything except the pain."

"Well, when we pray together tonight, we'll ask that God give you the strength you need to think of Him. Then the pain won't be so bad, will it?" Marge smiled. I was incredulous. Then Clarence staggered me all the more with his words.

"And, in any case, Cindy remember that it won't be long now."

Incredible. Even though Clarence had told me in the car that they had leveled with Cindy, I just wasn't prepared to see it with my own eyes, not to the extent that I saw. They had not only told a thirteen-year old girl that she was going to die, but they evidently kept *reminding* her of it. Prior to that moment, I had believed that only Indians did things like that. I had thought that the drill for other Americans was to lie right up to the end with a child. Or even with other adults for that matter. Sure, don't worry. The doctor says you're going to be just fine. Why, this time next year . . . and so I had only been in the Jones household for a scant five minutes before I saw that they were a most unusual family.

I got integrated into that family so fast it made my head spin. Hilda, the younger of the two Elkhounds, was the first to grant me total acceptance. That was after I'd been in the house for about half an hour. I was sitting in an armchair in the living room, and Marge and the kids were getting Clarence caught up on the latest household news. Hilda had been inspecting me, her alert brown eyes looking almost human, when, evidently satisfied, she rolled over on her back so I could rub her belly. First Friend.

By bedtime, I was astounded to find myself feeling comfortable in the house. Throughout Clarence's holiday vacation, as we did things as a family, bonds were even more strongly formed. By the end of the first week, even Heather, the older Elkhound, had accepted me, and that was something indeed. I have never seen, before or since, a dog like Heather. They say that if you work with a dog hard enough and really know what you're doing, you can get the dog to understand about 75 words. Heather knew about 500 words, and the Jones' told me they hadn't given her any special training.

The Jones family surprised me with a birthday cake on December 18, my twenty-eighth birthday. I helped Clarence Junior do some Christmas shopping for his father. Clarence and I took the twins ice skating. I could only act as a spectator on that trip, since I was unfamiliar with ice and didn't like it anyway, but I liked being with the kids. We all trimmed the tree together. We threaded chains of alternating popcorn and cranberries and strung them around the tree while listening to Bing Crosby's rendition of "White Christmas" on the radio. We also hung balls and gingerbread men and aluminum icicles. Naturally, one tree light bulb was bad, and it took us a good half hour or more of trial and error to find out which one it was. There was eggnog and there were carols and there was a Christmas turkey. And, for the first time in my life, I think I caught a glimmering of what the holiday is about in the hearts of Christians—it's a kind of euphoria that comes not only from a feeling of deliverance, but from a sense that makes peace and brotherhood seem as if they're actually possible if the world will only reach out to grasp them.

Cindy was as animated as any other kid about her Christmas presents, both those she received and those she gave. But particularly about the latter. You see, she painted with watercolors, and her present to each member of the family was a small five-by-seven watercolor portrait of the family, including her as she perhaps would have looked had she not been dying. In the portraits, she was standing tall and straight, and her cheeks were like roses. Each watercolor had been done separately, of course, so no two were exactly the same. We found that she'd been working on them since early October, and only her mother had known the secret. I knew, as did everyone else there, that they would treasure those amateurish little watercolors for the rest of their lives.

16

The six months I spent as a member of the Jones household went by quickly. I had never worked so hard in my life. Clarence and I would catch the 7:21 B & O commuter into Washington every morning after devouring a hearty breakfast prepared by Marge. From Union Station, I'd catch a bus to a CIA cover operation just off DuPont Circle. Wilros Travel Agency was a place that anyone could walk into without any suspicion being aroused. Say an embassy clerk on lunch hour, a member of a visiting trade delegation, someone on a cultural exchange program, and so forth. They could make a delivery or have a very private talk with a "travel agent," depart with a fistful of brochures, and leave no one the wiser. If any legitimate customers walked in off the street, there were a couple of real travel agents there to accommodate them, although the service was very bad and the prices exorbitant, so few returned.

It was in one of the small back rooms at the Wilros Travel Agency that I met Professor Kazakov, the renowned Talmudic scholar who was to teach me Aramaic. We didn't hit it off too well at first, and things kind of went downhill from there. Here he was, a professor of international repute, who could think of about a thousand other things he'd rather have been doing than spending half of his sabbatical teaching a class of one Aramaic. He had consented to do so only after the Secretary of State had asked him to do it as a personal favor. He was being well paid for it, but, like most men of genius, money meant nothing; it was his time that was important to him. No one could replace the six months that was being taken from his life, and he never had any particularly warm feelings toward the CIA in the first place. He felt certain that he was being used to prep me for a spy mission on which I would impersonate a scholar, and that once I was caught, this infamous incident would only serve to discredit genuine Talmudic scholars the world over, leading to a new wave of oppression against Jews. When we first met in that back room, he glared at me sternly over a pair of half-spectacles.

"Young man," he said with the expression of one who has just bitten into a lemon, "I am here to teach you. I am here against my better judgment, and only because a man whose integrity is beyond question assures me on his honor that what you are going to do is absolutely essential if we are to survive as a nation. I will do my best, my very best, I expect you to do the same. Do we understand each other?"

I nodded and we were off and running. Those were the very last words of English spoken in that room for the remainder of the six months. From then on, he spoke in nothing but Aramaic, and I either had to sink or swim. I understand that Berlitz uses the same method in some of their courses; it's called "total immersion," and believe me it's effective. You get instant results, and progress is rapid beyond belief. But it's mighty hard work. I left that room every day feeling like a limp, damp dishrag.

There were basically four languages in use in Palestine during the time of Christ. Greek was used by scholars, the aristocracy, those engaged in large volumes of trade with the other lands of the eastern Mediterranean. Hebrew was used by the Jews in all religious ceremonies as well as in prayer, but most Jews didn't use it as a base language any more than Roman Catholics in twentieth century America used Latin. Latin was spoken by the Roman occupation army as well as by Roman civil authorities, and all official matters of state were recorded in it. But Aramaic was the everyday language of the people. Everyone in Palestine spoke Aramaic, and, quite naturally, it was the language that Jesus Christ preached in. It was used in many different dialectal forms and used extensively from ten or more centuries before Christ until about five centuries after him. Even today, a form of Aramaic is still spoken in Syria and among the "Assyrians" living in Azerbaijan. In its eastern form, it's closely related to Syraic, and in its western form, to Hebrew.

It was tough. Learning any language is, of course. You can have all the language aptitude in the world, but you still don't build a vocabulary by grasping a concept. You don't learn irregular verb forms through osmosis. Sweat and drill and more sweat. But this comes as no revelation to anyone who's ever studied any language, so I guess none of you need me to carry on about it. You get the picture.

Meanwhile, Clarence spent his mornings sifting through the Library of Congress multimillion volume collection for background information on first century Palestine—the customs, laws, monetary system, climate, and so forth. He spent his afternoons at the White House, acting in his capacity as head of the Presidential Secret Service detail.

Clarence and I would meet in Union Station just in time to catch the 5:27 each evening, and supper would be waiting for us at home. Supper in the Jones house was always a lively affair, and it meant a great deal to Clarence. It was the only time in the day, he told me that you had the whole family in the same room at the same time and, consequently, the only time you had to reinforce the kids' conception of the family as a unit, a unit that hung together no matter what because each person was important.

First, there was the grace before meals; the family took turns leading that. Then, as the food was being passed and the meal began, Clarence made a point of asking each of the kids what had happened to them that day. What's more, he listened. I've had meals with many families since, but I have never seen the readiness with which the Jones kids cut their parents in on what was going on in their lives. They confided in their parents, sought their advice, and often even followed their advice. Why? I've given a lot of thought to the matter, and the answer is love. Simple love.

Now before I go any further with this book, I want to allay your fears. This book is not going to be devoted to extolling the Jones family and the love they showed for God, each other, and others, although one could write an entire book about that extraordinary family. But that isn't why I sat down to write this book, and it probably isn't why you sat down to read it. I sat down in front of this typewriter with a ream of blank pages and all the determination I could muster because I wanted to share with others the true story of what is surely the most remarkable adventure, the greatest quest in the history of mankind. I only wish that they had chosen a better man; a modern Homer would have been ideal.

But I learned a lot from the Jones family, and I'd be remiss if I didn't share a few thoughts with you before I resume the narrative proper:

Now love is a curious thing. There are so many different types and intensities of it that not even the Greeks had enough words for them all. We all want love, every one of us. And, the older I get, the more convinced I become that it's impossible for any of us to make that march from the cradle to the grave without getting our hearts broken at last once. Love is something you can neither buy nor sell. You can't rent it or borrow it. About the only thing you can do is give it away, hoping that you'll get some back in return, even though it doesn't always work out that way. It's truly the most powerful force in the universe, having launched thousands of ships and given many the courage to face torture and death unflinchingly. It's inspired men to write sonnets and symphonies that will live as long as man does, and driven others to stick their heads in ovens or put pistols to their heads. The power unleashed by the splitting of the atom pales into puny insignificance in the shadow of the power that makes a man use cardboard in his shoes to patch the holes so he can give his children a good education or buy his wife a special birthday present.

Despite the oceans of ink and blood and sweat and of tears expended in the name of love throughout the millennia, none of us really know much about it. It's odd, this love business. I don't profess to know any more about it except that I know it when I see it, and I saw many forms of it in the Jones household. I saw it in Clarence's eyes when he looked into Marge's, in Marge's secret smile when she looked at the kids. In the kids helping each other to recover from physical injuries as well as from disappointments. I saw it in the short evening Scripture reading and prayer that followed supper each night, when the Joneses thanked God for "all circumstances" because "in all things God works for the good of those who love him who have been called according to his purpose." There was love in that house. It hung, like something palpable in the air. It permeated the very walls themselves. It was all there—romantic love, brotherly love, paternal and maternal love, neighborly love, godly love; I even caught glints of erotic love sometimes in the glances that Clarence and Marge exchanged.

Before I leave the subject, lest you think that I'm describing people who were not really human beings, I want you to know that the Jones house was not some kind of magic never-never land. They had fights; there was some selfishness that surfaced from time to time. There were some thoughtless words sometimes, and some harsh words. Sometimes certain members of the household didn't like each other very much. Marge had moods when she felt she was being taken for granted. Sometimes the kids weren't completely straight with their parents. Sometimes Clarence just wanted to be alone. But the point is that they never stopped loving each other. And the kind of love that is independent of liking is the most precious love of all.

They put me up in the room that doubled as Clarence's den, and he and I would repair there each night, so he could brief me on all the research he'd done that morning. Using that amazing photographic memory of his and his keen analytical ability, he'd go through about thirty books each day and condense the material into a two-and-half-hour briefing each night. For the first few weeks, I had each Saturday and Sunday off. Then one night, Clarence told me he'd made arrangements for all the rest of my Saturdays before the mission.

"One other thing, Lightfoot," he said in an offhand way one evening as he was winding up the daily briefing, "I've arranged for some self-defense training for you. The CIA has an instructor who's one of the best in the world. I pulled all the strings I could to get him to spend his Saturdays at our Secret Service training site in Beltsville for the next several months. You'll be his class."

"Self-defense? But I'm not going on any military mission, Clarence. I thought the idea was for me to observe and report. Period."

"It is indeed," Jones nodded "but we're sending you back to a pretty rough-and-tumble era. A dead observer or an observer in prison is of no use to us. Remember, you're going to a country under the thumb of an occupation army. It's a country that's a hotbed of intrigue, plots, and counterplots—both political and religious. Even if you're in Herod's palace itself, you're not safe. You know, Herod the Great murdered a number of his own family members, including one of his wives and several of his sons because he suspected they were plotting against him. Caesar Augustus himself said that it was safer to be Herod's pig than Herod's son. His son, Herod Antipas, who is now," Clarence shook his head in wonderment, "now … who will be ruler when you arrive, is not a great deal better. He's not as nuts as his old man, but he has just as few scruples.

"As for crime, being out on the roads after dark in those days was not only dangerous, it was downright stupid. Palestine was a muggers' and highwaymen's paradise. There was no police force in any sense that we can relate to. That's why people traveled in caravans. The story of the Good Samaritan was a story that the people of the time could really relate to because it happened all the time. Robberies that is, not people stopping to help the victims."

"If you really think it's necessary."

"I do." Clarence stared off unto the distance for a long, silent moment. "Since I've been with the Old Man, during the war, and during the Cold War, I've seen a lot of people sent out on jobs they never returned from. The Old Man and I have talked about it a few times. When men don't return, you're haunted. Sometimes for a few minutes. Sometimes for a lot longer. Sometimes for a lifetime. Did I do everything I could have for him, you ask yourself. Did I make sure that he got the best training and enough of it? How about his equipment? Was it all he needed? Was there something else that I could have said or should have said to make the job and the dying any easier? Did I let him down?" He turned back to me. "That's not going to happen with you, old buddy. I intend to come through for you in every way. And you can take that to the bank."

17

★ ★ ★ ★ ★

The Department of Agriculture holds several hundred acres of prime farmland in the Beltsville, Maryland area, which is about ten miles due north of Washington. And it's on the grounds of the Beltsville Agricultural Research Center that the Secret Service has one of its training facilities. It's not used to train new agents; they all go to Glencoe, Georgia, for initial training just like all other federal law enforcement officers, with the exception of the FBI. It's used primarily for refresher and in-service training, so it's not very big. But it's more than adequate. The classrooms, auditorium, and gym are all housed in one long single-story cinderblock building, and the ranges are all one would expect. In fact, in autumn, when all the leaves are off the trees, you can see the mock-up of a city street off to your right at the Beltsville exit of the Washington-Baltimore Parkway if you're northbound. I had some fun with my Colt .45 shooting pop-up targets on that "street" every Saturday after my hand-to-hand training. At least that was some consolation or compensation for going eight hours of muscle straining, bone-crunching fighting with Tom Riley, the CIA expert Clarence shanghaied to train me. Tom was indeed an expert. A guy like him should be required by law to register his earlobes as lethal weapons. He knew every trick in the book and then some. It was the last Saturday in January that we drove out there to meet him for my first class. He was waiting for us in the gym.

As soon as we walked in, he scared me. He was built like a grizzly bear, only he looked more dangerous. In an instant, he was pumping Clarence's hand and thumping his back.

"Hey, stranger, where've you been hiding?" Clarence returned the big man's huge grin.

"Hi, Tom. I've been busy fighting for truth, justice, and the American way."

"Yeah, you and Superman and Batman. This the boy wonder here?"

"This is him, all right. Pretty poor material, but see what you can do with him, O.K.? He's not too bright, but his heart is in the right place." The giant gave me a long and frank appraisal.

"Hummm . . . uh huh . . . uh huh . . . umm," he intoned as he walked around me. I felt like a used car. "Well, they don't call me the 'miracle man' for nothing. I guess if I could teach you how to fight, Clarence, then I can do the same for this miserable wretch. His skull doesn't look much thicker than yours does. O.K.," he said, rubbing his hands together, "what'll it be? Karate, savate, kung fu, knife fighting, club fighting, boxing, wrestling, American street fighting, judo, tae kwon-do, jujitsu? Name your poison."

"Some of all the above, along with offensive and defensive work with a lance, also with a sword about yea big," Clarence said, extending his hands, Riley looked perplexed.

"You mean a saber that big. Nobody uses swords that size anymore."

"No, I mean a sword that big."

"You mean a bayonet that big."

"No, I mean a sword that big."

"The lance I can see, but, with all due respect, nobody uses swords that size any more. What you're talking about is the Roman short sword. Nearest thing anybody's used in the past couple of centuries is the machete, the cavalry saber, and swords used for ritual beheadings in the Middle East, and none of them are close at all."

"Where he's going," Clarence said, indicating me, "they use them." The wheels in Tom Riley's massive head began to whir. His professional curiosity was aroused. Clarence threw him a red herring.

"O.K., off the record. My friend here is going to, shall we say, visit the palace of a Middle East potentate. This personage is a bit eccentric. His palace guards are experts with these weapons, and my pal here won't be able to carry anything with him except a knife."

"Hmmmm. Roman short swords," he said, warming to the challenge. "Do they carry shields too?"

"Right. Convex rectangular shields, about so long and so wide," Clarence replied, gesturing, "made of leather over wood with metal reinforcements "

"Body armor?"

Clarence nodded. "Cuirasses of segmented metal on the upper torso, and iron helmets with extensions that come down over the temples, like so, and a flared extension that protects the back of the neck."

"Amazing," Riley muttered. "Look, this potentate has got to be some kind of screwball. Do you know what you've just described?"

"What?"

"The gear of a Roman legionnaire."

"Is that right?" Clarence said innocently.

"I like it," Tom nodded. "Yes, I do. It's a challenge. A break in the routine. I've been getting kind of tired of teaching college boys karate down at The Farm." He stuck out his hamlike hand to me. "Tom Riley."

"My name is Aloysius Lightfoot O'Brien."

"Clarence, when I finish with your boy," Tom laughed, "he'll be able to take on a whole Roman legion." Clarence and I joined in the laughter.

I was quite a novelty with the kids. They asked question after question about life on the reservation and Indian customs and beliefs. The American West was so far removed from their world that it may as well have been on the far side of the moon. Clarence Junior was interested most especially in flying. He knew an awful lot about aircraft of all types, but his passion was fighters. It was his ambition to become a fighter pilot. How did the MIG-15 stack up against the F-84E? Against the F9F-2? What was it really like to fly a combat mission? How good were the Chinese pilots?

The ground rules, Clarence told me, were that I could be as free and open with his family as I cared to be, as long as I didn't discuss the mission. He told his family that I was in training for an important job, but we weren't allowed to talk about it. They were evidently a well trained Secret Service family, because they took it in stride, and never asked a single question about my training or my job. Not even Cindy.

About Cindy. My first impression of her had been totally and absolutely incorrect. I'd seen her as a pitiable little waif. Well, she wasn't. I'd seen her in a very weak moment that first day, at a moment when the pain had been so bad as to be almost literally unbearable, and at a moment when her eyes were filled with tears because she was so happy to see her Dad back home.

The truth was that she had an inner core of steel, and a courage so great that it was of Apache dimensions. Apache warrior dimensions; even greater, for I doubt that I could have faced what she had to, and reacted with love, as she did. Nor had I ever met any other men who could have. It takes courage to face pain, suffering, and death with stoicism. It takes guts to face the Great Leveler with equanimity. But it takes courage bigger than the sky itself to face it with love.

We often make the observation that pain and suffering constitute a mighty crucible in which a person can either be strengthened and refined, or broken and destroyed. Cindy's will and character and her spirit had been tempered to an exquisite hard sparkling luster, not unlike a beautifully cut, many faceted diamond. It had made her much older and wiser than her thirteen years. Impending death finally makes philosophers of us all, I think, but it had outdone itself with Cindy. She had been an exceptionally bright kid to begin with, and her illness had given her even more time for reading and for reflection. She was easily more mature than most kids six or seven years older. I got very close to her, and I often had to remind myself that I was speaking to a child of thirteen, not a college student. Her eyes were older than the rest of her body, you see.

One evening, there was a curious look in those eyes as she regarded me at the dinner table.

"Daddy, is it all right if Mr. O'Brien reads to me tonight?"

"It's all right with me, if Mr. O'Brien doesn't mind." He had a most curious look in his eyes too. It took me completely by surprise. But I genuinely liked the kid so I didn't even think twice about it.

"Sure."

So, to make a long story short, after Clarence and Marge had tucked her in that evening, in I went. She looked so frail, so ghostly, her complexion matching the stark white pillow case. I drew up a chair and asked her what book she wanted me to read to her from, for there were many books in her bookcase. She pointed to the single volume on the nightstand. The Bible. I had gone through all twenty-eight years of my life without ever once opening that book, and here I sat, undone at the hands of a thirteen-year old. I thought briefly of telling her what I had told so many adults over the years. I had my own beliefs, thank you. Live and let live. Let everyone go to hell his own way. Isn't that what America is all about, after all? Thanks just the same. Adults know better. Then there was another very unique consideration.

Clarence had told me just two weeks before that the question of my reading the Bible had been the cause for some heated debate among the members of the Project Council. Some had taken it as a matter of course that the study of the Bible, particularly the New Testament, would be an integral part of my training. Others maintained that to study the Bible would be to prejudice the witness; that expecting to hear certain words said or to see certain things done, I might imagine I saw them happen that way. Extreme care had been taken in the selection of a witness, said Dr. Namuh, the leader of this faction on the Council. One had been found who satisfied the all important requirement of an established reputation of objective observation skills and honesty. The candidate was also neither an atheist nor a Christian nor a Jew but, in that felicitous phrase that Dr. Namuh used, "a seeker after truth." Why tamper with an ideal arrangement? It was a hard question. Ike had paced a few miles back and forth across the carpet of the Oval Office, and he hadn't yet arrived at a decision. Well, there it was. The book in question. Right in my hands.

Come on, I told myself, what was I, a grown man, afraid of? A book is a book, not a bomb. Or so I thought at the time.

"O.K., Cindy. Any particular part?"

"The Lost Sheep."

"Lost Sheep, huh? Which chapter is that?" I asked, flipping through the unfamiliar page headings.

"Start at Matthew, Chapter 18, Verse 12."

"Matthew . . . hmmmm . . ."

"Here, I'll find it for you, Mr. O'Brien," she said, taking it and deftly flipping to the spot. It's a very short bedtime reading, that. But you'd have to search a lot to find one more comforting.

> For the Son of Man is come to save that which was lost. How think ye? If a man have a hundred sheep, and one of them goes astray, doesn't he leave the ninety-nine, and go into the mountains, and seek that which has gone astray? And if he finds it, verily I say unto you, he rejoices more over that one sheep, than of the ninety-nine that didn't go astray.

"That's a pretty short bedtime reading, Cindy."

"It's not the number of the words that count, Mr. O'Brien. It's what they say. See, now I'll just lie here and think about those words and fall asleep."

"Oh, sure I see," I said. "Good night, Cindy," I said as I got up and turned out the light. I went back to my room and went to sleep thinking about those words too.

19

One Saturday, Riley handed me the wickedest looking blade I'd ever seen in my life.

"This, Lightfoot, is the British commando knife of World War II fame. It's also known as the Fairbairn-Sykes knife, after its designers, Captain William E. Fairbairn and Captain Eric A. Sykes. Both men had served on the Shanghai Municipal Police force when Shanghai was not a very nice place, and both were appointed to be the first instructors of close combat at the Commando Training Centre in Achnacarry, Scotland, in 1940.

"Now a lot of armchair knife fighters spend hours, days, even years, debating the relative merits of different fighting knives like the variations of the Bowie, the Arkansas Toothpick, the U.S.M.C. K-Bar, the 1918 combination trench knife and knuckle duster, and so on. They talk about metallurgical specifications, blade configurations, and a hundred other things, and they easily impress other people who also know nothing about knife fighting. Forget all that malarkey. I can tell you this without reservation. The Fairbairn-Sykes is the finest fighting knife ever made. Notice how it's grip-heavy so it sits well back in the palm yet it's still lightweight, so it's easily manageable. You can see how it has a double-edged, pointed blade of diamond cross-section 6-7/8 inches long with a square ricasso. The 'S'-shaped crossguard is two inches long. The checkered grip runs the entire length of the hand, diagonally across the palm, for maximum gripping power, and the small spherical 'pommel' further transfers the balance of the knife to the hilt. The tang is full length for maximum strength, and is threaded at the end to accommodate the top nut, which can be used in a skull-cracking mode on a down stroke. The bluing is, of course, to prevent any reflection of light. Clarence tells me that this is the only weapon you'll be allowed to take with you on your mission. I don't know why, and I'm not supposed to know why. I'm kind of partial to submachine guns myself, and I could show you how to take one down and successfully secrete it on your person even if you were wearing nothing except boxer shorts and a tee shirt. Time for action comes, I'd have trained you so you could reassemble it in less than fourteen seconds. But," he shrugged with resignation, "a knife is what they told me, so a knife it will be. And this is the very best. When I'm through with you, Lightfoot, and you head on out for your mission packing that blade, you're going to have absolute confidence in it, and with good cause. You're also going to be able to take on anybody with a Roman short sword and a lance. You're going to be a terror with your hands, your feet, clubs, and rocks. You're going to be one mean machine."

I looked down at the deadly razor-sharp commando knife in my hands and thought fleetingly of the gentle Galilean whom Cindy had introduced me to, and whom I was going to travel through two millennia and halfway around the world to see.

So that's how I spent all my Saturdays for nearly five months. Riley was a demanding instructor, and my muscles began to know the true meaning of the word soreness, but it wasn't as bad as all that. In fact, I came to look forward to Saturdays. After five days of intensive head-work each week, a good workout of about ten hours helped to calm me.

Meanwhile, back at the ranch house, Clarence's nightly briefings were alternately boring and fascinating. For example, when he explained how alluvial deposits along with narrow bands of clay and calcium carbonate came to accumulate on the fissured white limestone which lay under the surface of Palestine, my attention was less than total. On the other hand, when he talked about civil and criminal law, the judicial system, and the penalties, I hung on his every word. I had no desire to inadvertently disobey some obscure law, and so spend the rest of my life in a first century prison, or be stoned, burned, beheaded, strangled, or crucified. I also wanted to pass up flogging.

Each Sunday was a day of rest. While the Joneses went to church in the morning, I caught up on my sleep or did some reading. In the afternoons, we'd sometimes take in a movie, go for a drive, or, when the weather got warmer, picnic, go swimming, or play badminton in the back yard. One can never get enough of the fabulous institution known as the Smithsonian; we spent a lot of time there as well. All in all, it was a pleasant time. The only cloud, and it was an exceedingly dark cloud, was watching the steady deterioration of Cindy.

20

"Look, Cindy, it's easy for God to love you, and for you to be certain of going to heaven. As far as forgiveness of sins, I can't believe that a sweet kid like you even knows what sin is, let alone be a sinner," I said to her one evening. I read to her very often now, and we had even begun to discuss some of what the readings meant. She had just turned fourteen.

"What could you have done, Mr. O'Brien, that's so terrible that even God wouldn't forgive you for?" I avoided her direct gaze and felt as tongue-tied as a schoolboy.

"Adult things. You wouldn't understand. You're too young."

"Murder?" she asked. "Adultery?"

"And what would you know about those things?" I smiled uncomfortably.

"I read."

"You read," I echoed, nodding in what I meant to be a superior and patronizing way.

"Well, you learn a lot of things from reading too, Mr. O'Brien. Things you haven't experienced firsthand."

"Yeah, but . . ."

"Let me tell you about a story I read. A real high ranking military leader happened to see a totally nude woman on a roof. He caught an eyeful and had to have her. She was married to another man who was at the front fighting."

"I know the type who'd pull a stunt like that. They're low. They're nothing more than . . ." I stopped myself, suddenly remembering that I was in the presence of a girl who'd just turned fourteen. But I could see the Dear John letter at mail call, and . . .

"He got her pregnant, Mr. O'Brien," Cindy continued, "so then they had to try to figure out how to explain it to her husband."

"An abortion, I guess. That's what they ended up doing?"

"No, her lover ordered her husband back home, hoping that if her husband, ah, got together with her, then he would think that it was his child. Then everything would be O.K."

"You mean this guy was her husband's C.O.?" Cindy nodded in response. I became enraged. "Why, that makes the . . . swine even a thousand times more . . . contemptible!"

"Well, the man wouldn't sleep with his wife. He was so brave and so loyal to . . . his C.O. that the only thing he could think of was to get back to the front with his men." I grinned ruefully.

"So much for that solution."

"Now things are desperate. The commanding officer figures that the only way out now is to have the husband killed. He orders the man who's directly in charge over the husband to put the man in such a position during battle that it's certain he'll be killed."

"You mean the C.O. didn't have the nerve, the courage, to do his own killing? He had to have some other poor slob do his dirty work for him?" The answer was a grave nod. "Scratch what I said about him being a swine," I said, clenching a fist. "This makes him . . . hey, wait. Is this a true story?"

"Yes, Mr. O'Brien. But let me finish. Just as planned, the husband gets killed at the front. Do you think that God would forgive the . . . C.O.?"

"Never," I said with feeling. "There's such a thing as justice. If there is a Christian hell, that guy should fry in the hottest part of it." We were both silent for a long moment, then I realized once more that I was with a child. "Hey, Cindy, if your old man knew you were reading garbage like that, true story or not, you'd be in big trouble. I don't think you're old enough to handle . . . adult situations like that. And your mother would really hit the ceiling." The last response I expected was a twinkling of her eyes. Then she giggled, a child once more.

"So what's so funny?"

"There's nothing to worry about, Mr. O'Brien. You see, the story's in there." Her finger pointed to the Bible on the nightstand. "I just told you the story of David and Bathsheba." I shook my head.

"You're your father's daughter, all right. That's exactly the kind of trick he'd pull."

"I didn't tell you the story to trick you, Mr. O'Brien. I told it to tell you that when David asked forgiveness, God forgave him. Not only that, but Jesus was born in the House of David.

"I don't know what kind of 'adult things' you've done wrong, but I know that God will forgive you if you ask Him and if you're truly sorry."

"Cindy that just seems too . . ." I was going to say childlike, then the word simple came to mind, but the words that came out of my mouth were "good to be true."

21

The final pre-mission meeting of the entire membership of the Project Council was held March 15, 1959, in the conference room adjoining the Oval Office. Ike sat at the head of the table, of course, with Clarence sitting on his right hand and me seated to his left. As we sat watching the members file in, I began to feel like a pretty big shot. The Secretary of State, the Director of the CIA, the Director of the Oak Ridge Facility, the Chairman of the Joint Chiefs of Staff, the Secretary of Defense, the Director of the Smithsonian, and two of the most distinguished contemporary philosophers and Nobel Prize winners, Drs. Namuh and Shakhurin, all filed into the room, well aware that history was about to be made. Evidently, smiles are not permitted at such moments.

The room itself was imposing. The plush royal blue rug, the long rectangular table, a rich, deeply polished mahogany, the leather upholstered chairs, the view of the Washington Monument through the window directly behind the President, all this bespoke power.

The President glanced at his watch.

"Did Dr. Jankor phone to say he'd been held up?"

"No, sir," Clarence answered. Ike compressed his lips.

"He seems to have been unavoidably detained nonetheless. Let's give him five more minutes."

Everyone began to stare at the door, waiting for Jankor. I don't know what I was expecting, probably the stereotypical absent-minded, unkempt little guy with a thick German accent that Americans of the 1950's pictured all scientists to be—especially geniuses. When Erbil Jankor breezed in, that quaint little picture went out the window. He was a young man, no older than 35. He was tanned and fit, and dressed in a very loud aloha shirt, chinos, and loafers. Jankor carried no briefcase or notes of any kind.

"Hi, Mr. President, gentlemen," he beamed. "Sorry I'm late."

"I'm certain it couldn't have been helped," Ike said, "Isn't it still a bit chilly out there for . . . the way you're dressed?"

"It sure is. I just got off the plane from Vegas and didn't even think about where I was."

"Las Vegas?" asked the Secretary of Defense primly.

"Yep, a couple of days vacation. All work and no play and so forth. Did I miss anything?"

"Not at all," smiled Ike, in spite of himself. "Let's begin. Clarence, start with your report."

"Yes, Mr. President." Clarence leaned forward. "Captain O'Brien is midway through an intensive course in Aramaic, and his instructor, Professor Kazakov, assures me that his progress is excellent, and that the captain will be quite fluent by the end of June. We have been and will continue to be providing Captain O'Brien with daily area background briefings including, but not limited to principles of Roman administration of occupied territories, regional topography, flora and fauna, religious practices, customs and folklore, the economic system, social and class relationships, first century arts and sciences, and related topics. The captain studied classical Greek as an undergraduate at the University of Arizona, and has brushed up on his high school Latin. He is in excellent physical condition, and his Air force survival training, flight training, and war record all bespeak a highly intelligent man possessed of physical courage, inventiveness, and the ability to function independently under conditions of high stress. As you know, the President personally interviewed him. I have also interviewed him exhaustively, and have been overseeing his training. Everything is on target. Are there any questions?"

One of the distinguished philosophers addressed himself, and rather pompously I thought, to Clarence. "Mr. Jones, I'm sure that all this . . . shall we say, 'nut and bolts' training is all well and good. But I'm not at all satisfied that the single most important aspect of the entire project has been sufficiently made clear to the good captain. I speak, of course, of the very real danger of changing history, however inadvertently. As you all know, and I must remind you of this for the record, I have been against this project from the very outset. But, after being overruled, I remained on this council to at least help minimize the possibility of a disaster occurring." He adjusted his pince-nez, glared myopically around the table, cleared his throat, and continued. "Has Captain O'Brien been made to understand and appreciate the absolute necessity of being nothing more than an *observer?* The slightest change in his role could rewrite world history. Has it been sufficiently impressed upon him that he is neither to take lives nor to save them? Has it been sufficiently impressed upon him that he is not to introduce any new technology? Has he been made to understand, that, if he marries, he may not, under any circumstances, father any children? Has he been told that he must never make any references to the future or—"

"Mr. Jones and I have made things clear to the captain," Ike responded a little gruffly.

"For example," Dr. Namuh continued, as if he hadn't heard the President, "what if he should decide that he has a moral obligation to warn the people of Pompeii before Vesuvius erupts?" He glanced at a file. "The captain will be in his seventies, if indeed he is still alive at the time. Nonetheless. What if he has a child, and—"

The President was really gruff this time. "I have just told you that Captain O'Brien has demonstrated to my complete satisfaction that he understands all the implications of his actions or inactions, as the case may be." A tense silence hung over the table. The head of the CIA evidently felt an obligation to break it. He spoke to the group at large.

"With respect to materiel support to avoid anachronisms, our counterfeiting division has completed the necessary work. Captain O'Brien will be furnished with coinage appropriate for the time and place—Greek drachmas, Roman denarii, Phoenician minas (money of account current throughout the whole of the East Mediterranean), and, of course, talents and shekels. The money has been coined and worn just enough to make it appear that it's been in circulation anywhere from two to eight years. CIA tailors have taken measurements, and Captain O'Brien will be provided with an absolutely authentic wardrobe. Our people in Damascus sent us some fabric woven in precisely the same manner first century clothing was. It arrived in a diplomatic pouch last Thursday. O'Brien's bedding, cooking gear, and the very food he carries with him will all be indistinguishable from the gear worn, carried, or eaten by any other first century traveler. Everything's O.K. on this end. The only major item left is the dental work, and we can schedule that at Captain O'Brien's convenience."

Ike's brow furrowed.

"Dental work? Are you having dental problems, O'Brien?"

"No, sir. At least, none that I'm aware of." We both looked at the Director of the CIA, who in turn looked to Dr. Namuh. He received no help from that quarter.

"Yes, sir. Dr. Namuh called us about it. Our Clandestine Med Division is to rip out all the modern dental fillings the captain has. I was given to understand that you had O.K.'d it." Ike was getting extremely angry. He steepled his fingers and stared at Namuh as if the philosopher was a curious kind of insect he was looking at under a microscope.

"Pray tell, Dr. Namuh, why on earth do you feel the need to have this young man's dental work ripped out?" If Namuh was daunted, he sure didn't show it.

"Not just the dental work, but some of his good teeth as well.

If anyone in the first century were to examine the good captain's teeth as they are now, it would be obvious, obvious to anyone that the man is—"

"A time traveler from the twentieth century? Rubbish!" He turned back to the CIA chief. "Cancel that 'dental appointment.' And, by the way," the President smiled, "good work."

Clarence spoke. "And while we're on the subject of CIA support, I want to thank you again for lending Tom Riley to us on Saturdays."

"Thank you, Mr. Jones. We aim to please."

"Mr. Riley," asked Namuh, "is he also a teacher of languages?"

"Mr. Riley," Clarence answered, "is one of the finest instructors of hand-to-hand combat in the world."

Namuh's face flushed a beet red instantly, and he pounded a puny little fist on the massive conference table. "Have you taken leave of your senses? Hasn't anything we've said, any of the decisions we've made in the council gotten through to you, mister?!"

"I've been given charge of three mission-related assignments," replied Clarence levelly, "security, recruitment, and training. It is my judgment that, at the least, we owe this man some training in how he can protect his life."

"It's men like you who are turning this country into a police state!" Namuh shot back.

"That will be quite enough," Ike said irritably. "Next report? Owens."

The Director of the Oak Ridge Facility, a thin man dressed nattily in a three-piece tweed suit, removed his pipe from his mouth.

"All the equipment is in order, Mr. President. Everything's been checked and rechecked, then it's been rechecked again." Ike nodded, and Owens continued. "And the added security measures taken by Mr. Jones make this easily the most closely guarded secret in modern history. But," he said as his face clouded, "a bit of a problem has come up. Several days ago, three FBI agents burst into my office, asking questions about the project. I told them that they were not cleared for it. When they attempted to enter the L-2 Facility, they were denied access by the Secret Service agents Mr. Jones has stationed there. I got a call just yesterday afternoon from Mr. Hoover himself. In no uncertain terms he told me that internal security of classified defense projects is the responsibility of the Federal Bureau of Investigation and that the Secret Service was exceeding its authority as stated in its charter. He was extremely heated, sir, and he said that an FBI inspection team would arrive at L-2 tomorrow. He said that if the Secret Service agents attempt to deny them entrance, the FBI agents will arrest the Secret Service agents and charge them with interference of federal officers in the performance of their lawful duties." Ike was scowling. It just wasn't his day. He pressed the bar on the intercom.

"Miss Hotchkiss, please get Director Hoover on the phone for me immediately."

"Yes sir."

He was looking very much the five-star general now, and I was glad that it wasn't me who was going to be on the receiving end of his wrath. Once again the room was veiled in a heavy, uncomfortable silence. Finally, there was a faint crackle of static from the intercom.

"Mr. President? Mr. Hoover's secretary said to tell you she regrets that Mr. Hoover is indisposed at the moment but that he will call you back when he gets the opportunity." Ike set his jaw, but his voice was perfectly calm and soft as he answered.

"Please tell her to pass the word along to Mr. Hoover that I fully realize this is the time when he takes his customary after lunch siesta, and I know how much it means to him. But tell her that if he isn't on the line in thirty seconds, I am personally going over to his office and kick him off that couch. If I have to do that, it's going to make me very angry, and it's going to embarrass him, and we don't want either of those things to happen."

"Yes sir."

You could have heard the proverbial pin drop until the intercom crackled again a few moments later. None of us knew what, if any, expressions were playing across the President's face during the wait, for he had swiveled his chair around and had spent the time gazing out the window. All we could see was the back of his high-backed leather chair. The only words he said were addressed to me.

"Lightfoot, if you ever get the chance to run a government, any kind of government, pass it by. Not so much because it might play havoc with world history, but because you'll never know any peace, and they can never pay a man enough to deal with people who figure that they should be giving the orders instead of taking them. There are easier ways to make a living."

"Yes sir."

"Mr. President? Director Hoover is on 2."

"Very well, Miss Hotchkiss, I'll take the call in my office. Excuse me for a moment, gentlemen," Ike said, rising. "I'll be right back." He was gone for all of ninety seconds. I know, because I timed him with my father's pocket watch. When he reentered the room, he appeared to be totally unruffled, as though he might have left the room to get a drink of water.

"Next. Dr. Jankor?"

"I have run a myriad of computer simulations of the mission. All equations from which technical specifications were derived are accurate. I'm perfectly satisfied."

"Excellent. Gentlemen, I asked Dr. Jankor here primarily for the purpose of answering any questions you may have regarding the process. Clarence and I have only presented you with an encapsulated, extremely simplified explanation. Perhaps, an oversimplified account. Here is the one man who knows precisely how O'Brien's journey will be effected. If there are any questions, speak now or forever hold your peace."

Namuh glared at Jankor with undisguised contempt. The arts versus science. "I'm afraid that test tubes and Bunsen burners are not exactly my forte."

Jankor grinned and replied, "And I'm afraid that circumlocution and pomposity aren't mine, so it would appear that we have nothing in common. I'd be worried if we did. Do any of you other gentlemen have any questions or comments?" There were questions, and Jankor answered them clearly, simply, and in a style that demonstrated a wry sense of humor. It was old hat to me, because Clarence had done such a good job of briefing me and the President. Although I did have one question. It struck me as odd that I hadn't thought of it until now.

"Dr. Jankor," I asked, "I understand, at least in a rudimentary way, how you're going to transmit me through time by having me 'ride' the tachyon beam. But how do I travel from Oak Ridge to Palestine? How is the geographical move accomplished? What about the curvature of the earth? Doesn't the tachyon beam travel in a straight line?"

"A good question, and one that's easily answered. The beam does indeed travel in a straight line. We are going to bounce it off the moon. That's how it and you are going to get to your geographical destination." When I laughed, I got some strange stares from the men around the table, so I had to explain.

"Excuse me, it's just that when I was first interviewed for this mission, I thought it was connected to the space program. Now it seems that, in a sense, I was right. I'll be the first man on the moon." Everyone smiled except for Namuh, who sat glowering at Ike.

He was a man with a one-track mind, a little man in every way. Yet a whole generation of philosophers and scholars venerated him for his presumed wisdom. He was a professor emeritus at one of the finest universities in the country, and he was a Nobel Prize winner. It was a strange world.

"Not, apparently, that it will do any good whatever, but I do want to emphasize one last time for the record, that I object to this 'mission' most vigorously. And, to further compound the mistake, a military man is chosen. The military mind is simply not capable of—"

"Of what, Doctor?" Ike asked frostily. "I have a passing familiarity with the military mind myself."

"Mr. President, may I at least have your personal assurance that, excluding the canister, of course, the captain will carry no twentieth century objects back into time? No guns, hand grenades, binoculars, or similar paraphernalia military types are fond of and deem so essential?"

The President looked like he was one step away from having the philosopher thrown bodily out of the room, but he answered coolly. "You have, Doctor. What's more, he will carry no cameras (tempting though that idea is), ballpoint pens, watches, and so forth. I think, with that, we've exhausted that topic."

"Very well."

"Dr. Linstrom," the President said to the Director of the Smithsonian, "may we have your report next?"

"Of course, Mr. President. We'll have a crack archaeological team standing by in Tel Aviv. As soon as word is flashed that Captain O'Brien has departed, they will proceed to the excavation site. They will recover the canister, take samples of the dating elements embedded on the exterior, and send them to the laboratories of the British Museum, MIT, the National Museum of Natural History in Paris, the National Center of Scientific Research in Madrid, the Center of Forestry Research and Analysis in France, the Department of Prehistoric Studies at the University of Bordeaux, the Cairo Museum, and the National Scientific Academy of Japan.

"Although some of the dating elements consist of radioactive isotopes, most are samples of various types of wood. Wood, after all, is what we've been most successful in using to determine the age of an item. New techniques have already made Carbon 14 dating obsolete. We, along with the other institutions I've mentioned, have used four relatively new testing methods to date Tutankhamen's coffin, Egyptian canoes, and ancient wooden implements, with most impressive and extremely accurate results. I refer to measuring the degree of lignite formation, the gain in wood density, the degree of fossilization, and cell modification.

"As soon as the samples of dating elements have been dispatched to the Smithsonian as well as to the other selected institutions, the canister itself, seals unbroken, will be sent immediately to this room via Secret Service courier. We shall all convene again in this room at that point. The seals will be broken, and we'll read the captain's account. That will be approximately 3:00 p.m. Eastern Daylight Time on July 11, 1959."

"That's only less than three days after I leave!" I protested. "It'll take me time to locate Jesus and . . ." Dr. Shakhurin, the other philosopher on the Council, who had remained silent until now, broke in gently. "You're forgetting, Captain O'Brien, that the moment after you've been transmitted from the L-2 Facility at Oak Ridge, you will have been dead, and the canister will have been in the ground, for two thousand years."

22

Cindy. The kid was a real scrapper, and I saw more courage in this fourteen-year-old girl than I've seen in grown men with some pretty impressive medals on their chests. Now courage seems to come in two varieties. There's your basic single-heroic-act kind that the aforementioned men with medals have displayed, and the day-by-day grit-your-teeth guts kind that keeps you fighting on, often in unsung and unglamorous situations, when every fiber of your being tells you that you should have given up yesterday or last month or last year. The latter is generally unrecognized and unsung, and I think that's a crime. Sure, Rudyard Kipling spoke of forcing "your heart and mind and sinew to serve their turn long after they are gone and there is only the will which says to them, 'Hold on,'" but he was only one man, and the kind of courage he spoke of doesn't sell newspapers or magazines.

Someone once said that a hero is no braver than anyone else; he's just braver for five minutes longer. As a definition of heroism, I've never much liked it. It's glib and it's flippant, and real heroism is far more complicated. But it does do one thing; it brings endurance into the equation. It's one thing to, in a supercharged fraction of a second, throw yourself on a live hand grenade to save the lives of your buddies (and I don't mean to denigrate such acts of valor), but another thing entirely to deal with fear, grief, pain, or loneliness as a way of life. People are decorated for shedding blood, but not for shedding tears. Awards are given for limbs broken or shattered, but not for broken hearts or spirits. Much ado is made over the hero who dies in combat, but how often is the courage of his widow recognized? His worries are over permanently; hers have just begun. How about the courage, the fortitude, it takes for her to cope with heartbreak and grief, to face each gray dawn and get up to struggle to rebuild her life and her dreams, and those of her children?

It's often easier to die than to live. Very often. We all know this from our own experiences. Haven't we all, and more than once, when sunk deep in depression, pain, grief, or sorrow, wanted to be done with it once and for all? Some follow through. They are the suicides. The quitters. As an Apache, I was brought up to believe that Usen, God, doesn't like quitters. He has no use for them. The earth has turned many times on its axis since my youth on the Arizona desert, and I'm more certain than ever about that.

Well, Cindy was brave for five minutes longer, a lot longer than five minutes. Better than anyone else I've met before or since, she was the personification of what Paul E. Billheimer calls "the heroism of faithful endurance." He makes the observation, in his *Don't Waste Your Sorrows*, "It seems to some that a life which is ended swiftly by an act of martyrdom may be more heroic and a greater testimony of deathless love than ... patient endurance of ... sorrow, suffering, disappointments, heartaches, and pain." But may it not be, he asks, "that God is obtaining a similar quality of selfless devotion and sacrificial love" from the latter as from the former? "If so," he says, "then those who suffer triumphantly, accepting the 'things that hurt and things that mar' with submission, thanksgiving, and praise, may be enhancing their eternal rank in a similar way as did the martyrs." I can see so many things now so clearly that I couldn't see then.

Cindy and I got to know each other very well indeed during the six months that I was a guest in the Jones household. As the time

120

went by, she lost more and more strength. We had all expected it, of course, had known it was going to happen, but that isn't the same thing as being prepared for it. By the end of March, she was too weak even to use her wheelchair, except for very brief periods of time. She was losing weight like crazy, and by mid-April, looked skeletal. That's also when she began losing her hair. By the beginning of May, she could no longer sit up and so could no longer read. We all had Marge schedule us to read to her at various times throughout the day. As might be expected, her remarkable precociousness was revealed in her choice of books. Just a few we read to her were *The Thousand and One Nights*, the works of Mark Twain, *Don Quixote*, *The Last of the Mohicans*, the *Odyssey*, everything Arthur Conan Doyle ever wrote about Sherlock Holmes, and *Plutarch's Lives*.

I've already mentioned that Cindy wasn't your average kid. She thought a lot. About a lot of things. As I said before, impending death finally makes philosophers of us all.

Sunday mornings, when the rest of the family went off to church, was when we'd have our long talks. I'll never forget one of the very last we had. It was toward the end of June, and the final countdown for the mission was in progress. I'd begun to get cold feet, but I was too scared to back out. At that stage, I was given to emitting long mournful sighs and to spells of depression. That particular Sunday morning, I paused for a moment before climbing the stairs to Cindy's room. I stood looking at the watercolor family portrait in the beautiful oak frame that Marge had bought for it. Marge had put it up over the living room couch on Christmas day. Since she'd been in on Cindy's surprise, she'd had the frame in the attic, ready and waiting. The Jones family, dogs included, smiled at me from behind the glass.

The thing that really got to me, and I'm sure to everyone else, was that she'd painted herself as she would have looked had she not been dying. What a heartbreaking contrast between that image and the poor, pain-racked little girl wasting away upstairs. I gave another of the long sighs for which I was becoming famous around the house and, like an old man, slowly trudged upstairs.

"Hi, kid."

"Hi, Mr. O'Brien." The doctors had said that, by all rights, she should have been dead a month and a half ago. They couldn't understand it. She kept hanging on with an iron-willed tenacity that defied belief. It was as if she were waiting for something. As if she knew something would happen if she could only hold on long enough.

"What'll it be today? Want to pick up where we left off in the *Last of the Mohicans* or where we left off in *Romeo and Juliet?*"

"Can we just talk for a little while?"

"Sure," I said, sitting down.

"Mr. O'Brien, you're not going to be with us for too much longer, are you?"

"No, I'm going to have to go very soon now."

"I hate to see you go when you're feeling so sad." Just like the kid. She's dying, and she's worried about me. I forced a laugh.

"Oh, I'll survive. It's just that I'm nervous about starting a new job, moving to a new place, wondering how I'll fit in with the new people, and stuff like that. It's normal."

"If it's normal, how come it's a secret?"

"Well," I waved a negligent hand, "you know how we adults are—self-important, going around making mountains out of molehills all the time."

"Have you prayed about your new job?" Great. Leave it to a kid to be direct. An adult would know better than to ask a personal question like that.

"I envy you your faith. I really do, Cindy. I only wish I could have that kind of faith."

"What's stopping you?" Another one of my sighs.

"I've seen a lot of things. A lot of bad things. A lot of things that a loving God like you say yours is, just wouldn't allow to happen. I believe in God, I guess, but mine is different from yours. He's not much given to listening to prayers. Sometimes He intervenes in human affairs, and sometimes He doesn't. Mostly He doesn't."

"Why doesn't He?"

"I don't really know. I guess maybe He just has more important things on His mind. Anyway, when He does intervene, it's to take up for the brave, the strong. He has no use for the weak or the irresolute. He stands by the man who's true to himself and his beliefs, true to his family, his tribe. And even then, Usen sometimes deserts such a man and allows the forces of evil to triumph. Why? Who can say? He's a hard taskmaster. He is the stern Judge to whom you must finally account. He's not your God, A God of love, forgiveness, and mercy.

"Cindy, I've seen a lot of things that a loving God like yours just wouldn't allow to happen. You really haven't seen that much of life. If you'd seen or been through some of the things that I've been through," I said, thinking of a senseless barroom brawl in Globe that left my father dead, a stretch of highway near Safford where a leering Death took the lives of the only two women I loved, the stupidity, the futility of the war in Korea . . .

"What *you've* been through, Mr. O'Brien?" Cindy flashed. "What about what I'm going through? Do you think its fun to die a little more each day? To know that you'll never see your fifteenth birthday? To see the terrible, heartbreaking pain in the eyes of your mother and father every time they look at you? To hear your sister cry herself to sleep nights because she loves you so much that she can't handle your death?" The sudden unleashing of such powerful, pent-up emotion took me aback. It took her aback too. She made a fist and bit on it hard, blinking back the tears. "Oh, Mr. O'Brien, I'm sorry. I truly am. But we've all known pain, disappointments, and the feeling sometimes that not even God cares." Her eyes searched mine with urgency. "But don't you see, God *uses* pain to refine us. It's all part of His plan. Don't go away without knowing that."

"Cindy, I'm the one who should be apologizing. I feel terrible for being so insensitive. But I'm not going to lie to you. I just don't see any pattern."

"And because *you* can't see it, it can't exist?" It was uncanny. That was how her father had answered my incredulity as Gettysburg, during my initial briefing. When I started to tell him that time travel was impossible, he'd said that everyone else on the Project Council had reacted in the same way at first. "But," he had said, "that just proves how limited, how small, our own minds and imaginations are. It can't be so because we can't conceive of it. Rubbish," he had said. Cindy was a chip off the old block.

A good point though. Which was harder to believe in? Einstein's time dilation effect or a loving God? At the time, both were equally incomprehensible to me.

23

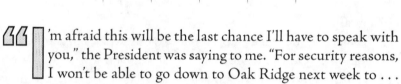

"I'm afraid this will be the last chance I'll have to speak with you," the President was saying to me. "For security reasons, I won't be able to go down to Oak Ridge next week to . . . see you off, as it were. Too much attention has already been drawn to the project."

"I understand, sir,"

"Good." He smiled tightly and got up to look out the window at Lafayette Park, where brown-baggers from the various federal agencies were contentedly eating their lunches and taking full advantage of the idyllic summer day. His hands were clasped behind his back, and he stood there silently for a very long time before turning to face me again.

"O'Brien, I've spent many a long hour trying to find the right words for this occasion, but they've consistently eluded me . . . I don't know what to say. You're a bright young man, and I know how much hard work you've put into your training. The sacrifices that you've made and will make for the sake of the mission are . . . heroic. To risk your life for your country in battle is one thing. But to do what you're doing is another. You're quite an unusual young man.

"But I felt I couldn't let you leave without one last exhortation on how vital this mission is. How very vital. For me to let you go without my being absolutely certain that you understand the full implications, the gravity, of this mission would be nothing short of criminal." He turned back to look out the window again.

"O'Brien, what is your personal opinion of Jesus Christ?"

"Well, sir, I guess I won't really know until I meet him."

"Touché, but you're not getting off the hook that easily."

"Well, Mr. President," I hedged, shifting uncomfortably in my chair, "I think that, regardless of whether he was the Son of God or not, he was a very good and wise man and a great teacher. The principles he espoused were . . ."

"Very glib," Ike said, spinning around to face me again. "A very enlightened, neutral, and inoffensive way to answer that question. And, oh so open-minded. Well, it won't wash, O'Brien; it won't wash at all.

"You see, either Jesus Christ was exactly what He claimed to be, the Son of God, the Messiah, or He was not a wise and good man at all; He was a raving lunatic or a liar or both. There simply is no in between." He folded his arms and leaned back against the window sill. "With this mission, we have the opportunity to settle the question once and for all time. And, regardless of what the answer is, the world will never be, can never be, the same again.

"All of western civilization, whether people like it or not, is either directly or indirectly influenced by Christianity—our laws, our art, our literature, our music, our customs, our social contracts, our very calendar itself, all show the tremendous influence of the Galilean we know as Jesus Christ. With you, we have the opportunity of knowing beyond all doubt." His voice softened, and he looked directly into my eyes. "A lot is riding on you, son. Perhaps more than either of us could possibly imagine."

"Sir," I replied, "I'll either accomplish the mission, or I'll die trying." As soon as the words came out of my mouth, I was embarrassed. Straight out of a Grade B melodrama. But I meant them, and he could see that I did. I guess that's all that really mattered.

"Good," The President smiled, "I know you won't let us down.

Now there was one other thing I wanted to talk to you about. Is there anything at all I can do for you? Is there anything that needs to be done or that you'd like to do before . . . your departure? Clarence tells me that all your training has been completed. Perhaps you'd like a week's vacation? We could fly you anywhere you'd like." He'd carefully avoided the term "last request," but that's what he was asking about. It was an unexpected offer, and I hadn't given any thought to it. The training had been so intensive I hadn't had the time to do any thinking along those lines. "We could fly you anywhere." Hmmmm. Fly. That was it!

"Sir, I wonder if I could take just one last flight."

"Can do!" Ike beamed enthusiastically. "Clarence can arrange it though the Commanding Officer at Andrews. You name the plane, and if the United States owns it, you can fly it."

"Thank you, Mr. President."

"Just be careful."

"Yes, sir," I answered, unable to suppress a smile.

On the way home, I mentally ran through the planes in the United States inventory. Any plane! I felt like a kid poring over a toy catalog during the Christmas season. Would it be the F11F Tiger that the Navy Blue Angels aerobatic team used? Made by Grumman, it clipped along at 890 mph and had a ceiling of 50,500 feet. Or how about the F-106 General Dynamics Delta Dart? Designed from scratch to Area Rule principles for minimum supersonic drag, its mighty Pratt & Whitney J75-P-17 afterburning turbojet moved the beauty along at a spritely Mach 2.31, or 1525 mph. How about an F-104 Lockheed Starfighter? Or the F-101 McDonnell Voodoo? By the time I reached home, I had decided. It would be the Delta Dart. Speed.

Speed. That was always one of the things I enjoyed most about being a jet fighter pilot. Watching the earth flash by below you at speeds faster than sound itself could travel. Going into fantastic, eye-popping power dives, then barrel-rolling out of them. It's a job for men who refuse to grow up completely, and I freely admit it. You're not supposed to admit it. You're supposed to maintain a solid, sober demeanor at all times, somewhat like a corporate tax accountant, and pretend that it's not fun. The motto of the Strategic Air Command is "Peace Is Our Profession." And according to some unwritten law, a man who enjoys that profession is viewed with extreme circumspection, especially by civilians. Image. You must maintain the correct image.

One of the biggest disappointments of my life was reaching the age when I had to pretend to be grown-up. Once you pass your teens, you have to act like an adult, and I think that having to hide the child in you is a deplorable shame. Still, it's far better to hide the kid in you than to lose him. Some are successful in the latter. You meet them all the time. They're uniformly stuffy, pompous, and dull. They don't enjoy life, and they seem to be dedicated to making sure that no one else does either.

I was home quickly and wasted no time in dragging Clarence to the phone to make the arrangements for my last flight. It took only two short phone calls. He used that Top Secret Cosmic code stored in his head, which verified and authenticated the fact that this was at the direct and personal order of the President of the United States, that it was covered by the highest security classification, that no questions were to be asked, and that it was to be accomplished immediately. Having that code (which changed daily at midnight, Greenwich Mean Time) in hand or, in Clarence's case, in brain, was better than having Aladdin's lamp.

The following morning, at 11:00 a.m., two very solicitous bird colonels and a bevy of junior officers escorted me and Clarence to a brand-new, sleek F-106A General Dynamics Delta Dart. The very first production units had only entered active service two weeks before. It was equipped with the new Hughes MA-1 interception system, which was designed to be integrated with the nationwide SAGE (semi-automatic ground environment) defense system with a digital computer used to track and select targets, and aim and fire the weapons. It was armed with four Falcon AAMs and two Genie nuclear-tipped air-to-air unguided rockets. And it was the hottest fighter plane in the world.

I drank in its beauty as we approached it. I was in my pressure suit but per Clarence's security measures, had ripped off my name tag and insignia of rank. In addition, by this time, my beard was in its full glory. I was getting some strange looks from our escorts. I ran an awed hand over its smooth metal skin. This baby had a service ceiling of 57,000 feet (10.8 *miles*) and a top speed of Mach 2.231 (1525 mph). Clarence eyed it with frank, if unprofessional, interest. He kicked one of the tires on the landing gear.

"Hmmmm," he said, addressing our entourage thoughtfully, "how many miles does this thing have on it?" In the brief glance he shot at me, I caught the twinkle in his eye, and even then, that's only because I'd been living with him for more than six months. One of the colonels frowned; the other was nonplused.

"You mean hours, sir," piped up a young second lieutenant. "We use hours of operation to measure engine wear, not miles."

"You mean like a taxicab?" I asked, putting on my best village idiot expression.

"No, no!" Clarence exclaimed in mock exasperation, "taxi-cab meters run by the quarter mile."

"Except when they're standing still," I fired back heatedly. "When you're idling with the flag down, the meter clicks a nickel off every minute! I should know! I drive one!"

"O.K., O.K., Mr. Know-It-All. Do you think you can drive this crate?"

The bird colonel who'd been frowning was now scowling, and his face was a bright cherry red. No sense of humor, I thought. The other officers stood immobile, like men carved from stone. Clarence and I were playing to a tough audience.

"I guess," I replied to Clarence with a careless shrug, "seen one plane, and you've seen 'em all."

The nonscowling colonel spoke. "Excuse me, gentlemen, but this is the newest, most advanced and sophisticated jet fighter in the world. Might I suggest that another plane be more suitable for . . . whatever it is you have in mind?"

"This farce has gone far enough," exploded the cherry red

colonel. "O.K., 'Mr. Jones,' I want to see some identification, and I want some questions answered right away. I'm entitled to that and—"

It was the one and only time I'd ever seen Clarence erupt. He terrified *me*, and I wasn't even the object of his fury.

"No, you are not entitled, Colonel. You are interfering with an activity classified at the Top Secret Cosmic level, and ordered by the President himself. You're entitled to nothing but the coded authentication, which you've already received. But if you want identification, mister, O.K., you've got it." Clarence flipped open the small leather case that held his Secret Service badge and I.D. He shoved it under the colonel's nose. "That's right, Jones is the name. Now after my colleague takes off, you and I are going to have a little discussion on the chain of command." He turned to me. "O.K., let's get you up in the driver's seat of this heap."

A junior officer stepped forward and whispered into the ear of the other colonel, who then spoke to Clarence. "Ah, excuse me, Mr. Jones, but it's just come to my attention that your friend hasn't filed a flight plan." Clarence looked at me.

"That right, Junior?" I nodded in response.

"Yes, that's true, Colonel. He hasn't." Turning back to me he said, "O.K., son, the keys are in the dash. Don't bring it back too late. Your mom and I want to go out dancing at the Elks Club. And don't forget to put gas in it."

"I can dig it," I smiled. He clapped me on the shoulder, and we climbed up onto the left wing.

"Boy, Clarence, you really blasted that guy."

"I guess I did, didn't I?" he said with genuine regret. "Come on." To my surprise, we climbed back onto the runway. Clarence beckoned to the colonel, and he came over.

"Colonel, please excuse me for losing my temper. I'm truly sorry. It's just that if you knew who this man is and knew what he's already done for his country, along with the things he's going to have to face, the things he's volunteered to face . . . well, you'd be shaking his hand and, along with me and the President, offering to help him in any way you can." Clarence squinted off into the horizon before continuing. "Heroes are hard to come by these days, and we did a lot of searching before we found this man. He's a good man, and, what's more than that, he's become a good friend. We were just trying to have a little fun. A defense mechanism, I guess. Nevertheless, the fun wasn't intended to be at your expense. I'm sorry if it turned out that way."

"I'm sorry too, Mr. Jones. I was out of line." He shook my hand then Clarence's.

As I was settling into the cockpit, I knew I had to ask. "Clarence, you didn't need to do that. The guy acted like a jerk. He deserved to be put in his place. Why the apology?"

"You don't know?" His sad face searched mine. "You really don't know?" I shook my head. "Because, Lightfoot, if you treat a jerk like a jerk, he'll just become a vicious and embittered jerk. You've got to treat him the same way you'd want to be treated . . . Abe Lincoln once said that the best way to get rid of an enemy is to make him your friend."

"Now you've put *me* in *my* place." He smiled and handed me my helmet.

"Enjoy, Lightfoot. Get up there above the clouds, and just forget everything for a while."

In a few moments, I was off and thundering down the runway. The plane was a dream. I streaked directly for the ocean, acclimating myself to the ultra-sensitive controls as I went. At full throttle, I reached the Atlantic in minutes, and then my world consisted of nothing but shades of blue. Blue ocean and blue sky. Aside from the brilliant white heaps of cumulus clouds, there was nothing else. I corkscrewed, did lazy barrel rolls, put the craft into screaming eyeball-popping power dives, skimmed across the ocean at a speed of 1300 mph and an altitude of twenty feet, and climbed higher than I'd ever climbed before—to more than ten miles above the earth's surface. I was a free creature of the sky, existing only to fly, to soar, to glide.

The words of John Gillespie Magee, Jr.'s exquisite sonnet, which

I hadn't read for years, slipped into my mind as clearly as if I were reading them at that moment.

> Oh! I have slipped the surly bonds of Earth
> And danced the skies on laughter-silvered wings;
> Sunward I've climbed, and joined the tumbling mirth
> Of sun-split clouds . . .
>
> And, while with silent, lifting mind I've trod
> The high untrespassed sanctity of space,
> Put out my hand and touched the face of God.

24

I didn't know how to say goodbye to the Jones family, the family that, in a very real sense, had become my own. Clarence was the brother I'd never had, and Marge the sister. The kids were my nephews and nieces. So I resolved the problem in a way I'm not particularly proud of; I stole away like a thief in the night. As soon as everyone was asleep on the night before Clarence and I were scheduled to leave for Oak Ridge, I crept around the house, "executing my will," such as it was.

A large lump rose in my throat as I left my Colt .45 Peacemaker on Clarence's nightstand, along with a note that didn't say nearly enough. Going around to the other side of the bed, I covered Marge with my mother's blanket. Then I went into the room across the hall and left my father's railroad watch on Cindy's nightstand. She'd often admired it and, even though she had only about two weeks of life left in which to enjoy it, well at least it was two weeks. As I walked out of the room, I smiled to myself in the darkness. What a grandly ironic farewell gift from me—a timepiece.

Then I quietly left the house and walked around the block to where I'd secreted the rental car. I jumped in and hit the road to Tennessee. I had, of course, no baggage, and I didn't look back.

Road signs on the outskirts of Oak Ridge identify it as

"America's Secret City," and so it was for years. Construction on Oak Ridge began on November 22, 1942, and proceeded at a fantastic pace. Vast resources were urgently needed to produce enriched uranium 235 and a pilot reactor for the production and processing of plutonium. The Manhattan Project had top priority from the beginning, as well as top secrecy. Even though, a scant two and a half years after ground was broken, Oak Ridge was the fifth largest city in Tennessee with a population of 75,000, it appeared on no maps. All roads to and from it were controlled by military checkpoints, and no one either entered or left the city without the express permission of the military commander. Huge fences topped with barbed wire surrounded the entire city. The perimeter was ceaselessly patrolled by men who were told to shoot first and to ask questions later. All it inhabitants were sworn to secrecy. Finally, on August 6, 1945, the existence, as well as the role of the city, was revealed. Nevertheless, it wasn't until March 19, 1949, that the checkpoints were dismantled, the fences came down, and Oak Ridge became an open city.

I parked the car and walked Oak Ridge's clean, quiet streets aimlessly, feeling quite sorry for myself. I'd tried to sleep and couldn't, tried to read and couldn't. I couldn't even think straight. Kaleidoscopic images just kept flashing and tumbling across my mind's eye—supersonic aircraft and camels, electric power plants and millstones, Clarence, Amanda Clearwater, the U.S. Marines storming a beach defended by Roman legionnaires—my mind was spinning. We were coming right down to the wire now, and, after all the careful preparation, after all the time spent in psychological acclimatization, I realized that I just couldn't handle it. The human mind is by far the most complex and sophisticated thing that man has ever run across. It can adapt to practically anything. But it had finally met its match, I thought. It could not adapt to traveling two millennia back into time to meet the most important figure in all of human history. Son of God or not, he had changed the world for all time to come. I was a simple man who felt most at home on the desert with a canteen of water, some beef jerky, a knife, my blanket, and my Colt. I was way out of my league this time.

But I was half-Irish and half-Apache. That made me all crazy. They'd picked their man well. Not only that, I didn't have any better offers at the moment. When I heard a church bell chime 6 p.m., I shrugged resignedly and began walking toward the L-2 Facility. When I was ushered into the operations booth, it was 78 minutes and counting until H-hour. Technicians flipped switches and turned knobs on consoles that looked like something out of Flash Gordon, only a thousand times more advanced. Dr. Jankor and Clarence stood conferring with two important looking men I'd never seen before. Jankor was the first to see me. He grinned with relief, then Clarence turned and saw me. They excused themselves and came over to me. Jankor spoke first.

"You scared me, Captain. You really scared me. I was getting ready to send the U.S. Cavalry out after you."

"I told you he'd show on time, Doc," Clarence said heartily.

"Piece of cake. I'm an old time traveler from way back," I replied airily in a tone I hoped matched Clarence's. My breathing was shallow and rapid, my skin pale and clammy. I wasn't fooling anybody, and we all knew it.

"O.K., pal," Clarence said briskly, "let's go into the conference room and get you suitably attired for the occasion. We'll also go over the rest of your gear."

He and I walked into the conference room in silence. It was dark and cool inside, with a huge air conditioner churning away for all it was worth. My clothes were laid out on the table. They were woven by hand in precisely the same way all first century Palestinian clothes were. The hand stitches, the type of thread used—everything was absolutely authentic. Not only that, but the clothes had been "aged" and covered with road dust, so as to give the impression that the wearer had been traveling a great deal.

"Cheer up, Lightfoot. There are hundreds of thousands, maybe hundreds of millions, who'd do anything to be in your shoes."

"In my sandals you mean," I said, shrugging into the outfit. "Whew! Did they have to make the clothes smell so bad?"

"Atmosphere. Authenticity. Trust them."

"The CIA?" We both laughed.

"Look, you don't have to go through the rest of your gear. I've gone through the checklist five times. It's all there."

"O.K."

"We've still got a bit of time. Let's just sit for a spell. Try to relax."

"Easy for you to say."

"Maybe this will help," Clarence said, producing a hip flask. He wasn't a drinking man, so I was surprised. He unscrewed the top and held it under my nose. Then I was even more surprised.

"Tulapai! Where in the world . . . how . . ." Clarence held up a hand.

"I'm in the Secret Service, remember? We have our ways."

I took a mouthful. "It's tulapai," I confirmed. I haven't smelled or tasted any since some old men on the reservation brewed up a batch once when I was home from college on vacation." I passed the flask to him, but he waved a hand.

"How do they make it?" he asked, trying to take my mind off things.

"Well, I only saw it done once, and now only the old ones know how. As I understand it, first you soak corn thoroughly in water, then put it away to sprout. Then you dry it and grind it by hand on the metate or grinding stone. Then comes the tricky part—knowing which and the correct amounts of weeds, roots, root bark, seeds, and other stuff to add to it. Each good tulapai maker has got his own secret recipe. Anyway, the mix is poured in five-gallon cans, water is added, and it's boiled for hours. Then its transferred into empty cans, and the mash is reground. The residue is added to the liquid again, and then more hours of boiling. You set it aside for about a day to ferment, and there you are."

"Sounds like mighty potent stuff." I shook my head.

"Only if you drink it in large quantities."

"What's a large quantity?

"About two gallons." I passed the flask back to him after I'd taken a second mouthful. "Thanks."

"You don't want anymore?"

"No thanks, Clarence. I'm driving."

"Cigarette?" he asked uncomfortably.

"Blindfold?" I countered. "Clarence, take it easy, you're more nervous than I am. If such a thing is even possible."

"Sorry, Lightfoot. Look, I have a favor to ask."

"Name it."

"If this works, if you do see Him, get to speak with Him, please ask Him . . ."

"About Cindy?" I interrupted. Startled, he could only nod.

"I was going to do that anyway, Clarence. I figure nothing ventured, nothing gained."

"Thanks. I only wish your attitude was a bit more positive."

"You guys selected me because I have a neutral attitude."

"True. But I know that if you ask Him, and, if He says the words, Cindy will be healed."

"I'll ask him . . . about Cindy . . . Clarence, I guess you don't need me or anyone else to tell you this . . . but Cindy's some girl. There are some people who can never be defeated. You can kill them, but you can't defeat them. Cindy is such a person. She would have made a fine Apache, Clarence."

"Thanks, Lightfoot," He stood up. "Ready?"

"Now's as good a time as any, compadre. I don't know how much longer I'll be able to maintain my mandatory Apache stoicism." I grabbed the document canister, and Clarence took the bag that contained my gear. Dr. Jankor and two others were waiting for us right outside the conference room door. We followed them in silence, our footfalls echoing hollowly in the cavernous building. We went through a maze of ductwork, transformers, switching consoles, and lead shielding, traveling in an ever diminishing spiral, getting ever closer to the core of the cyclotron itself. Finally we ascended a flight of stairs to a platform. We gathered around an opening in the ductwork. Inside the ductwork was a metal grating measuring about eight feet square.

"O.K., Captain," Dr. Jankor said, "just lie down on your back in the middle of the grating. That's right, just put the canister alongside you. Now, Mr. Jones, if you'll just put the captain's gear on his other side. Good. All right. Now here's the drill. O'Brien, first we're going to be closing the overhead cowling. You'll then be sealed in a spur of the cyclotron. Next, thousands of small jets of air will come up from below. You and your equipment will be suspended on a cushion of air. We'll accelerate the stream of tachyons to the precise speed we need to send you back to your target time slot. Then we'll focus the beam on that part of the moon's surface we're going to use as a reflector. Next, we'll divert the stream through your spur, much as one would use a railroad switch, and you're on your way. Next stop Galilee. God willing."

"Well put, Doctor," I replied.

"Look at it this way. If the worst happens, and, if we're completely wrong, or, if there's an equipment malfunction, you'll never know what hit you," he said jovially. "Remember, we're talking in terms of two ten-millionths of a second."

"Thanks."

There was an awkward silence, while everyone, including me tried to think of something suitably inspiring to go into the history books along with this moment. Clarence whispered something in Jankor's ear, and the doctor nodded in response. He motioned to his two colleagues, and they descended the steps, leaving me and Clarence alone together. He extended a firm hand, and I shook it. Then, without ceremony, he grabbed the cowling and began to lower it.

"Today is a good day for dying," I said.

"Only the mountains live forever, my brother," responded Clarence with the words of the Apache Death Chant that had a strange comforting effect on me. Just before the cowling closed completely, I saw a solitary tear run down the cheek of the Secret Service agent. Then all was blackness.

25

Have you ever accidentally rolled out of bed in your sleep? Suddenly there's a rude thump, and you lie there for a moment in the darkness, trying to figure out where you are, what time it is, and what happened. Well, that's exactly what my trip was like. I could spend hours or days with a thesaurus and possibly succeed in making it sound more exciting. In fact, I almost feel an obligation to do just that. But then it wouldn't be the truth. The truth of the matter is that the greatest journey of all time lasted two ten-millionths of a second and was as anticlimactic as can be.

Evidently, I had materialized a few feet above ground and fell the rest of the way. No damage, fortunately. I just had the wind knocked out of me. But I lay there a long time, more from psychological shock than from anything else. The Rubicon had been crossed. I was fully committed. Now there could be no turning back. I lay there for perhaps half an hour before I sat up, looked around me, and took stock. It was twilight and getting dark fast. The all-important canister had survived the trip, as well as my traveling bag. There were no signs of any humans or animals about. The terrain was rocky and desolate, there was a chill to the air, and an unfriendly wind whistled eerily through the hills.

I knew that if everything had come off as planned, I was now on a small plateau overlooking Chorazin, a village situated on a bluff north of and approximately 885 feet above the Sea of Galilee. As I said, it was growing dark quickly, so I got up to reconnoiter. First things first. I had to locate the prearranged burial site for the document canister.

It took me no more than five minutes to locate the peculiarly shaped rock formation that I'd spent so many hours studying from photographs. Studied so much in so many photographs taken from every imaginable angle in every possible lighting condition, that I would have been able to recognize it in my sleep. I paced off the designated twenty paces and began to dig. They'd provided me with a small spade about the size of a U.S. Army entrenching tool, but made of first century materials in a first century fashion. After I'd buried the canister, I sat trying to decide whether to hit the road then or to get some sleep and wait for the daylight before moving. I decided on the latter and was rummaging around in my traveling bag when my hand felt something cold and metallic. Dumbfounded, I pulled out my Colt .45 Peacemaker. It was in a shoulder holster, and I found a note with it:

Lightfoot—
In addition to a multitude of human beings who can bring you to harm, first century Palestine is also populated with wolves, big cats, the Syrian brown bear, and several species of vipers. I thought you might have some use for this.
The Jones family sends love and prays that God will watch over you and protect you.
Clarence
P.S. Inside you'll also find your blanket.

What a guy, I smiled to myself. I took off my cloak and tunic and strapped on the shoulder holster. Then, after I put my tunic back on, I used my British commando knife to slit an opening that gave me ready access to the gun. After I replaced my knife in its neck sheath and put my cloak back on, I tore Clarence's note to shreds, then watched the wind blow the pieces away. "Good-bye, old friend," I whispered.

It had long been one of my boasts that I could go to sleep anytime and anywhere I chose. My mother used to poke gentle fun at me by telling me that it was the Irish blood in me. But try as I might, I couldn't get to sleep that night. I was just too keyed up. So after an hour or so of restless tossing, I rolled up my blanket, put it in my traveling bag, and, after taking my bearings from the stars, struck out eastward. In that direction I knew, lay the Jordan, and once there, I'd simply follow it south, hopefully running into numerous people along the way, since it was a major artery for trade caravans and pilgrims. From other travelers I'd be able to get the latest news about the whereabouts of Jesus Christ.

It was true that Clarence had cautioned me never to travel alone at night. In fact, in some areas, it wasn't even safe to travel alone in broad daylight. But I just couldn't help myself. The moon was full and the sky cloudless and bright with light from a thousand stars. That being the case, even though the terrain was tricky, I told myself there was more than enough light to ensure that I wouldn't stumble and fall into some abyss or walk off some cliff. And as for human and animal predators, was I not Aloysius Lightfoot O'Brien, a Chiricahua Apache warrior? Was I not trained in armed and unarmed combat? Didn't I possess sound judgment, experience, and a Colt .45 Peacemaker? There was no way I was going to be the first Apache in history who was afraid of the dark. A man has his pride.

As I worked my way eastward and downhill, I intersected a narrow game trail, which in turn led me to a road. It was not much of a road by twentieth century standards, but it is what passed for a road in that time and place, which is to say that it was wide enough to accommodate an ox cart, and it was fairly level.

If anything, the sky seemed to grow brighter with each passing moment, so I relaxed and began to let my mind wander as I walked along. Why, I asked myself, have men voluntarily put themselves in dangerous situations since the beginning of time, why? What ever possessed me to agree to do such a thing? In my case, I could rule out a lot of the obvious and usual motives right away. Not for the money. They had supplied me with enough gold to see me through a couple of years of walking around (hopefully with Jesus Christ), plus a rather large cache of gold and precious stones in the canister that I was to remove when I put in my records and reburied it. That cache was more than enough to set me up in a nice business of my own after the job was completed. But it wasn't the money. Of that I was sure.

For glory then? No way. If my mission was successful, the only people who would ever know about it wouldn't even be born for another two thousand years. Why did I do it? I had no theological ax to grind. I didn't care much one way or the other about the man known as Jesus Christ. I was after no Holy Grail. For mankind? For the pursuit of knowledge? No. I was a simple man, and, despite Ike's and Clarence's pep talks about the importance of the mission in terms of the influence of Christianity on world history, art, literature, philosophy, music, laws, and so forth, they were speaking about concepts that I had neither the equipment nor the inclination to grapple with. No, I hadn't volunteered because of any lofty dedication to expand the frontiers of human knowledge.

As I plodded on through the night in first century Palestine, I came at last to the reluctant conclusion that it was nothing more than line proximity. There is an old, indeed, an ancient theory, as old as the hills and man and danger. Perhaps it's been around for so long because it's true. There is a line between life and death, goes the theory, and the closer one gets to that line, to sudden death, the more intense one's experiences become. All the perceptions are heightened, thoughts come with crystal clarity, colors are more vivid, and the ranges of the senses of smell, hearing, and touch are multiplied a hundredfold. When a man has looked leering Death full in the face and experienced that strange exhilaration that comes with it, all subsequent experiences are anticlimactic. Some men get hooked on that feeling and spend their lives going back to the line in constant attempts to recapture it. That's what drives a man to volunteer for more combat missions that he has to, or a cop to *want* a tough beat, or a man to race automobiles, or walk a circus tightrope, or skydive, or any of a number of things that no rational person would do.

Perhaps it was the Theory of Line Proximity that was at work here. In flying combat missions, I'd approached the line many times. When I was shot down and fighting my way back to Allied positions, I came as close as a man can get without actually crossing the line. In those days, I drank in the wonderful multicolored sunsets like a man dying of thirst attacks a canteen of cool water. I saw distinctly each shade and hue and tint. I marveled at the symmetry of tree leaves, acutely aware of each tiny branch in the incredible networks of veins. I felt, reveled in, really *appreciated* the warmth of the sunlight on my face. Such were the thoughts that were going through my mind when I heard a voice come from immediately behind my right shoulder, only about fifteen yards back. I was getting careless; I should have heard him approaching at forty or fifty yards on a night like this.

"Wait, friend! May I journey with you a way?" There was a false heartiness in the voice, and, as he got closer, I decided that I didn't much care for his small and beady ferret-like eyes either.

"Certainly, friend," I replied, matching his phony smile. Both of us were sizing each other up, although I'd like to think that I was less obvious about it than he was. The syphilitic sores on his forehead didn't do much for his looks either.

"Where are you bound?" he asked me.

"Southward toward Capernaum, where I hope to find a teacher, one Jesus of Nazareth." Ferret Eyes looked at me quizzically.

"Your speech. Your accent. I have never heard the like of it before. Where are you from?"

"A far-off land," I replied, gesturing vaguely to the west.

"Are you a merchant of some sort then?"

"No, friend, Just a humble seeker after truth," I answered honestly.

"Aren't we all?" he mumbled distractedly, peering at a dense thicket just ahead. In a casual gesture, I scratched my back and felt the reassuring presence of my knife in its neck sheath. I waited for him to make the first move.

"I have heard him speak, this Jesus," Ferret Eyes said unexpectedly. "Frankly, if you have come a great distance just to see him, you have wasted your time."

"What makes you say that?" We were getting closer to the thicket, and the tension was mounting. I should have listened to Clarence.

"Oh, he is a holy man. Of that, there can be no doubt. But he speaks nonsense. Half of what he says is in riddles, and the other half naïve, childish prattle. Nonsense. You and I are men of the world, are we not? We know the ways of the world. This Jesus has evidently led a very sheltered life, and does not. He babbles foolishly of loving one's enemies, of his kingship in another world, of . . . nonsense." He waved his hand in a deprecating fashion and gave a very bad portrayal of a man suddenly struck with an idea. If he'd been a cartoonist, he would have drawn a light bulb over his head.

"My new friend, let us travel no further this night. You are new to this area and perhaps know little of the dangers that can befall a traveler in these parts. Thieves and murderers abound. They lie in wait for the unwary. I know of a small hut but a stone's throw away. Though it is small, it is snug and comfortable. I have used it often when making this journey. It is just through there," he said, indicating the thicket. Although this guy didn't put much stock in what Jesus said, he was obviously a disciple of P.T. Barnum if he thought I was going to follow him into that undergrowth. It was a set-up, and it was clear that he had at least one accomplice.

"I think not, my friend," I said, "but I thank you for your concern."

"But," he urged, "if you'll forgive my saying so, you appear ill equipped to defend yourself. I noticed immediately back down the road that you carry no sword or spear, no club or bow." I'll just bet you did, I thought.

"I am a man of peace. I don't believe in violence."

"All the more reason to wait for dawn and to travel with me." His rotted yellow teeth were bared in a predatory smile.

"No," I said firmly, "I appreciate your concern, but I must be moving on. Peace be with you."

"Very well," he said. "Then I insist upon accompanying you for your own protection."

"It's hardly necessary, but do as you wish," I replied, casually putting my right hand on the back of my neck.

"Then it's settled! But before we continue, please allow me to ah . . . attend to the call of nature first." He motioned for me to sit on a large rock. "I'll be back in just a moment." Then it was certain. He had at least one accomplice hiding in there. Before he disappeared into the thicket, he gave a quick look up and down the road. All clear.

He had tried the easy way first, attempting to lure me off the road, and have me set upon from behind while I followed him through the blackness of the thicket. I hadn't risen to the bait. Now he and his friend or friends were going to do it the hard way. I didn't need my Apache blood to know that the attack would be lightning fast and that they didn't plan on letting me live. I sighed heavily and once again berated myself for not listening to Clarence. Only seconds after I took out my Colt Peacemaker, the three of them came boiling out of the thicket like giant, crazed hornets. Speaking of giantism, one of them was easily six and a half feet tall. He was as hairy as a gorilla and wielded a club three times the thickness of a baseball bat. He scared me. The second had a spear poised, and my faithful traveling companion had his Roman short sword in his hands. I could have taken any two of them on, armed with only my knife. That's how good and how thorough my training had been. But all three at once? Colonel Samuel Colt was going to have to save the day.

My first shot caught Goliath in the forehead, felling him like an oak tree, and the second shot hit the man with the spear squarely in the center of the chest. Automatically I lined up Ferret Eyes in my sights, but eased up my pressure on the trigger. The two deafening explosions and their consequences had rooted him to where he stood, frozen in shock. His bulging eyes were riveted on the Peacemaker, which he had seen belch fire and thunder and death twice in one second. He dropped his sword. Neither of us moved for a very long time. My mind was spinning. I had really gone and done it this time. I had really botched things up. Not here in the past even a day, and I had already killed two men through my own stupidity, and before me stood a man who had just had nineteenth century technology demonstrated in such a graphic way that he was never going to forget it. Did this mean that I'd have to kill him too? Dr. Namuh would probably insist upon it. I had never killed a man in cold blood. Without exception, from Korea on down to the two men who now lay at my feet, the only times I had ever killed were when I had to to save my own life. Wait a minute. Forget what Dr. Namuh would say; what would Clarence do? I uncocked the gun and replaced it in my shoulder holster.

From my traveling bag I extracted the entrenching tool and tossed it over to Ferret Eyes. "Bury them, say nothing to anyone of this, and you may live."

He got down on his knees. "Oh, yes! Yes, mighty sorcerer! Had I but known you knew the secret crafts of the Egyptians and the Chaldeans, we would have never . . ."

"Obviously," I observed drily. "Now I charge you most solemnly never to speak of this to anyone. If you do, you will surely die."

"Never, mighty sorcerer," he sniveled, prostrating himself before me. "On my mother's grave, I . . ." The rest of his babbling was lost on me for I had spun on my heel and continued down the road, leaving him to bury the dead.

I went on my way in remorse, beset with a strange and heavy disquietude that I could not dispel for the life of me. Within *hours* of my arrival, I had violated three rules of time travel. I had killed. I had demonstrated advanced technology. I had let the witness live. Well, I told myself, the man was terrified; he probably never would speak about the incident to anyone. Even if he did on some occasion, his fears allayed by the influence of the grape, tell someone, he'd never be believed. Even if he were believed, the listener would chalk it up to magic. It would never occur to them to try to make their own firearms.

But in killing those two men, had I altered history? Had they lived, might not one of their descendants have become a factor in some important historical event? Might not one of the descendants they now would never have be a da Vinci? A Bach? A Hitler? Or, would these two men just have been killed by travelers or other highwaymen stronger than themselves anyway? My head began to spin. But wait, I asked myself, the fact that I was still here—didn't that in itself prove that I hadn't altered history? All thoughts of this nature ultimately lead in circles, and entertaining them for any appreciable length of time is an excellent way to lose your marbles. Thrusting them out of my mind with a great effort, I gazed up at the full moon as I walked along and wondered about the man from Nazareth and who and what he really was.

26

I saw no one else along the way as I followed the road paralleling the Jordan until the river emptied into the Sea of Galilee; then I struck westward along the coast and hit the outskirts of Capernaum at about dawn. A bustling fishing port on the northwestern shore of the Sea of Galilee, it was the logical place to start. Although they were originally from Bethsaida, it was here that Jesus was supposed to have recruited Peter and his brother Andrew, along with their business partners, James and John, the sons of Zebedee. It was at Capernaum's quayside, while Matthew was bent over his customs ledger, that Jesus had simply said, "Follow me," to the tax collector, and the man immediately rose and did just that for the remainder of his life. In addition, Capernaum is but twenty miles from Nazareth, where Jesus spent the first thirty years of his life, a period remarkable for the fact that no one really knows anything at all of it. If time and circumstances permitted, I could do a little research in that area. Most importantly, though, Capernaum was Jesus' base of operations, the place to which he always returned, the place, Mark says, where Jesus felt most "at home."

The nervous energy that I'd been running on since I'd left Clarence's house and drove down to Oak Ridge was finally beginning to give out on me. You can only run on adrenalin for so long. Sleep. That was the first order of the day.

Even at this early hour, the town was starting to stir. There were a number of women in the street carrying pitchers of water gracefully balanced on their heads, and tough and swarthy looking fisherman with bleary eyes were heading down toward the docks. I stopped one of the latter and asked him where I might find a good inn. Eyeing me suspiciously (I think it was my very unusual accent), he directed me to a rather large affair, whitewashed, and built around a central courtyard, with small rooms opening onto it. The roof was composed of red tiles, unlike the roofs of the dwellings around it; no humble roof of wattling covered with beaten earth for this edifice. Clearly, had there been a first century Michelin Guide, this place looked like a good bet for a five-star rating.

An attractive but stern-looking young woman answered my knock. Her complexion was dark and smooth, and her raven hair framed a face that would have even been beautiful had it not been for the hardness in her dark appraising eyes.

"Yes?"

"I'm a traveler in need of lodging. Have you any rooms available?" She didn't answer my question; instead, she seemed to only intensify her scrutiny.

"For how long?"

"That I cannot say," I replied, spreading my hands. Silence for a time, and then, with those shrewd black eyes still measuring me, she responded a second time, yet still not answering my question.

"You are a merchant then?"

I should mention here that, in those times, it was not at all unusual for a trader to travel to a distance province or country and spend a year there negotiating sales before returning to his home to execute the orders. James even refers to this in Chapter 4, Verse 13.

"No, I am not," I smiled. "I am more of a pilgrim, actually." She frowned and began to close the door. I put my foot in it.

"I would, of course, pay you in advance."

"The daily rate, Sir Pilgrim, is two denarii," she said in a supercilious way. "It has been my experience that few self-righteous, prayer-babbling vagabonds are able to afford our accommodations." Those black eyes watched transfixed as I extracted two shiny silver shekels from my bulging coin bag.

"Excellent," I said, not batting any eye, "please permit me to pay you for four days in advance. If I leave before then, you need only give me my change, and needless to say, should I decide to stay, I'll continue to pay you in advance. Will that arrangement be satisfactory?"

"Most satisfactory, sir," she replied smiling, every inch the transformed woman. "Welcome to my humble inn. May your stay be a pleasant and prosperous one."

"Peace to all in this house," I intoned as I crossed the threshold.

My room was clean by anyone's standards, and the mat upon which I was to sleep was almost new. Good, I wasn't yet enough of a first century man to peacefully coexist with lice. I used my bedroll as a pillow, and under it stashed my Colt.45, journal, and money. I slept like a baby for a solid eight or nine hours and, when I awoke, felt completely refreshed and relaxed. Just plain old fashioned sleep is, and has always been one of the most potent wonder drugs around. It's cheap too.

I walked into the front room of the innkeeper's quarters to find a slightly overweight young man with a shock of prematurely graying hair preparing to go out. He turned and beamed.

"Ah! You slept well, I trust? Anna told me she took in another guest early this morning. You would be he, according to her description."

"Yes, I slept very well, thank you. You are . . .?"

"Bartholomew," he replied with a friendly bob of his head, "master of this inn. Anna is my wife. At least," he paused to consider in mock seriousness, "I *think* I am master of this inn. I must ask

Anna about it. I get confused sometimes." His eyes twinkled. I liked him.

"I am Lightfoot. I come from a land far to the west, which I'm quite sure you never heard of. In any case, that's unimportant. My king has sent me here to learn all I can about a man—one Jesus of Nazareth, a preacher. Perhaps you can help me." At the sound of Jesus' name, Bartholomew became very animated.

"Perhaps we can help each other. Please accompany me on my constitutional before the evening meal, Lightfoot." He rolled the name awkwardly around his mouth. "Lightfoot . . . what manner of name is that? Egyptian? Phoenician? Syrian?"

"Western."

"Just so. Western," he nodded, satisfied. We went through the door and began walking at a sedate pace, passing many fishermen going home for the day. Bartholomew walked with his hands clasped behind his back, his eyes gazing thoughtfully off into the distance.

"Yes, perhaps we can help each other. You see, we've had many travelers, pilgrims one might even say, stop at the inn. This Jesus has suddenly come out of nowhere, out of complete obscurity, and has begun a ministry of some sort. He came through here several weeks, no; it's been closer to two months ago now, and even recruited some local men. I regret that I did not hear him speak the few short days he was here. I was off visiting my brother and his wife in Baskama. By the time I'd returned, they'd all gone. They traveled south and have picked up many followers, or so I'm told. Of late, many of our guests who have come up from Samaria and Judea tell quite remarkable tales of this Jesus. The stories grow more frequent and, might I say, more incredible with each passing day. The passion that the man arouses, both for and against him, is powerful indeed. Now scarcely an evening meal goes by without heated arguments erupting among our guests. I have consistently remained neutral though. A prudent businessman must.

"A professional innkeeper must never favor one side over another in a debate among his clients. You, Lightfoot," he was

still having trouble pronouncing my name, "are obviously a man of
the world, a man who has traveled far, a man of much learning. I
perceive that you have spent much time in many inns. You know
how important the role of the innkeeper is." I nodded gravely, and
he continued.

"You see, the professional innkeeper must never stifle the free
exchange of ideas. On the contrary, it is his sacred duty to society
to encourage it. It is only through learning from his fellows that
man progresses." Bartholomew's manner approached pomposity,
but you just couldn't dislike the little guy. He was exactly the
kind of character that Don Knotts has always been so good at
portraying. "An innkeeper," he went on, "must be a philosopher to
be sure, but he must also be an excellent moderator, ensuring that
everyone has his opportunity to be heard, a Solomon-like judge
who sees to the proper presentation of each case, a listener with
the patience of Job of old, a referee to prevent physical harm from
befalling those who get, ah, shall we say, overenthusiastic in their
arguments, a man with the wisdom and insight of—"

"You said we might be able to help each other?" He frowned at
the interruption, but only for a fleeting instant.

"The last few weeks have been like no others in memory. I have
talked with people who have claimed that they have seen Jesus heal
the sick, restore sight to the blind, cleanse lepers, and perform all
manner of miracles. Others say that they have seen him, and all
they beheld was but an ordinary man, except that this one speaks
in riddles, making no sense. Some say he is a great prophet surely
come from God; others say that he is a blasphemer who must be
put to death. Some even say," and at this, Bartholomew stopped
in the middle of the road, dramatically looked over his shoulder
and around in all directions, then stage-whispered, "that he is the
Messiah!"

"What do you think?"

He put an index finger to his temple and resumed walking.
"I don't know. Even in my short lifetime, I have seen several men
who have held great sway over people, men who claimed to be the

Messiah, who worked wondrous ways with words, much like a fine musician does with the notes on the scale. Artistry. Sheer artistry. Yet, alas, all of them turned out at last to be frauds that had to be stoned. I have seen eight or ten such men like this; perhaps I shall see eight or ten more. This particular man seems to be the least likely candidate of all. He keeps company with tax collectors, drunks, thieves, and prostitutes. Hardly what one would expect of the Holy One of God, the Messiah," He shook his head. "I don't know. I cannot say. I only know that *if*, I mean to say, *what if* he *is* the Messiah? What if, only a few days journey from where we now stand, the most momentous events in the history of the world are now taking place? I can't bear it, Lightfoot! I must find out!"

"Then come with me," I said. "We're both after the same thing." He shook his head ruefully.

"It isn't as simple as that, my friend. You don't know my Anna. I have brought up the matter several times recently, and she becomes enraged. I was hoping that perhaps you might intercede for me. You are obviously a man of means, or so my wife says, and she is always right about such things. In addition to that, now it turns out that you are a highly placed advisor to a king in a foreign land, come here solely to seek out and observe this Jesus. You," he coughed nervously, "could perhaps discuss the importance of your mission with my wife. That may well influence her enough to accede to my request to let me seek out this man so that I may see him for myself, since it is well known that a woman respects a stranger's opinion more than her own husband's."

"I'll be happy to. But what if this doesn't work?"

"Perhaps you could tell her of your intention to hire a guide, a local person who knows the country and the people and the language better than yourself." I stared at him. It wasn't a bad idea. Not a bad idea at all. Misunderstanding the reason for my silence, he hastily added, "Not that your knowledge of our language is bad, you understand. It's just that your accent may make it difficult for some to understand you. Then too, my knowledge of local customs and so forth may well prove to be quite useful to you."

The more I thought about it, the more convinced I was. Bartholomew could be useful. Not only in the ways he was suggesting, but also as a man Friday of sorts. He could take care of the logistics, procuring food and lodging, transportation, and the like, leaving me more time to devote listening to and observing Jesus. Yes, I thought, it wasn't a bad idea at all.

"Oh," he waved a negligent hand, "you wouldn't have to pay me much. A nominal sum would suffice. To be honest, I'd do it for free. It's just that Anna puts so much stock in money that I fear, in the end, that will be the only argument that will win her over."

I was still lost in thought, trying to analyze the additional complications a companion might pose to a time traveler. As long as he didn't go rooting through my belongings, and as long as he respected my right to privacy when I needed to work on my reports . . .

"You needn't really pay me at all, Lightfoot," he blurted. "Just tell the woman that you'll be paying me, and, when I return home, I'll just tell her that on the way back I was set upon by bandits, and that all my wages were stolen!" He looked at me anxiously.

"I'll pay you. What do you think would be a reasonable price?"

He beamed and spoke briskly. "Ah, well. That would depend to a large extent upon the length of the trip. When I've considered going by myself, I've thought that a month should be more than sufficient to determine whether or not this man is really the Messiah." I frowned in reply.

"That's a pretty optimistic estimate for such a serious endeavor. I was figuring on a lot longer."

"What can be so difficult about it?" Bartholomew shrugged. "We listen to see if he makes sense and that he does not contradict Mosaic Law. We speak to members of his entourage as well as to him. The Pharisees, the Sadducees, the Zealots, agents provocateurs of Herod Antipas as well as of Pilate himself will be bombarding him with questions, trying to trip him up. We'll see how well he acquits himself in the defense of his teachings. We'll see if he is in fact fulfilling the prophecies as set forth in the Scriptures, and, lastly, we'll see with our own eyes whether or not he is enabling the deaf to hear, the blind to see, and the crippled to walk. What could be simpler? A month at most—that's how I see it."

"I intend to follow him to the end."

"To what end? Surely not until the end of your life?" Bartholomew was incredulous.

"I was thinking more along the lines of until the end of his life."

"But that amounts to about the same thing! He is a young man—about the same age as you, certainly not a day over thirty I'm told. You could spend three decades following him!"

"I think not, Bartholomew. In any event, you will be free to return home at any time. I will pay you two denarii a day in addition to all expenses, and you may go home whenever you have satisfied yourself about the man. If you still want to." Bartholomew shook his head wonderingly.

"You must be truly dedicated to your king to accept such a mission."

"I am dedicated to truth. Nothing more; nothing less."

Bartholomew studied me curiously for a few long moments as we walked along. "You are a peculiar man, Lightfoot, and your king and your countrymen are no less peculiar, I warrant. But I accept your commission."

What a character. He was suddenly like a kid being let out of school for the summer, eyes dancing with thoughts of adventure to come, but he was trying at the same time to make it look like *he* was doing *me* a favor. Well, who knows, I thought; maybe he was.

"It's done then," I smiled.

"Yes, Lightfoot, and now all we have to do is to tell Anna. You are so good with words, my friend. I wonder if you'd mind . . ."

I told her all right, and it was like being caught smack dab in the middle of the desert when a thunderstorm comes barreling in from the northeast. About all you can do is to stand there and get wet. I got a good two and a half sentences out of my mouth before she darkened, and the verbal thunderclaps broke over us like a string of atom bombs.

"Who is the bigger fool?" she demanded of me in what was clearly a rhetorical question. "An imbecile or the man who hires one? You men," she spat vehemently, "you disgust me! None of you ever grow up! Can any of you ever be long content with responsibly meeting the demands of everyday living? With mending the roof, with plowing, with tending to the animals, with acting like adults in the real world? No, you become easily bored and want to escape into a pretend world. You run off like children after one adventure or another. You start a war, dress yourselves up in silly costumes, and go marching off to foreign lands. Can women do thus? No! It is we who must pay for your folly. If it's not war, it's 'seeking truth.' How noble!" she mocked. "Ask the *women* of Capernaum what they think of this Jesus! It's the scandal of Galilee! Those so-called 'disciples' he recruited here left their boats and nets at the docks and their wives and children to fend for themselves!

Those irresponsible bums simply walked off to follow their 'Lord and Master.'

"I appeal to that pea-sized brain of yours, Bartholomew: would any good man, let along the 'Holy One of God,' encourage men to desert their own families, to forsake their duties? Go then!" she said, her dark eyes flashing. "Go!" she shrieked, picking up an earthenware platter and throwing it at us. We ducked, and it sailed over our heads and shattered against the wall behind us. We backed off.

"This fool," she shouted at me, pointing at Bartholomew, "not eight months ago, wanted to follow the Baptist! A grown man wanting to be dunked by a lunatic in the Jordan so that his 'sins could be washed away.' And just where is the Baptist now? Imprisoned at Herod's fortress of Machaerus! What will happen to him? He will be put to death, Bartholomew, just as this Jesus will be. Mark my words: no good can come to him or to any who follow him!

"How childish you men are! You cannot leave well enough alone. You cannot be content with what you are and what you have! There must always be the Great Cause, the Crusade, the Search for Truth! How utterly like children you are, wanting to run away, seeking glory, honor, and meaning, wanting to believe in romance, mystery, and magic. GO!" she screamed, hurling a pitcher. We ducked again and, although we were still unscathed, backed up some more.

"Would that the world were ruled by women! Would that the world were ruled by practical creatures who are closer to nature and to reality! We live in the real world, with the pain of childbirth, with nursing our young, tilling the garden, preparing meals, washing clothes, curing ailments . . . with real life!

"You worthless scum, Bartholomew! You are good for nothing! You inherited this inn from your father. It was his energy that built it, not yours. Just as it is my energy and business sense that run it! When you are not sleeping, you are daydreaming, and, when you are not daydreaming, you are in the midst of silly philosophical discussions over wine with your other air-headed friends. Be off with you then! It will make my lot easier!" With this, she picked up a five-gallon urn. We headed for the door fast and were through it and swallowed up in the cool dark night when we heard the urn crash inside. Bartholomew looked at me and said, "She's Assyrian," as if by way of explanation. He stroked his beard thoughtfully for a moment, considering the situation. "At least we were almost through with the meal when you broached the subject. It's best to begin any journey with a full stomach."

I nodded.

"I'd hoped for a good night's sleep before continuing, though," I said.

"I also, Lightfoot. Anna? Anna, my sweet dove? The good gentleman is *paying* me for accompanying him. Do you hear me? It is a *job*, my little nightingale. I will be paid in gold, Anna. GOLD, do you hear? I am to be a guide." Silence. "Anna?" Emboldened, he approached the door. "I will be bringing home *money*, my beloved." Our bedrolls and my bag were thrown out.

"Bartholomew, if you're gone for any longer than a month, or, if you come home with empty pockets . . ." the threat hung heavily in the night air.

"Thank you, my little treasure," Bartholomew called out cheerfully as we picked up our things. "I will be counting the moments until we're together again."

And so we set out for Gennesaret, the next town further south along the shores of the Sea of Galilee. We reached it in no time at all, and, since I was so wound up, I insisted we push on further south to Magdala, the home town of Mary of Magdala, better known as Mary Magdalene. But along about 11 p.m., Bartholomew began dragging, so, since we were on the outskirts of Magdala anyway, I called a halt and we sacked out in an olive grove. I was beginning to get excited and so slept little.

28

"All, right," I said to Bartholomew as the sleepy town began to stir in the bright early morning sunlight, "let's split up and meet back here in about two hours. You go to the market place and get us some food; here's the money, not only for today, but for several days of travel. At the same time, ask as many people as you can about Jesus, when he came through here, when he left, where he went, and so on. If you have the time, talk to anyone who had direct personal contact with him."

"Where are you going?"

"To find a prostitute." I caught the upraised eyebrows and quickly added, "A certain very special prostitute."

"Aren't they all?" the little innkeeper remarked drily.

"Look, Bartholomew, I'll explain later. But, believe me, my reasons have nothing to do with my glands. It's just that I understand that there is a certain prostitute in this town who is, or is about to become, very close to Jesus." Bartholomew shook his head sadly.

"And he is supposed to be a holy man of God."

"This shouldn't come as any surprise to you. You told me yourself that he is known to associate with sinners."

"And I also told you that that is precisely one of the things

159

that casts serious doubt upon his claim to be of God. As Anna has reminded me on more than one occasion, her people have a saying. 'He who lies down with dogs, gets up with fleas.'"

"Very catchy. I must remember that. Now let's get moving. See you later."

Where does one go to inquire about the whereabouts of prostitutes, I asked myself. Why, to the docks, of course, I responded. I walked up to a crowd of fishermen on the quay, who were deep in consultation, alternately scanning the sky and pointing at several different places on the Sea of Galilee, obviously conferring over the best places to fish that day, considering the weather, the temperature and condition of the water, and similar factors.

"Excuse me," I said, interrupting the pontifications of a swarthy man who was clearly a leader of some sort. He glowered at me. "I was wondering if you fellows could direct me to a prostitute." Guffaws and raucous laughter rang out in the chill morning air. It was accompanied by much rib-poking and not a few lewd remarks.

"Isn't it a bit early in the day?" leered a squat Neanderthalic type, displaying a mouthful of rotten teeth. I flushed.

"You misunderstand me. This woman, I'm searching for a particular one, you understand, has information that . . . will be useful to me."

"What is the woman's name?" growled the leader, whose dark complexion only served to highlight the stark-white puckered four-inch scar on his right cheek.

"Mary."

"Mary, you say." He scratched his left armpit reflectively. "There are ten towns on the shores of the Sea, and Magdala is by far the largest. Of prostitutes we have plenty. In addition, Mary is a very common name. Is she called by anything else?"

"Not to my knowledge. 'Mary' is all I know."

He shook his head. "What does she look like then?"

"I have no idea."

"Indeed," he said, now pensively running his hand over the stubble on his face, trying to give the impression of a man of infinite patience even when confronted with a village idiot. "How old is she then?"

"I don't know."

"You do not," he observed with heavy irony, "give us much to go on." There were barely suppressed smiles all around, and I felt the perfect fool.

"That's true," I admitted, "but I approached you because men of your obvious worldly wisdom might be expected to know of such matters. There was a marked change in the atmosphere. They'd been prepared to scornfully dismiss me. Now they'd received a challenge.

"Stranger, how can you possibly expect even us to guide you to a certain wench when all you know is that she's called Mary and is a wanton? You don't know her by any other name. You don't know what she looks like. You don't know how old she is. Do you know if she is now in Magdala, or whether she is called a Magdalene because she *once* lived here? What is her father's name? His occupation? Her mother's name?"

Well, he had me, of course. Not only did I not know the answers to any of those questions, but it suddenly occurred to me that she might be called Magdalene because she was *going* to be taking up residence there before she met Jesus, and that that hadn't happened yet. Although he'd been through here once, he'd be through here several times during the course of his three year-ministry. It could be entirely possible that Mary just hadn't yet come to Magdala. Or it could be that the Bible refers to her as a Magdalene, not because she had lived there, but because her family lived there. She may have been visiting them when Jesus came through. Perhaps that had already happened, and she was following him even now.

At any rate, I certainly couldn't go to the nearest telephone booth and look under "Magdalene, Mary" in the directory. Once again it was brought home to me that my job was not going to be an easy one. Clarence had told me that one of the most important requirements for the job was resourcefulness. He was right.

"You are, of course, right," I responded to the group. "I'm sorry." As I began to leave, the leader spoke.

"Wait! Friend, it is clear that you are on a most unusual errand and, further, that there is a great deal you're not telling us." When I turned back, his probing, intense eyes locked on mine, and I could see the high intelligence that resided behind them.

"It's simply that I have a great deal of interest in the iterant preacher named Jesus. I was told that this Mary I seek knows him well. It is really nothing more complicated than that."

"The Nazarene," the scar-faced man said softly, thoughtfully, "ah, yes. The self-styled 'fisher of men' who netted a number of our brothers in Capernaum."

"That's the man."

"We heard his words. He stood on the deck of a boat in this very place and preached to a multitude. His words are . . . powerful. Scores left to follow him south."

"But you did not."

"We did not," he acknowledged, his eyes dropping to the ground for a moment.

"But if his words were so powerful . . ." I left the rest of the question unspoken. The crowd began to murmur. The incident had changed, all in the space of a couple of minutes, from making sport of a funny-looking foreigner with a thick accent who was in search of a prostitute to being asked to account for turning away from a strange Nazarene who spoke to their innermost heart of hearts. Their leader spoke for them, speaking with a passion that suggested he was also trying to convince himself.

"We have wives, children, old people to take care of. We have responsibilities. *We* must work for a living, my friend. We live in the real world, not a dream world of prophets' visions! In the real world, a man must eat, and he must labor to earn his bread!"

"What you say is true as far as it goes," I said. "But I cannot help but feel that it is now you who is not telling all." Our eyes locked again. He opened his mouth to protest but then shifted his gaze to the south, to the direction Jesus had taken.

"His words are too hard," he said sadly, almost plaintively. "Too hard," he whispered. "We are only men."

I nodded, knowing exactly how he felt. A strong wind came up as I turned and walked away.

29

† † † † †

The Horns of Hattin is an extinct volcano that dominates a large basalt plateau 860 feet above the town of Magdala and just west of it. Eons ago, a shifting of the Earth's crust caused adjacent surfaces of the hard, dense, dark volcanic rock to be differentially displaced parallel to the plane of fracture. The effect is breathtaking in more ways than one. The fissure, or rift, is known as the Valley of Doves, and, as Bartholomew and I toiled up it, I felt some of the same kind of awe I felt when I first saw the Mogollon Rim in the Arizona uplands. The cliffs here were every bit as sheer, dangerous, and visually dramatic, the northern wall rising to 320 feet, and the southern to 600 feet. When we reached the summit, we could see the village of Arbela below, and it was here that I called a halt for the day. The sun was beginning to set.

I began writing my report on the following morning before we moved out. Writing my report at dawn was to become standard operating procedure. At dawn I was not in a hurry to scribble the report down quickly, racing against the fading light of the sunset. In addition, my mind was fresh. The trouble was that until we caught up with Jesus, there was little to report. All the research Clarence had done was right on the mark. There were few surprises in my journey across the face of first century Palestine. The construction of the dwellings, public houses, and places of worship; the way the people dressed, what they ate, how they earned their livings—it had all been described in the chronicles of the times. Nevertheless, like a good military man, I entered every detail in my report every morning. Everything. The date, time, weather conditions, place names, people's names, the prices of food and lodging, the flora, the fauna, everything. A friend has urged me to publish my report, but it is my feeling that that document would be of little interest to anyone except a handful of archaeologists and historians.

Somehow I still couldn't believe, really believe, that I wasn't going to be coming back from this mission. My mind just wouldn't accept it. I still pictured myself being debriefed by Clarence back in his home or sitting in Ike's den back on the farm in Gettysburg, showing him on a map the places I'd been, telling him what Christ had said, my observations, and so on. I still saw myself returning to my squadron at Nellis Air Force Base. I still saw myself watching television, flying, driving a car, flipping an electric light switch, and doing a thousand everyday things that my conscious intellect knew very well I'd never do again. Palestine in the first century was no more or no less "civilized" than many parts of the world were in the mid-twentieth century. I guess that's what made it so hard to believe that I wasn't going back again. Subconsciously, I was looking at this as a tour of duty in an underdeveloped country, not unlike my tour of duty in Korea. Well, I knew I'd have to face the truth and come to grips with it sooner or later, but foremost in my mind was getting the mission accomplished, my investigation completed, and my report back in the document canister under five feet of earth. Then I'd face it. In the meantime, if it made things a little easier to believe that, on the other side of the world, people were watching the "Ed Sullivan Show" on Sunday nights, I could see no harm in it.

Bartholomew was not an unpleasant traveling companion. He was exuberant, like a kid playing hooky from school. I guess if I were in his sandals and away from that shrewish wife of his, I'd feel the same way. At any rate, he was a good little guy, and his infectious high spirits made the miles melt away. As we journeyed along, we met a number of people who had seen Jesus, and most, at least most of those whom we'd asked, were of the opinion that he was clearly a major prophet, perhaps even on the same order as Elijah. Since my interviewees were not by any means part of a statistically validated sampling anyway, I varied my line of questioning, with some interesting results. Of some who were most glowingly enthusiastic, I asked point blank, "Do you think he is the Messiah?" In most cases, the eyes would suddenly become guarded and furtive, darting about, possibly to see if there were any Teachers of the Law within earshot. Remember, blasphemy was a capital offense. "Of that, I am not qualified to pass judgment," would be the usual cautious reply. It was in the afternoon in the village of Arbela that we met an extraordinary exception.

Bartholomew and I spent all morning at the well talking to people, for Jesus had spent some time here and had made quite an impression. It is perhaps important to point out here that, for the most part, there were no individual wells in Palestine. Water was extremely scarce and digging a well was a big undertaking. For this reason, there would usually be a single community well where the people tended to congregate, not only to draw their water, but to meet, rest for a spell, gossip, and socialize. We took a light snack and a siesta at noon, which was the custom in those days. It was after we awoke that I saw the old man approaching, and there was something about the way he walked, something about his eyes.

"Yes, I have seen Him," he answered in response to my question. He pointed due south. "You'll find Him no more than a day's journey in that direction." His smile was so benign, so serene, and his eyes so incredibly clear. Eyeglasses were a long, long way off, so it was nearly always the case that old people squinted. One reason was simple presbyopia, a hyperopia for near vision which develops with advancing age. It results from a physiological change in the accommodative mechanism by which the focus of the eye is adjusted for objects at different distances. As a person grows older, his lens substance gradually grows less pliable and eventually can't change shape in response to the action of the ciliary muscles. That's why you see so many old people who aren't wearing their glasses looking like they're doing a trombone act when they're trying to read. Other ways in which age can wreak havoc on the eyes is the development of cataracts, glaucoma, and spots. The man standing before me was seventy if he was a day, and his eyes were as wide and clear as those of a child.

I had started out the day in high enough spirits but, as time had worn on, found myself drifting off, only half listening to the people we were interviewing. It may sound strange, but I'll tell you why. True, we had talked to person after person who either had received or observed a physical healing of some sort, and true, these people had nothing to gain by lying to us about it. I did not question their sincerity; I questioned their judgment, their objectivity. Every healing we had heard of until then could have been explained in nonsupernatural terms. Every type of healing we had heard of until then was being performed by numerous faith healers in America of the 1950's (and is still done today, I might add). I'm talking about the lame walking, the deaf hearing, and so on. Plenty of people even in twentieth century America have risen from wheelchairs, or thrown away crutches or hearing aids in faith healing services. And I know doggone good and well that none of those healers are the Messiah. How then are those people healed? As near as I can tell, all physical healings can be attributed to three broad causes. First, the person healed had never had anything *physically* wrong with him in the first place. As more and more research is done in the area of psychosomatic medicine, we are finding that, despite outward symptoms, there is absolutely nothing physically wrong with anywhere from ten to twelve percent of the people admitted to hospitals. Their psychogenic pain is real enough, their illness or disability real enough. But only in the sense that they believe it is real and believe they have no control over it. A charismatic authority figure, medical or religious— it makes no difference as long as the patient has complete faith in him—can therefore "cure" such a credulous and disturbed person instantly. Could some of the people I had met or heard about who were presumably cured by Jesus fall into this category? As a completely impartial observer, I had to allow for that possibility.

There was a second and very real possibility. We know that under extreme stress or emotional turmoil, the human body becomes capable of seemingly incredible feats of strength. You see it in the violently insane. You also read about 110-pound women lifting the front ends of automobiles to free their injured children, or about ordinary people bending iron bars with their bare hands, or running or jumping enormous distances when the chips were drown and there was nothing else they could do to save their lives or the lives of those dear to them. We're even quite used to such stories. We simply chalk them up to the amazing power of adrenalin and the wonder that is the human body. But that's only the tip of the iceberg. Modern scientists are only now discovering and isolating even more subtle and remarkable defense mechanisms. For example, there is a certain complex biochemical compound that the body begins to manufacture under extreme pain and extraordinary emergency conditions. It's a powerful pain killer, and its properties are strikingly similar to those of morphine. Researchers are trying to reproduce this "natural narcotic" synthetically primarily because, with the proper dosage, it can be every bit as effective as other narcotics but has the added advantage of being nonaddictive. We know now that it is probably due to its presence in the bloodstream, rather the presence of adrenalin, that makes it possible oftentimes for a man to be seriously, sometimes even mortally, wounded in combat and yet not even realize it until the battle is over. There have been cases of men running on broken legs or driving a bayonet thrust home with broken or shredded arms during the heat of battle. Even dying men have been known to summon up near superhuman strength for one last valiant act.

Naturally, there is a price to pay when one draws strength from these marvelous biochemical wells. It's not a free ride. As soon as the crisis is over, the effects of further strain heaped on a body already suffering from torn muscles and ligaments, loss of blood, shattered nerve endings, and fractured bones, are felt with full force, sometimes causing permanent disability or death. Could it be that these or similar biochemical phenomena are responsible for some "healings?" Could it be that, in an emotionally supercharged state, when a vibrant, forceful, and enigmatic figure lays a "healing" hand on some people, that, responding in a burst of pure faith, they unknowingly unleash or tap into these biochemical springs, enabling them to feel no pain, but instead a surge of power and exhilaration? Could this biochemical lift last for a few hours, a few days, a few weeks? As a completely impartial observer, I had to allow for that possibility too.

The third possibility, of course, was that the healings were truly of supernatural origin. If so, from whence did this power emanate? From a munificent Creator, from the Christian God, the embodiment of Good? Or from, as the detractors of Jesus suggested, a malevolent Force of Evil, Satan? Although theologians tell us that one of Satan's favorite tactics is misleading and deceiving people, I couldn't figure out what his angle could be in giving enormous power and its attendant credibility to a man who spoke out so forthrightly against him, to give power to a man who told people to love their enemies. It was crazy. There was no percentage at all for Satan in a set-up like that. No, clearly if the healings were indeed supernatural, and, if Jesus continued to fulfill the prophecies concerning the Messiah as set forth in the Scriptures, then Jesus of Nazareth was exactly what be purported to be: the Son of God, the Christ.

But that brings me right back to my point. Up until we met this old man, we'd had no clear evidence that the supernatural was involved. All of the healings we'd investigated could have been explained away in other ways. The old man's clear eyes glowed, and his whole face was radiant with joy.

"Yes, I have seen Him," he repeated. "Only a week ago I was dying. Even breathing was rapidly becoming so laborious that I knew I couldn't keep it up much longer. I had become a frail, pitiable skeleton racked with terrible, unendurable pain. For years before, I had been almost totally blind, able only to discern lightness, darkness, and shapes. I had no teeth, not a one. Any real hearing acuity had also fled years before. It was just when I was experiencing what I was certain was the final viselike tightening in my chest that I suddenly felt a strange peace flood over me. Peace, well-being, and a powerful compulsion to go outside, to the source of the peace and light. I felt a Force, a Power . . . ," he shook his head. "I can scarcely begin to describe it, and, to my surprise, I was able to get to my feet! I had not been able to do that unassisted for the previous three years! I had to get outside, that's all I knew. I groped toward the Light, tripping over things, yet never wavering in moving toward the Light. Then suddenly I was outside in the street in the midst of a huge and tumultuous crowd. I was being jostled around by the eagerness of a hundred bodies all with the same goal as I—to get closer to the Light. Then a woman's voice said, 'Make way! Let the old one through!' I felt dozens of hands lifting me, passing me over and through the throng until I was at last lowered to the ground at the very Source of the Light. A Light brighter and warmer and purer than any I'd ever known.

"'Grandfather,' the Light said, 'your sins are forgiven you, all of them. And, as a sign that my Father in heaven has given me the authority to do this,' I felt His gentle but firm hand on my forehead, 'I bid you arise and begin a new life.' My eyes were opened instantly, and I saw Him kneeling over me. An indescribable joy washed over me, and I sprang to my feet like a boy of twenty. 'Master,' I said, 'let me follow you, for you are, I know, the Light of the World.' He lay his hand on my shoulder and addressed the now hushed crowd. 'Do you hear this man? It is not man who has revealed this to him, but my Father in heaven.'"

"'Then may I come with you, Master?' I asked. He shook his head. 'No, grandfather. I would have you remain here as a witness that the Son of Man has passed this way, healing the sick, forgiving sins, and, to as many as received Him, giving them the power to become sons of God.'"

The old man had finished his story. As I said before, we had already heard a number of stories similar to it, so many that listening to them had been rapidly becoming a wearisome task, not unlike that of a man working in his third week as a department store Santa Claus. But still, there was something about this man. Something I couldn't quite put my finger on. He stood before me smiling, displaying a set of perfect teeth . . . TEETH! That was it! It wasn't so much his excellent vision that had been gnawing at me as it had been his teeth. What in the world was a man of seventy-odd years doing in first century Palestine with a set of perfect teeth?

"Excuse me, but I couldn't help but notice your teeth. May I?" He smiled strangely, sat on the edge of the well, and opened his mouth for my examination. Evidently he was used to people asking for a look. Now, thanks to Dr. Namuh's desire to have some of my teeth yanked out so I'd fit in better with the populace, my interest in first century dentistry had been piqued, and I'd asked Clarence to do a little research on the subject. So it was that I knew that the replacement of lost teeth with artificial ones of gold, silver, and wood was indeed done in those days, at least by the well-to-do. The very first artificial dentures were made by the Etruscans around 450 years before the birth of Jesus. They used the teeth of oxen held together by gold bands. The Phoenicians, slightly more advanced (if you want to look at it in that way), had the teeth of their slaves extracted to make dental bridges, and the bridges were held together by gold wire. The Greeks had artisans carve ivory teeth to replace lost originals. What I saw when I looked into the old man's mouth, though, defied belief. A perfect set of thirty-two gleaming original teeth. There weren't even any plaque or tartar deposits. I tugged and pulled and practically stuck my head in his mouth, examining them closely. They were his teeth.

"Impossible," I said softly.

"They came to me at that moment He healed me. When my eyes were opened, my hearing restored, and all illness left me." He stood up.

"Thank you," I mumbled, turning to look off toward the south. He began to walk away but turned and came back.

"Son," he smiled sadly, "you and your friend are going about this in the wrong way."

"About what?" I asked shortly, preoccupied and angry for having my thoughts interrupted.

"Why, your inquiry into Jesus, of course."

"Oh?"

"Yes. I don't mean to be critical, but if you confine your investigation to only those things that can be seen and touched, you will be missing the whole point of what Jesus has come among us to do. You see, curing my blindness, my deafness, giving me new teeth, renewing my whole body—all those things are as nothing compared to the biggest change He makes in men . . . He changes their hearts. He changed my heart, and my life will never again be the same. I know a peace and a joy now that is far more precious than the healing and renewal of my physical body. He has renewed my soul. That has made all the difference." So saying, he turned and walked away. I felt a chill at the base of my skull.

Bartholomew erupted in jubilation. "Then it is true! He is the Christ! The Anointed One!" He shouted, beaming at me. "Just think, my friend, soon we will come face to face with the Messiah!" I said nothing in reply.

"What is the matter? We have found what we sought!"

"Perhaps. Perhaps not."

"How can you possibly say that when—"

"When at second and third hand strangers relate incredible things to us? When a peculiar old man tells us a tall tale?" I interrupted harshly. "You are too ready to accept, Bartholomew. You've already decided what you want to believe. One cannot seek truth with an attitude like that. We must deport ourselves as if we were judges in a court of law. There is much at stake here, more than you could possibly know." He looked hurt, and I softened. "Look, Bartholomew, would the unsubstantiated testimony we've heard so far stand up in any court? Be reasonable, use your head, not your heart."

"Friend Lightfoot, isn't your heart after all, the only court that matters?" I looked into the eyes of a man whose words I could not answer.

"Let's get going, Bartholomew. Southward. We should be able to get a good piece of distance behind us before the sun goes down."

30

That night I lay gazing into the small campfire lost in thought. This was lunacy. First, time travel was impossible. Second, even if it were possible, no sane man would volunteer to be marooned for the rest of his life in a remote and, in many ways, still primitive province of the Roman Empire in the first century merely to scribble down notes and make observations on an itinerant Galilean preacher. Perhaps he was what he claimed to be and perhaps not. Did it really matter at all? As long as millions *believed* he was and followed his teachings, what did it matter? The important thing, I thought, was that men should live together in harmony, in peace. The important thing was that most people cared about justice and honor. The important thing was that most people had compassion for those less fortunate than themselves. Whether this state of affairs came about through people following the teachings of Ghandi, Confucius, Mohammed, Jesus, or whomever, was of little or no consequence. (Little did I realize at the time how radically my opinion would be altered in the coming weeks.) Well, it was too late now, I thought, sighing deeply.

"Lightfoot," Bartholomew said, responding to the sigh, "you're troubled?"

"I'm just having some trouble getting to sleep."

"Sometimes talking helps."

"And sometimes it doesn't," I replied irritably. At that moment, further talk with Bartholomew was the last thing I wanted. He was an O.K. little guy, but he just talked too much. I had tuned him out several hours before on the trail and had begun searching the skies for even a single jet contrail to prove that I was still in the twentieth century. In a backward and primitive place to be sure, but still in the twentieth century. Bartholomew spoke again, evidently deciding he knew what was best for me.

"Tell me about the land you come from, what it is like, and so forth."

"What it is like," I repeated, still staring into the fire. "It is a big country, and one must make a long ocean voyage to get there. Our government is similar to Rome's, but our Senate has much more real power than the Roman Senate has in comparison to the Emperor. Our . . . emperor attains office by popular vote rather than through heredity. All citizens aged twenty-one or over may vote. I . . . don't quite know what to say, what to tell you." I shrugged. "There is so much to say and yet so little. We are a people like any other. We have our philosophers, our farmers, our statesmen, our merchants, our thieves, our poets, our murderers, our architects, our teachers, our holy men and sinners, our great men of vision and courage, our knaves and fools. We are not so different from any other people in any other place or time. We just try to make it from our mothers' wombs to our graves with as little pain and as much happiness as possible."

"Your land, what is it called? You haven't yet told me."

"Since it is composed of a union of separate provinces, or states, we simply call it 'The United States.'"

"From what you say, your land seems to be much like Greece. You have your city-states and the idea of democracy."

"Yes and no, Bartholomew," I said, my gloom subsiding as I found myself unexpectedly warming to the conversation. "As you undoubtedly know, the civilizations of Egypt and Sumer began with a number of independent city-states, each one a city with a few

175

miles of dependent agricultural villages and cultivation around it, and, out of this phase, they passed by a process of coalescence into empires. But the Greek city-states, for hundreds of years, remained totally independent; they did not coalesce. Even though the Greeks shared a common language and a common heritage, they had no strong feeling of national identity. They thought of themselves as Athenians or Spartans or whatever first and foremost. It took nothing short of a revolt against King Darius and the mighty Persian Empire to finally unite them.

"Now a somewhat similar situation existed with respect to my country, which originally consisted of thirteen separate and distinct provinces, each going its own separate way for many years. Like the Greeks, a man thought of himself first as a member of his province or region—say as a Pennsylvanian or a Georgian, or as a Northerner or a Southerner first, and only secondarily, if at all, as an American. But our revolt against our king, who was named George III, and his empire changed that, just as a revolt changed that for the Greeks. This is not to say that all conflicts between states or provinces or regions ceased, but it did bring us all together. And we have stayed together in spite of everything, but that is another story. As for democracy, we not only borrowed the idea from the Greeks, but the very word itself. Only we went still further. In the Greek city-states, slaves could not vote, freedmen could not vote, women could not vote, non-Greeks could not vote, Greeks originally from another city-state could not vote in the city-state in which they resided, even Greeks born in the city whose *fathers* had come from eight or ten miles away from the city beyond the headland could not vote. In addition, many of the city-states demanded that one must be a land owner in order to vote. So it was that even in Athens, the most democratic and freest of them all, out of a population of 315,000, only 43,000 were eligible to vote."

"In your country slaves are permitted to vote?"

"In my country we have no slaves."

"No slaves?"

"No, we did away with slavery almost a hundred years ago." Only a hundred years ago, I thought ironically. Progress.

Bartholomew was shaking his head in wonder. "And you allow women to vote?"

"Yes, we gave women the vote nearly forty years ago." Again. Progress. Why had it taken so long for such elementary reforms to have come about? Here I was, talking to a man two millennia removed in time from my own, and I was suddenly struck with the uncomfortable realization that I couldn't boast of two millennia worth of social progress. We were on the right track to be sure, but mankind had not exactly been moving down that track with any dazzling speed.

"A most remarkable land," Bartholomew opined.

"Most remarkable," I agreed.

"Have you then subjugated many people, as have the Romans?"

"Only the original inhabitants of the land, my mother's people. We have fought wars in other lands and on other shores but, after we win the wars, we always pack up and go home."

"Why?"

"I . . . don't know. I guess we just aren't the subjugating type."

"How odd."

"I guess so. I never thought much about it before," I shrugged.

"Your people sound most peculiar."

"Oh, people are people, Bartholomew. As I've said, we're no different than anyone else. We're born and we die, and in between those two events we spend our time trying our best to make sure that we experience more happiness and contentment than pain and suffering. We make friends and enemies; we love and hate, buy and sell, get married and have children, learn and forget, spend and save, succeed and fail, and laugh and cry. Once every generation or so, we go off and fight a war. We're no different than anyone else. Once I thought we were unique, but that was before I did some traveling."

"All my life I have wanted to travel," said Bartholomew wistfully. "I was born in Capernaum, raised in Capernaum, and will surely die in Capernaum. Lightfoot, you can't even begin to understand what it's like—day after day, week after week, month after month, year after year, to see travelers come and go and to always remain behind yourself. To hear them tell of the great and wondrous places they've been, the exotic sights they've seen, the . . ." he broke off suddenly. "Lightfoot, I've never even been to Jerusalem! Anna resents every moment that I am away from the inn. She doesn't understand anything. She thinks that I'm always trying to shirk doing any work around the inn.

"The moment I met you though, I knew the time had come. I immediately recognized you as a kindred spirit, as a fellow seeker after truth. And, as if that were not enough, you too were intrigued by this man called Jesus. Clearly, it was the appointed time to make my move. No more daydreaming. I decided on the spot that this time I would translate thought into action. I want it to be said of me, and, which is vastly more important, I want to be able to say to myself, that at least for once in my life, I was not Bartholomew, the dull, timid, and henpecked little innkeeper, but Bartholomew the Adventurer, Bartholomew the Bold, a man who left home and safety behind him to embark on a glorious Quest . . ." he stopped dead and looked embarrassed. "At least once in his life, a man must do something like this. Do you know what I mean? Do you understand the feeling?" Did I?

"Yes."

"Tell me, Lightfoot, your king, your emperor, is he a Jew?"

"No," I replied, momentarily taken aback by the unusual question.

"Then your countrymen are? Or at least the majority of them, they are Jews?"

"No, only about three out of every hundred."

Bartholomew's brow wrinkled in the flickering firelight. "Then why are your people interested in the Jewish Messiah? This is a matter of great importance to Jews, of course, because the Messiah will free us from the oppressive yoke of Rome. But why should a mysterious and far-off land of Gentiles consider this to be such a momentous issue?"

I moved my gaze from the campfire to the vast blanket of stars overhead, and it was a long time before I finally spoke. "Most of my countrymen, as well as the people who inhabit the countries we have allied ourselves with, say they believe in the teachings of Jesus. It is entirely possible to do so without being a Jew. At any rate, most profess to believe in the teaching of Jesus. Now a few are lying, and a few really do believe, but most merely think they believe; in their hearts, they are not really sure. Therefore, they don't make as serious or as concerted an effort to live up to the teachings of Jesus as they would if they *knew* beyond any shadow of a doubt that he is who he says he is. Jesus, along with the things he has said and the things he stands for, pervades our entire Western civilization—our literature, our laws, our art, our music, our customs, our codes of ethics, everything."

"But how is it possible that one man, a man who is not yet widely known in his own country, have such a far-reaching effect on a land so far away?"

"Believe me, there has been enough time for such a thing to happen," I said, brushing aside his question. "At any rate, because of his vast influence over my land, if I can deliver absolute proof that he is or is not the Messiah, either way, then it will profoundly change our Western world." Suddenly, I realized that I had just parroted Ike's initial speech to me. Bartholomew's eyes grew large as he looked upon me with a new respect bordering on awe.

"A tremendous responsibility must surely weigh heavily on your shoulders."

I felt uncomfortable under his stare and not a little inadequate. He was right. This was serious business, more serious than anything else in the history of mankind. I felt a twinge of guilt when I remembered that only a few short moments ago, I'd been feeling very sorry for myself. I continued to stare at the countless stars and galaxies in the infinite vastness of space. For the first

179

time, I really believed in what I was doing. This was no longer just an adventure or a challenge.

I had to know.

The next morning our path put us on a main trade route leading almost due south toward Jerusalem. It was here that we fell in with a caravan, and, during the course of the day's march, I pumped as many people as I possibly could, trying to get as much information as was available concerning Jesus. In the evening all the men sat around the campfire and tried to impress one another with stories about their business acumen, strength and endurance, success with the ladies, and learning. Nothing much ever changes, I guess. Except for the clothing and the language, it could just as easily have been a meeting in an Elks Lodge in Poughkeepsie.

Since trees were so scarce, wood was seldom used to fuel fires in Palestine. Camel dung was used instead. Centuries later, the Plains Indians would use buffalo chips for the same reason. The aroma left something to be desired, but it sure burned pretty well, and there was plenty of it.

During a lull in the conversation, I brought up the subject of Jesus, and immediately I caught some guarded looks being exchanged in the flickering firelight. A silence hung like a pall over the group.

"Friend," said one of the ugliest men I'd ever seen in my life, slowly drawing a wicked looking curved knife from his belt, "you show an uncommon interest in our opinions of the Nazarene." There were nods of assent all around as the man brought out a sharpening stone and methodically began to hone the blade. Out of the corner of my eye I saw another meditatively fingering the handle of a Roman short sword.

"You appear to be a most curious man," the first went on, almost crooning as he worked the already impossibly sharp and gleaming blade back and forth across the surface of the stone. "A most peculiar stranger comes among us and begins to ask all manner of questions of us about a most controversial public figure. Some say that such a stranger could well be a spy for that fox, Herod Antipas." He spat, punctuating the sentence. "Others are of the opinion that such a man could be a spy sent by the Sanhedrin or by the Procurator."

In what I hoped was a casual gesture, I brushed my right hand against my left side and felt the reassuring thirty-seven ounces of steel that was my Colt .45 Peacemaker. Reassuring? No. There were too many. Besides, there had already been too much bloodshed. I was tired of killing, and that wasn't what I'd been sent here to do anyway. I let my hand fall away. There was nothing for it but to try to talk my way out of the situation. And, if that didn't work, well, Aloysius Lightfoot O'Brien's final resting place would be a shallow and unmarked grave in the desert. People have done worse.

I began to mentally frame a reply to the accusations. The words and the tone would have to be just right. This crew was a hair's-breadth away from turning into a lynch mob. Things were so volatile that I'd just as soon have been playing catch with a bottle of nitroglycerin. I decided to use some body language for a start. I slowly spread my hands, palms up, in the universal gesture of a harmless and innocent man who has been seriously misunderstood. Next, summoning up all the tact, diplomacy, and practical psychology at my command, I opened my mouth to speak, when Bartholomew thundered, "Ignorant dogs! How dare you accuse my colleague of being a spy for Herod or the Sanhedrin or Pilate? He is nothing of the sort!" Bartholomew puffed out his chest importantly. "He is a spy for a foreign country of great proportions lying far to the west across a great ocean!" The effect of his impassioned outrage was stupefying in the sense that no one there, including me, believed that anyone could be stupid enough to come out with a pronouncement that placed his neck as well as that of his traveling companion's in the noose so neatly. We, all of us, were so dumbfounded that we sat there in a frozen tableau that might have made an excellent diorama for the halls of the Smithsonian. Mouths were agape, and the ugly man with the nasty knife had stopped sharpening it in mid-stroke. I can't be sure, but I think my heart also stopped.

It was then that a most remarkable thing happened. Into the mouth of my pal with the knife, flew a large moth. He leaped to his feet, spitting out sticky pieces of moth and dropping his knife and sharpening stone in the process. Then somebody laughed, then another, and yet another. Bartholomew and I even joined in. It doesn't sound so funny as I write these words though. I guess you had to be there.

When the laughter had at last subsided, I spoke. "To the extent that wandering and impoverished scholars who have many questions and few answers are considered spies in your country, then to that extent, I must confess. I am a spy. I mean no harm. My country is interested in many things. It sends out many people in many different directions to learn. To learn of foreign plants, animals, cultures, science, everything. We want to know what kind of creatures dwell in the sea, what the air is made up of, how old different artifacts are . . ."

"Let us not cloak or dissemble our speech and its meanings before these men," interjected an elder whose hair and beard were snow white. He spoke with gentle authority as he continued, "For dim though my eyes may be, it is clear that they mean no harm. I perceive that they only seek truth, and since such men are few, all men have an obligation to help them. Let us help then. Let us speak frankly and openly of what we have seen and heard of this Jesus and give them the benefit of our conclusions."

A portly trader in his late forties needed no further invitation. He began speaking in sonorous and self-important tones. "How can a man who profanes the Sabbath be *any* kind of holy man or prophet, let alone the Messiah? Did not the Creator *Himself* rest on the seventh day? The Scriptures are clear, 'Keep Holy the Sabbath.' Yet the Nazarene preaches on the Sabbath, heals, undertakes journeys—in short, treats it like any other day. No, this Jesus is not a godly man."

"But," a youth of about seventeen interrupted, "how can healing the sick, on *any* day, be an evil? Isn't healing doing God's work?" The trader cast him a baleful glance.

Another man broke in. "The crime that eclipses all else though, is his blasphemy! He calls himself the Son of God!"

"Perhaps," another said in the voice of one who is always ready to reason, "he means it in the sense that we are all children of God. Are we not the Chosen People? All of us are Sons of God. Yes, I think perhaps he is just using a figure of speech."

"No! I've heard him! I've heard him, and I can assure you that he means that he and he alone has some sort of special and unique relationship with the Almighty. That he claims special power and station. He even has the audacity to speak of his 'Kingdom.' He is a blasphemer pure and simple," the man exclaimed heatedly. "and if the Sanhedrin doesn't sentence him to death, then others will!" There was a chorus of hearty murmurs. So we were back once again into the lynch-mob mentality. These guys scared me. It was most inopportune for Bartholomew to chime in, so he did.

"My friend and I think he may truly be the Messiah." Dummy, I thought. "In fact," he went on, as all eyes swung toward us again, "almost all of my colleague's fellow countrymen are followers and believers in Jesus. That is why he was sent here on a special mission from his king—to consult with Jesus." Double dummy, I thought, if we ever get out of this alive, I'm going to . . .

The ugly man with the curved and shiny knife stroked his beard slowly and looked at the old man with an I-told-you-so expression on his face. "Indeed," he said, and a whole lot of meaning was put into that one word.

"It is as I've said," I replied, "I have come here only to learn."

"And precisely where *do* you come from?"

"It is a confederation of states far to the west. No one here," I said truthfully, "has ever heard of it."

"Stop it!" the elder said. "Enough of this! These men are here to learn; let it be so. I told you that it is our bounden duty to assist them. Would anyone else speak of the Nazarene?" The words of the frail old man had a powerful and instant effect on the mob, not unlike the words of a man reprimanding a young child. The men became subdued, the mood softened.

"This Jesus," said the man with the reasonable voice, "his words sound well and good when one is seated on a grassy slope and the sky is blue, and a gentle breeze refreshes you, and there is food in your belly. But his way cannot be followed every day in the real world. The story of how he intervened in the stoning of the adulteress is well known and will serve as an excellent example. Are you familiar with it?"

I had, of course, read it in the Bible but shook my head because I wanted to see if there were any other versions extant. Bartholomew also shook his head. The man nodded and began, "Well, it seems that a crowd had gathered to stone an adulteress who had been just caught in the very act. There could therefore be no doubt of her guilt. So, in OBEDIENCE TO THE LAW, a group of right-minded citizens prepared to stone her. It was at this point that some addlepated fellow took it upon himself to ask this Jesus of Nazareth what he thought of the situation. Do you know what the reply was? Never in ten thousand years could you guess what he said."

"He said not to stone her," piped up Bartholomew hopefully.

"Wrong," smiled the speaker. "He is much too clever, too cunning, to openly tell people to disobey the Law. He said, 'Let he who is without sin cast the first stone.'"

"And then what happened?" whispered Bartholomew, his eyes open wide.

"First one man, then another, then a few more, then all dropped the stones that were in their hands and walked away. The woman went unpunished."

"And then what happened?" Bartholomew asked eagerly.

"Then nothing! That's all! Nothing! Justice was not served!"

Bartholomew's blank expression seemed to enrage the man all the more. "You stupid fellow! Don't you understand the implications? If only sinless people can punish the wicked, then the wicked will never be punished! Then all of our laws should be torn up, our prisons and courts done away with! A man commits a crime, a murder say. If only a sinless man can execute him, why arrest him in the first place? A man steals. If only a sinless man can imprison him, why have prisons? They can be of no avail if we are to take the Nazarene seriously."

"He is a clever one, all right," another said. "A man recently asked him if it was lawful to pay taxes to Rome—a straightforward question, is it not? Well this Jesus wriggled out of that one by asking to be handed a coin. Then he asked whose picture appeared on it. 'Caesar's,' was the reply. 'Then render to Caesar the things that are Caesar's, and to God the things that are God's,' he answered. Now, I ask you, friend," he said to me, "no, I challenge you to tell me what his meaning was. Are we then to give all our money to Caesar, or only those coins that bear his image? As you may or may not know, the Law says, 'Thou shalt not carve images, or fashion the likeness of anything in heaven above, or on earth beneath, or in the waters under the earth.' Consequently, no devout Jew would be caught dead in the possession of coins that bear the graven image of men or animals. This is why all the coins struck in Jewish mints bear only the likenesses of various plants, fruit, or symbols. Even the arrogant Herod the Great did not dare put his likeness on coins; instead, he had only the words, 'Herod King' on one side, and a design of one kind or another on the reverse side, depending on the denomination. Sometimes a cornucopia, sometimes flowers, sometimes fruit, a shield, and so forth. Herod Agrippa put a parasol on his coins. Even the Romans respect our feelings in this matter. The coins that they strike in Judea bear only the *name* of Caesar, with a laurel crown and various other symbols. Good Jews do not go about carrying coins with Caesar's graven image on them. Of that I can assure you."

"The man who handed the coin to the Nazarene," said a suspicious voice, "was it perhaps one of his own men?"

"Of that I cannot be sure. I was not there and only relate the tale as it was told to me. Supposedly it was a Pharisee, although I suppose it could have been one of his men posing as a Pharisee."

I mentally thanked Clarence for all his research and jumped in. "Does anyone here have a silver piece?" That drew some nasty looks, for they all knew what was coming. I stared down the man next to me, and he grudgingly handed me a shekel. I held it up in the flickering firelight. "Don't each of you carry such coins? I am told that this is the most common coin in this part of the world." The answer was grumblings of assent. "And yet whose graven image appears on it? Melqart, a Phoenician god."

"We are traders," said the man defensively. "We have no choice in the matter. Phoenician silver is what we *must* deal in; it is recognized everywhere . . . besides, even the Temple priests have sanctioned the use of shekels for payments to the Temple."

Another voice broke in raucously. "Perhaps then, if we are to be true followers of the Nazarene, we should render our shekels to Melqart!"

"Do you see," said the man, "what foolishness this leads to?"

"Perhaps," I said, "you are taking him too literally. From what you've told me, it seems clear to me that he often is speaking symbolically and using figures of speech."

"Perhaps," said a richly vibrant voice from the darkness beyond the campfire, "you are not taking him literally enough." But when we all turned to peer into the black night, we could see no one, and the only sound was the passage of the wind.

32

Since we were now on a major trade route and in the company of the relatively fast-moving caravan, we started making pretty good time. Late the following afternoon, we found ourselves in Nain, a small village located on a plateau on the lower northwestern slope of Mount Moreh. What made this tiny, sleepy, little, insignificant settlement suddenly so important was this: the residents claimed that the day before, the man, Jesus of Nazareth, had raised a widow's son from the dead.

The merchants in the caravan expressed a mild interest but were anxious to feed and water themselves and their animals and move on. The business world hasn't changed much in two millennia, I guess.

But Bartholomew and I greeted the news with great excitement for two reasons. First, because we were now only one day behind Jesus; we would surely catch up with him the next day. Second, because of the nature of the miracle. I spoke earlier of being unimpressed, for the most part, by the many healings I'd heard of. There were too many other possible explanations. But for a man who was truly dead, there could be only one possible explanation for this rising at the words of another. This was really important, I knew, for there are only three recorded instances of Jesus raising the dead—this young man, Jairus' daughter, and Lazarus. Bartholomew and I let the caravan pull out without us because we immediately began interviewing everyone in sight.

By this time, we had established our standard operating procedure. Bartholomew interviewed eyewitnesses, while I, whenever and wherever possible, interviewed the principals. The young man, Silas, was twenty years old and his mother's only child. Her husband had died three years before. Silas was able to tell me nothing except that he had been deathly ill for about twenty days prior to his apparent demise. The last week, he had been running a raging fever and slipping into and out of a comatose state. From the symptoms he described, I gathered that it was some kind of viral infection of unknown origin. At any rate, he told me that he had grown gradually weaker, then died.

"How do you know that you died?" I challenged. "You were slipping into and out of consciousness quite a bit. You could have just been in another coma."

His belief was unshakeable. "Have you ever been dead?"

"What kind of question is that? Of course I haven't," I shot back in exasperation.

"Well, believe me, when you die, you'll know it."

So much for the son. "Could you," I asked his mother, "could you *possibly* have been mistaken? Could he have still been alive when you were taking him off to bury him?" She looked at me as if I were a madman.

"You have no children," she replied. It was not a question. I shook my head. "If you had a son yourself, you wouldn't need to ask such a stupid question. He is my only son, my flesh and blood. I gave him life. I fed him at my breast. I watched him grow into a young man. He is my son, my only child. Never would I consign him to the grave if there were even the slightest possibility of his being revived. Never."

Next I spoke to the woman's sister-in-law, the one who had actually prepared the body for burial. It would have been she who would have washed the body and anointed it with nard and with a mixture of myrrh and aloes. It would have been she who would have tied the hands and feet with linen strips, veiled the face, and wrapped the body in its shroud. It would have been she who would have been the last person to see or handle the body.

"Sir, with all due respect, your questions are silly. We all know the difference between a live man and a dead man."

"Mistakes have been known to happen."

She looked about furtively, and, after assuring herself that we were alone, declared, "When I put him in the shroud, he was dead. Of that there can be no doubt."

"How can you be so sure?" I pressed.

"You'll not tell my sister-in-law? May I have your word?" I nodded impatiently and she continued. "You see, she would be offended if she knew I had departed from the Jewish custom. But I am not a Jew. I was brought up in Egypt, where proper reverence is shown for the deceased. Here in Judea they are so backward in so many ways. I would not, could not allow my only nephew to be buried with as little ceremonial preparations as the Egyptians would show an animal."

"Of course not," I mumbled, glancing up at the ceiling. What a waste of time.

"So I prepared his body for burial in the Egyptian manner."

"You did what?" I asked, feeling a strong, powerful, and eerie tingling start at the base of my neck and run down the length of my spine.

"I removed his brain, intestines, and other vital organs, washed them in palm wine, and placed them in canopic jars filled with herbs, then—"

"Are you telling me that all the vital organs had been removed from that boy when Jesus of Nazareth stopped the procession and raised him?"

"Yes sir. You see, I left them in the canopic jars, and the jars were in my home. I had intended to go out to the grave later on that night, and inter the jars with the body under cover of darkness.

Many find the Egyptian ways . . . strange or even offensive. I only wanted to make sure the boy had a civilized burial."

"But when you saw the boy raised . . ."

She nodded. "The first thing I did, once I recovered my wits, was to run back to my home . . . where all the canopic jars were right on the shelf where I'd left them . . . only they were now completely empty."

"Thank you," I replied. Then I stumbled out into the street in a daze, where I literally bumped into Bartholomew. He was beaming.

"Lightfoot, I have talked to no fewer than eighteen people who saw the miracle. Following your instructions, I interviewed each person separately to preclude the possibility of one witness's account influencing another's. The accounts agree in all respects. They all saw the dead man raised to life by Jesus."

"Good," I mumbled absently.

"Is something the matter? You don't look well."

"My interviews," I said guardedly, "have also given indications that the event that occurred here was . . . most curious."

"Curious?" Bartholomew exclaimed incredulously. "Curious? A man is raised from the dead, and you find that only curious?"

"There could be other explanations," I said with little conviction.

"But I have personally talked to eighteen people who saw the thing with their own eyes, who saw Jesus raise him up!"

"How could those spectators be sure that he was in fact dead?"

"Well . . ."

"Could they not have been mistaken? Could they not have been tricked? Could they not be intentionally lying for some motive of which we know nothing?" I challenged him.

"Friend Lightfoot, why would anyone, let alone a large group of people, lie about such a thing? By saying what they do, they invite only ridicule and scorn from most, charges of blasphemy from others, and, from others such as yourself, sharp questioning.

"As for their being mistaken or deceived, I allow that it could be so, but do not for a moment believe it. This is one of the many wonders Jesus has worked, and one, however clever, cannot trick all of the people all of the time. Neither can people mistake all that they see and hear of Jesus and yet their stories be so consistent.

"But enough. You spoke to the boy himself, as well as to his mother and her sister-in-law. You are perhaps in a better position to judge than I. What are your conclusions?"

I suddenly felt all of two thousand years old as I looked up at the bright, starry night sky. I thought of the billions of stars in the firmament, of the inexorable wheeling of the enormous galaxies, of the boundlessness of the universe.

"My conclusion, Bartholomew, is that we are on to something so big that . . ." Words failed me at that point, and the silence was so intense that when I resumed speaking, I found myself speaking in a hush.

"But we must be sure. We must be sure."

33

On the road the next day, right after we finished a midday snack of lentil soup and bread, I stretched out on a large slab of rock for a short nap. The custom of a daily siesta was one to which I had no problems adapting, and I think if modern Americans took it up, there'd be far fewer ulcers, divorces, and heart attacks.

I had been minding my own business, content to just lie there soaking up the warm rays of the sun like a big old lazy iguana and was just beginning to doze off when Bartholomew spoke.

"Lightfoot, have you always been a spy?"

"A researcher," I snapped angry for being so rudely snatched from the arms of Morpheus. "Don't use that word 'spy' anymore, Bartholomew. You almost got us into some big trouble back there in the caravan. I'm a researcher. Remember that."

"Just so. A researcher. Have you always been a researcher?"

"No," I answered, putting my hands behind my head and interlacing my fingers. "I've spent most all of my life as a warrior."

Bartholomew rolled over and put his hands behind his head. For a long time we both did nothing more than gaze up at the impossibly blue, blue sky. The only thing I could be certain of was that we weren't thinking the same thing, for, in my mind's eye, I was in the cockpit of an F-106.

"I have often wondered what the life of a warrior is like. I myself have never been to war and at times feel that I am the poorer for it. It must be exhilarating—the camaraderie with your fellows, seeing strange lands. Yet, at the same time, it must be terrifying."

"It is both," I admitted, "but mostly the latter. It is also a very sorrowful thing—seeing innocent people turned homeless because of what you yourself have done." I thought of the bombing runs over Korean towns and villages and of the sickening, sinking feeling in the pit of my stomach as I thumbed the bomb release, sending a rain of napalm down on the thatched roofs of a people, who, for the most part, were guilty of nothing more than being in the wrong place at the wrong time. In a place where there were North Korean or Chinese troop concentrations or next to a strategic bridge or weapons production factory.

"It is also," I continued, "a sorrowful thing to see young men and women and children on both sides, who had their whole lives ahead of them, and who had so much to offer, cut down like so many weeds. The world will never know how many great writers, scientists, artists, inventors, and poets died by the sword before they could even have a chance to display their talents. Cut down. Cut down like so many weeds." I thought of the motto of one of the squadrons of fighters that specialized in close air-to-ground support, particularly in built-up, populated areas, "Kill 'em all; let God sort 'em out."

"Believe me, Bartholomew, you have missed nothing."

"Do you mean that if you had it to do all over again, you wouldn't choose the life of a warrior?" A fair question, that. I considered for a moment.

"No, I would do it all over again."

"Even though it is terrifying?"

"Yes, even though it is terrifying . . . you see, there are worse things that can happen to a man than death."

"My friend, what could possibly be worse than death?"

"Experiencing the death of the things you love, whether they are people or ideas."

"Ideas?"

"Yes, it's hard to put into words . . . I, like many others, see my country not so much as a place but as a noble experiment. When I fought, I wasn't fighting for its mountains or plains or valleys; I was fighting for what my country stands for. For the conviction that a man has the right to speak his mind, to worship God as he sees fit, to be secure in the privacy of his own home, to enjoy due process under law, to be free to pursue his dreams. If these things were to be destroyed, well, that would be worse than death."

"But, friend Lightfoot, most of the people in the world don't have those freedoms. Yet life goes on. Yet life is worth living."

"It wouldn't be for me."

"Fighting for those things is indeed most commendable. But what if you could not hope to win? A hundred years ago, for example, Spartacus challenged the might of the entire Roman Empire. He was doomed before he started. Surely you don't advocate the same kind of extremism?"

"One must fight whether he will win or not. These things are too precious to surrender under any circumstances." Out of the corner of my eye I saw Bartholomew shake his head.

"You would fight a war you could not win?" he asked in sheer disbelief.

"Of course, Bartholomew, I would prefer to fight a war I could win, but . . . look, of all the things worse than death that can happen to a man, the worst of them is this: to live with himself after he has forsaken the things he loves, the things that give meaning and purpose to his life. To see his reflection in a looking glass after he has betrayed the things he believes in—this is the worst thing of all."

In the long silence that followed we both dozed off, each to his own dreams.

I t came suddenly, and it wasn't exactly the way I'd pictured it would be. But then I guess that's characteristic of all the most important moments of our lives. None of us is ever really prepared. Although much is made of man's imagination, it is, nevertheless, always a poor match for reality.

Bartholomew and I topped a rise and beheld a virtual living carpet of people covering the next slope. There were between 6,000 and 6,500 of them clustered in a gigantic semicircle about the man who stood at the top of the 500-foot hill. We just stood there for a moment, frozen in our tracks, gawking. There, in the distance, stood the man who had changed the whole of human history in a way so powerful, so through, and so far-reaching, that the world even dated all its events in terms of years before or after his birth. There stood a man for whom tens of thousands who had never met him would go cheerfully to their deaths rather than renounce him. There stood either the biggest fraud in the history of mankind, a lunatic, or the Second Person of the Triune God. *Ecce homo;* behold the man. My knees began to shake.

Neither of us spoke. It was a moment too big for words. We kept our silence as we moved to join the crowd. We got to within 250 yards before the density of the crowd prohibited any further forward movement, then we sat down with the rest to listen. Needless to say, I couldn't distinguish any of his facial features at that distance, although I could hear quite well. We'd been sitting there for all of five minutes before I realized how extraordinary the latter condition was. *We could hear quite well!* He was speaking in a normal conversational tone, yet we, 250 yards away, could hear him as easily as if he were three yards away. He wasn't shouting and used no voice amplification devices, electronic or otherwise. Yet all who came to hear him heard him. Now this was the first physical phenomenon in connection with Jesus of Nazareth that I had personally witnessed, and, while it might seem unimpressive or even trivial compared to other things reported in the Gospels (or later in my own reports), it was my first on-the-scene experience with miracles, and I can still remember it as if it were yesterday.

There have been many famous and infamous men in the history of our planet who have been great orators, who could sway crowds or whole nations. Men, who through the skillful use of words alone, could make people laugh or cry or move them to show generosity or mercy or cruelty or heroism. Who could move people to build or to destroy, to heal or to kill. One thinks of such widely disparate personages as Patrick Henry and Adolph Hitler, as Demosthenes and Winston Churchill, as Mohammed and Daniel Webster. But Jesus was not like anyone else. He did not speak in the flowery multisyllabic eloquence of a Webster or a William Jennings Bryan, nor with the frenzied gut wrenching passion of a Hitler or a John Brown. No, he had a way of stringing plain, simple, everyday words together in a quiet but powerful and authoritative way that reached deep down inside you, where you really lived, and made you know that you were hearing the Truth, whether you liked it or not.

And a lot of times you did not, for the scar-faced fisherman in Magdala had been right. His words were hard. This is the Way. Choose it and live; reject it and die. The choice is yours, and you cannot straddle the fence. I was sent to die that you might have that choice. God's love for you, for all of you, is that strong.

The Way is hard, and, if you should choose it, I can assure you that you will suffer and be persecuted. Father will be set against son, mother against daughter, brother against brother. I did not come into the world to bring peace, but to bring a sword. To follow me, you will need all the courage and strength you possess, and still that will not be enough. You would still fail without the Holy Spirit. But I will send Him to you, and you only need ask and He will come into your hearts. If you think it's going to be easy, forget it. Choose now between the things of this world, the pleasures of this life, and the Way. It must be one or the other. It cannot be both, for you cannot serve two masters. It cannot be done, and in your hearts you know it.

His words were powerful, and they were hard. Oftentimes when he spoke, I would see people get up and, eyes guiltily downcast, slink away. Sometimes there were tears on their cheeks. For them the words were too hard.

I will not, in this book, report all of his talks verbatim for several reasons. Even the Gospels don't give the full text of each speech because there would be much redundancy. Jesus talked about the concept of the Good Shepherd, not once, but many, many times. The same thing is true of the story of the Prodigal Son, of the parable of the Sower, the parable of the Workers in the Vineyard, the story of the Ten Virgins, and of the Good Samaritan.

Before I move on, I'd just like to mention how the tale of the Good Samaritan rankled the nerves and offended the sensibilities of the Jews who heard it. It was not just a nice little story about how people should be kind to each other. It was flung out as a challenge. Some were shamed by it, still others insulted. You see, the hatred between the Judeans and the Samaritans dated back to almost a thousand years before Christ, when Solomon's empire was divided into two parts—Judea and Samaria. The Samaritans were a mixture of various peoples who had settled in that area after the Israelites had been exiled. And although they had, for the most part, adopted the tenets of Judaism, they hadn't adopted them as completely as the Israelites considered to be proper. Therefore, when the Israelites returned from exile, there was big trouble.

Feelings ran deep, and around 340 B.C. the Samaritans built their own temple on Mount Gerizim, claiming that theirs was the true Temple, not the one in Jerusalem. The people of Judea considered them to be unclean, heathens, and worse. Even the Talmud says, "A piece of bread given by a Samaritan is more unclean than swine's flesh." So you can imagine what a bombshell it was for Jesus to hold up a Samaritan as one whose actions were to be emulated. People thought of and talked a lot about that. As of course they were meant to.

As I was saying, for me to re-report the messages contained in the Gospels would serve no useful purpose. If you've read the Bible, you already know them; if you haven't, Bibles can be bought in any bookstore, and I urge that you buy one. The primary objective of my mission was to verify the accuracy of the writings, the testimony, if you will, of Matthew, Mark, Luke, and John; this I did. Although I did not follow Jesus for a very long period of time, I saw many of the events recorded in the Gospels happen exactly as described. In the nineteen weeks that I followed him, I saw not a single event occur otherwise than it was reported in the Bible. I saw some events that are not recorded, and, of course, there are things that were recorded that I was not around to see. But one need not see all to believe all, a point that Jesus would make to me later on, on the shore of the Sea of Galilee.

Before I leave the topic of the parables, I want to tell you how much I came to appreciate their importance. The genius of the parables, I would later come to realize, lay not in the fact that they were short and easily remembered. The genius of the parables lay in the fact that they represented the condensation of enormously broad and deep theological concepts and usually had more than one meaning. A man could hear the words of a parable, walk away, and two months later, as he was tilling his field or tending his sheep or mending his nets, realize in a flash of inspiration what Jesus' deeper meaning had been. How do you teach theology to non-theologians? Jesus had the answer. He implanted psychological time bombs in people's souls, bombs that would automatically be triggered when the listener was ready to understand.

That day, along with the nineteen weeks that followed it, was to literally change my entire life. Just as the world dates all its events in terms of B.C. and A.D., so I was to come to view my own life. Before Christ and After Christ. It was not a sudden thing, to be sure. No Saul-on-the-road-to-Damascus sort of thing. But day by day, as we followed him, the words of the Nazarene made me think. His words were like meat that one gnawed on; they spoke to the innermost heart, and the heart knew it.

But let's return for a moment to the question of physical evidence, of supernatural manifestations. Of tangible proof, that Jesus was indeed more than mortal man. It was not as easy as you might think to collect such evidence. For, while I and all the others who crowded around Jesus had no problem in at least literally hearing his words, it was usually quite difficult to get close to him, sometimes even impossible. In his chronicle of Jesus' ministry, Luke (8:19) tells of an occasion when even "his mother and his brothers . . . could not come at him for the press."

The accounts of Matthew, Mark, Luke, and John are replete with other references to the multitudes that surrounded him wherever he went. In the third chapter of his Gospel, Mark tells us of one of the times when the crowds literally backed him right into the Sea of Galilee, and the disciples had to evacuate him by boat. In his fifth chapter he tells of another occasion when "much people gathered unto him, and he was nigh unto the sea." Luke, in his twelfth chapter, talks of a time "when there were gathered together an innumerable multitude of people, insomuch that they trode one upon another."

It certainly made my job tough. Jesus was always in the center, of course. The twelve formed a core about him, and about a hundred dedicated disciples were in turn deployed about them. (Seventy-two of these latter would later be sent out as the first missionaries.) Well, these hundred and twelve or so people did their level best to protect Jesus, not only form physical harm, intentional or otherwise, but also from stress and fatigue. They saw to it that he had the opportunity to take his meals and to rest. They made sure that he had the privacy he needed to pray, to sleep, to meditate, and to instruct them. Not that they didn't let people through; they let plenty of people through when they saw the need and when they felt that Jesus had the time. Or when he himself told them to let people through, which was almost all the time.

He always wanted the doubters, the haters, and those who were attempting to discredit him around him. He wanted the vaunted Teachers of the Law right at his side, asking their silly questions designed to ensnare him, witnessing the healings, listening to his words. He also wanted the blind, the crippled, the deaf, and lepers to have free access to him. And then there were the thousands of ordinary people like Bartholomew and me. No, getting to his side was no easy matter. I considered faking blindness or deafness so I could make it through the screening process of the disciples, but after I thought about that idea for eight or ten seconds was ashamed of myself.

I've always believed that, to a large extent, you make your own luck. Also, that all things come to he who waits. Bartholomew and I doggedly followed him, day after day after day. And, as those at the center of the throng had received their healings or had their questions answered or just had to return home, we moved closer and closer to him all the time. The Chiricahua Apaches are justly famed for patience and perseverance. Apache braves of old, when stalking, could sit as immobile as rocks under the desert sun for twelve hours or more. Or, on the other end of the spectrum, could run for twenty miles across the burning sands with a mouthful of water, and spit out the water at the end of the run. We like to think we haven't changed. I have my mother's blood in me, and it's served me well. We haven't changed. I was determined to get to his side, whether it took me two weeks or two years.

Eleven days after we had first joined the throng, we had finally penetrated the screen of the hundred or so and were only yards away from him. But there we stayed for two days. It was almost insanely frustrating. We could hear all his words, of course; we had been able to do that from the beginning. But we couldn't see what was going on. One of the biggest things I was after was physical evidence, and I wasn't getting anywhere at all. The hundred and the twelve had a mysteriously efficient way of making sure that the crippled, the blind, the lepers, the deaf, the diseased had first priority, but even many of those sometimes had difficulty in getting to his side. Son of God or not, he was but one man, and there were only twenty-four hours in every day.

I tried some bombast on Thomas and on Andrew, but I may as well have been whistling an aria to the deaf. Thomas, somewhat self-importantly, I thought, merely sniffed that *everyone* wanted to see the Master and that *everyone* said it was urgent and that they had traveled a great distance. Andrew was very sorry, very sorry. But surely I could see that it was impossible at the present time, could I not? He wished that he could help me, he sincerely did. He would if he could, but he couldn't. Peace be unto me.

I can't begin to describe how frustrating those two days were. I constantly caught glimpses of him through the press and heard his words, but I needed to get to his side. Sure, I saw people who were apparently infirm make it through to the center of the crowd and saw many come back through, apparently healed. But evidence like that was useless, for reasons I spoke about earlier in this book, i.e., the possibilities of the infirmities being psychogenic in origin or the "cure" being a temporary condition brought about by the body's producing exotic and as yet, little understood biochemical pain-killing compounds under high stress. Add to that the fact that I seldom had the opportunity to examine any of the "healed" both before and after. Some I saw before and some after, but, those I did, well you could hardly say I examined them as they were borne past me in the milling multitudes; I saw them. That's about all you can say. And, as far as the lepers were concerned, nobody saw them too closely. The crowds parted like the Red Sea for them, leaving a very wide corridor indeed.

Then there were those who were not healed immediately or were seeking healings for people other than themselves. Jesus would say to some, "Return home and you'll find that your son (or daughter or wife or whatever) has been healed." To some others he'd say, for example, "Go, show yourselves to the priests," at which time presumably, they'd be healed. Such healings, of course, were impossible to validate since that would have required our going off and following those people, thereby giving up our hard-fought-for places in the crowd, something neither Bartholomew nor I was willing to do. And, unfortunately, almost none of those who received such healings ever returned. Did that mean that the promised healings never took place or that the people were just too ungrateful to come back and say thanks? Or, perhaps, there were some in each category. As an objective reporter and a scientific observer, I could make no speculations; as a man, I had to ask myself—if I were blind or had leprosy, and if a man healed me, could I imagine *not* going back to thank him who had miraculously given me a whole new life? I thought I knew the answer to that question until Jesus told ten lepers to go and to show themselves to the priests. One came back. Jesus asked if the other nine had been healed also; the man replied that they had. Where then, Jesus asked, were the others? The man shrugged and cast his eyes upon the ground. In the silence only the wind was heard.

And, oh yes, the one who came back was a Samaritan.

Finally, on the third day of being so close to Jesus, yet still not close enough to really see what was going on, I screwed up all my reserves of energy and willpower, and seeing a small break in the crowd, hit it like a crazed fullback on the three-yard line with four seconds to go in the game and tie score. Bursting through a tangle of flailing arms and legs, I suddenly found myself face-to-face with him and barring his way. Two of the disciples grabbed me, prepared, evidently, to "escort" me away most unceremoniously. He stopped them with a hand motion. They released me, and I imagined that the whole earth had stopped turning on its axis.

He was about 5'9' and weighed about 165 pounds. His features were markedly Semitic, and he was dressed quite simply. He looked to be three years older than I and in excellent physical condition. His outward appearance was unremarkable except for two things—his bearing and his eyes. The man whom millions would call King of Kings did in fact have a regal bearing. He carried himself with the assurance of a man who knows exactly who he is and what he must be about. But neither before nor since has the world seen a ruler like him. Instead of pride there was compassion; instead of pomp, humility; instead of imperious demands, there was only self-sacrifice.

Then there were those eyes. Luminous brown eyes from which, you were certain, nothing could be hid. I forget who it was who said that the eyes are the windows of the soul. Try if you can, to imagine looking through warm, soft, benevolent, and loving living windows into the soul of God Himself. That's how it was, and it was at this very point that I began to believe. I say began because full belief would not come until I had heard more in the coming weeks, and until I had collected my physical evidence.

Physical evidence. Only much later would I see and begin to understand the tragic, heart-breaking irony of it all. I, like the great masses of people who surrounded him, couldn't see beyond the physical world. When he spoke of healing, we could think only of the healing of bodies. At the time, few if any thought in terms of redemption and of being made whole spiritually. Jesus told us time and time again why he had come, and we heard his words but did not listen to them. Instead we, who were so obsessed with physical phenomena, regarded his ministry as little more than a traveling medicine show. How stupid we all were. How very stupid.

After what seemed like an eternity, during which I was transfixed by his probing gaze, he smiled a secret smile and spoke a single word to me.

"Come."

Swallowing hard, I moved on rubbery legs over to his side. He pointed to a pitiable blind man, who knelt before him in supplication. "You have heard the words. I have been asked who sinned, this man's parents or he himself, that he was born blind. I know of your interest in such matters," again he gave me a secret smile, "for it is exceedingly obvious. Who do you say sinned?"

"Sir," I said, "I know nothing of such matters."

He looked up and addressed the entire assemblage. "Neither this man nor his parents sinned, but this happened so that the work of God might be displayed in his life. As long as it is day, we must do the work of Him who sent me. Night is coming when no one can work. While I am in the world, I am the Light of the World."

I was right at his side when, using the index fingers and thumbs on each hand, he gently pried both the man's eyelids open. No wonder he was blind! He'd been born without pupils or irises! His eyeballs were stark white! Jesus gave me that strange, secret smile again and asked, "Could the thoughts or the actions of man alone heal him?" His eyes bored into mine, and my reply was long in coming, since it took me a while to calm my swirling maelstrom of thoughts. I stood on the edge of a metaphysical precipice; the Nazarene knew it and I knew it. Finally, I found my voice.

"Only God Himself could heal this man," I replied, and the crowd began to set up a murmur. Jesus inclined his head.

"You have said it." So saying, he knelt beside the blind man, spat on the ground, and began to make a paste of mud. There was an absolute hush as he worked the mud in the palm of his left hand, then applied it to the blank, stark-white eyeballs. After this, he placed a hand on the man's shoulders. "Go now, and wash in the pool of Siloam." Then, yet again, Jesus looked at me. I nodded. No words were needed. I took the blind man's right arm, and Bartholomew his left. We helped him to his feet and started for the pool. The crowd parted to let us through.

Now even I didn't need to be given directions on how to get there. Clarence's briefings were very thorough, and the pool has an interesting background. Seven hundred years before Christ, Hezekiah revolted against Assyria. Among the many extensive preparations he made in order to ready Jerusalem for siege was to have an underground water tunnel dug to bring in water from the Gihon Spring in the Kidron Valley. The 1750-foot tunnel was chipped through solid rock using only the simplest of hand tools. A monumental task indeed. The tunnel empties into the Pool of Siloam, which is still in use even today.

We had gone no more than an eighth of a mile when I noticed that we were being followed closely by a group of five men. They constantly stayed no more and no less than fifty yards behind us. Clearly, they were Pharisees. They were usually the only Jews to wear their talliths at all times. Then too, they also wore small cases, tefillin, made from the skin of ritually clean animals, attached by leather thongs to their foreheads and left hands. Inside each case, I knew, were four passages inscribed on parchment from Deuteronomy and Exodus. I told Bartholomew and the blind man to stop. Then I turned and stared them down. There was a hurried consultation among them, after which they walked up to us. I didn't like their looks.

"Nice of you to offer to help," I said with pronounced irony, "but we've got the situation well in hand." The barb bounced right off them.

"We come not to help but to observe," said the eldest pompously.

"Suit yourself," I shrugged. Bartholomew, the blind man, and I started off once again, with them dogging our steps whispering among themselves.

"Are you not," came a question in a accusatory tone, "you two, followers of the Nazarene?"

"Yes," said Bartholomew simply.

"Depends on what you mean by followers," I replied more moderately.

"Do you believe that he is the Messiah? The Holy One of God?"

"Yes," Bartholomew said for the second time. I kept my peace.

"And you?" they demanded of me.

"I believe," I answered slowly "in the things I can see." To my surprise, Bartholomew exploded.

"Then, friend Lightfoot, by that way of thinking, the man whom we are now guiding can believe in nothing, for he can see nothing."

"That isn't what I meant, and you know it," I shot back angrily.

"I have listened to the words of Jesus long enough to know that there is more than one kind of blindness," Bartholomew said sadly, looking first at me, then at the Pharisees. An uneasy silence fell between us, one that wasn't broken until we reached the pool.

We carefully led him down the steep and narrow steps, and all of us held our collective breath as he knelt and began to wash the mud off his eyeballs. His sudden scream echoed off the damp walls.

"I can see! I can see! I can see!" The Pharisees and I all looked at each other in confused amazement, while Bartholomew threw his head back and laughed in joy. Then the blind man turned to look at us with his new eyes. It was a sight I shall never forget. Not as long as I live. I was standing only a yard away, and I looked into the clearest brown eyes I'd ever seen, with the exception of Jesus! The hair on the back of my neck stood up, and the involuntary words that came out of my mouth were, "My God."

"Exactly," Bartholomew beamed.

The term "devil's advocate" comes from the Latin *advocatus diaboli*. In the Roman Catholic Church, the devil's advocate is someone who is appointed to be a type of prosecuting attorney in canonization proceedings. He is the one who attempts to dig up all the evidence he can to *disprove* the candidate's alleged saintliness, involvement in miracles, and so on. It was in the days following this incident that I began to see the value of the Pharisees in this role. They knew full well that all they had to do was to find a single incident that wasn't what it appeared to be, the most insignificant miracle that Jesus worked that could be explained away in terms of natural causes, the slightest utterance that they could trap him into making that could be twisted into blasphemy or treason against Rome, anything, anything at all that could be used against him. They knew that in such a turbulent land in such troubled times, it wouldn't take all that much to turn the admiring crowds into a single howling mob. The people had been disappointed and misled too many times in the past. It would take little to turn them into a lynch mob.

But it took something; they had to find *something*. And I've seldom seen men try harder. Their efforts in this particular case began at the very moment I've just described.

When I'd recovered sufficiently from the sudden shock at the pool, I turned to the Pharisees. "What do you think of *that*?" I asked more or less rhetorically. The rest began to gulp and stammer, but the eldest didn't blink an eye.

"I think that it is a clever ruse, but clearly this man before us now was never blind in the first place."

"Are you crazy?" I thundered. "You've been with us the entire time since we left Jesus!"

"I'll grant you that it was a very skillful and crafty maneuver."

"Maneuver?" I echoed in disbelief.

"Yes, switching the genuinely blind man for this look-alike as we were passing through the crowd. Very clever indeed, but you are not dealing with credulous country bumpkins or with children. We are Teachers of the Law and know full well how to spot deception."

"You *are* crazy! You have been watching us the whole time! The whole time since the Nazarene put mud on this man's eyes! I've not let go of this man's right arm, nor my friend let go of his left since!"

"The man whom this . . . substitute purports to be has been blind since birth. This is not he," he said with an air of finality, then, he turned and began to walk away.

"Wait! What would it take to convince you that this is not a sham?" He and his companions continued walking away. I yelled a challenge that echoed off the damp dark walls as they began to ascend the steps.

"Are you sincere seekers of the truth or not? You are not! You are afraid to face the truth! You are intellectual cowards, all of you! Go then and hide from things your little and narrow minds cannot or will not accept!" (Some objective witness *I* had turned into.)

My words had the desired effects though. Their leader stopped dead in his tracks. After a long moment, he turned. He was a proud man. I had banked on that, and it had paid off.

"Very well. Let it never be said that justice was not done. What would you have us do?"

"Do you admit that this man can now see?"

"Of course."

"Then we need only prove that he could not before the healing he received at the hands of the Nazarene. If we can do so, you would be forced to reevaluate your opinion of the Nazarene, isn't that so?

He looked very uncomfortable, even trapped. He knew better than to answer my question directly.

"But you have no such proof."

"What about witnesses? This man must have friends, family, neighbors. Why don't we find them and talk to them?" At this, the blind man broke in excitedly.

"I have been begging at the same gate to the city since I was a young child, and I live no more than a half an hour's walk away from the spot where we now stand. Since childhood, every day my father has guided me to the gate at sunrise, and come to bring me back home at sunset. Let us now surprise him! Let me guide you all to my home! I want to see . . . yes, to *see* the expressions on the faces of my father and mother when I walk through the door!"

"Sounds like a good idea to me," I said, staring at the Pharisees, who began to look even more uncomfortable. The former blind man, whose name was Ezra, bubbled on, oblivious to the charged, hostile atmosphere that was developing.

"Not only to see the expressions on their faces, indeed to see their faces, for the first time! What God has wrought!"

At this, the eldest Pharisee placed both hands on the high collar of his tunic, screamed, and made about a six-inch tear in the fabric. The others followed suit. "Blasphemy!" They wailed like banshees. "We will not stand by and see the Almighty's Name taken in vain!"

"Come," said the eldest, wheeling away, "brothers, associating with the ungodly has already defiled us enough. Let us go to the Temple to present offerings." Once more they began to walk away.

"Now it is you who are being clever," I said. "It seems you will do anything to avoid coming with us to face the truth." Again they stopped and turned, and again my eyes and those of the eldest Pharisee locked on each other.

"We will go with you," he finally said softly.

The stir that our little procession caused once we arrived in the man's neighborhood is hard to describe. When people saw *him leading us*, a crowd quickly gathered. "Look, it's Ezra!" some cried. Others, quite understandably, said, "That's ridiculous! It can't be! This man can see. It must be a man who looks like Ezra." The closer we got to his home, the denser the crowd became. "Is it really you, Ezra?" a woman called. Others took up the refrain. Ezra just kept beaming and embracing people. "Yes," he answered, "it is truly me, Ezra. Jesus of Nazareth has healed me."

His parents ran out to meet us, and he instantly recognized them by their voices. Ezra kept repeating to his parents and the crowd the story of his healing, and the complexions of the Pharisees grew more empurpled with each retelling. Finally, we were all in his home. His mother just kept weeping with joy.

"I charge you to tell me in the Name of the Almighty, the Everliving God," said the eldest Pharisee in sonorous, majestic tones, "is this man your son?" The parents were nonplused.

"Of course," answered his father. Ezra's mother stopped weeping and stared at the Pharisee as if he were a creature from another planet.

"There can be no mistake?" persisted the Pharisee.

"Sir," she said, "with all due respect, may I ask why you ask such a strange question?"

"Because we were given to understand that your son was born blind."

"He was," she nodded.

"This man is not blind."

She nodded again.

"Therefore, this man cannot be your son," said the Pharisee, as if he were patiently trying to explain an obvious fact to a moron.

"Sir, all I know is that this is my son, that he was born blind, and that now he can see," she said in a tone that matched his.

"Do you know that your son, I mean this man, has blasphemed? That he claims that Jesus of Nazareth, a false prophet, has healed him?"

"Well, *somebody* had to have healed him," the father said reasonably, while he stroked his beard thoughtfully. "It may as well have been this Jesus."

"Are you then saying that Jesus of Nazareth healed your son?" thundered the Pharisee.

"We weren't there," the father shrugged.

"Our son is thirty-one years old and is standing right here," said the man's mother. "Ask him yourself."

"We already have," said one of the Pharisees. "He claims that Jesus, whom he considers to be a prophet, healed him. That he was born blind, but Jesus gave him his sight."

"We have even seen it happen," chimed in the youngest among them, who promptly received a baleful look from the eldest and two others. The fifth spoke up.

"As for me and my friend who has just spoken, the question is not so much the matter of whether there was a healing or not, for we had," he paused before going on judiciously, "perhaps a better vantage point than did our colleagues and so saw more clearly. As for us, the concern is that he violated the Law by healing on the Sabbath. This makes him a sinner."

"But how," interjected the younger, "could a sinner perform a miracle?"

The eldest, correctly surmising that the situation was getting away from him, wrested control again. He turned to the blind man.

"I solemnly adjure you," he said with feeling, pointing his quivering index finger at Ezra, "in the Name of the Living God, to tell us exactly what happened and who this Jesus, whom we know to be a sinner, is."

"Whether he is a sinner or not, all I know is that he gave me my sight."

"Now tell us, from the very beginning, everything that happened. This is your last chance," he said menacingly.

"But you were there; you yourself saw what happened. Not only that, but you haven't ceased asking me the same questions. One would think that you want to be one of his disciples too!" Ezra said somewhat sarcastically. And that did it. The eldest Pharisee howled.

"*You* may be a disciple of his, but we are disciples of Moses! There can be no doubt that God spoke to Moses, but we know nothing of the Nazarene."

Ezra only grew more sarcastic. "Well, how about that! You know nothing of the Nazarene, yet you know that he healed me. Never since the world began has anyone ever given a man born blind sight, but Jesus does, so you are at a loss as to who he is, as to whether he is a fraud, a sinner, or whatever. Even a simple man like me knows that if he were not from God, he could do nothing."

"How dare you," demanded the Pharisee, "you, who were steeped in sin at birth, how dare you presume to lecture us in such matters?" There were some other less than gracious remarks the Pharisee made as he led his men through the door.

37

We spent a wonderful and festive evening in Ezra's home. Friends and relatives mobbed the house, and the laughter, wine, and tears of joy flowed freely. Nevertheless, we set out at dawn the following morning to catch up with Jesus. Ezra was one of the few who took the trouble to go back to thank the Nazarene; most of those he healed figured they had more important things to be about.

We had caught up with him before the sun was halfway across the sky, and, recognizing us from the day before, the disciples cleared a path through the crowd for us. Before we could utter a word, Jesus looked at Ezra and spoke.

"Do you believe in the Son of God?"

"If you'll just tell me who he is," Ezra replied fervently, "I'll believe in him."

"You have seen him. He is speaking with you."

"Lord," Ezra said, falling to his knees, "I believe."

Bartholomew too fell to his knees, "Lord, I believe," he said, his face wreathed with a beatific, almost otherworldly smile.

The Nazarene's eyes turned toward me. My mind, my universe, whirled crazily as I looked into the depths of those eyes. It had been possible to believe for a moment back at the Pool of Siloam.

It had been possible at Ezra's home when I saw the jubilant look on his mother's face. It had even been possible on the way back, as I quietly mulled over the words that I'd heard Jesus speak, and reviewed what I'd been seeing and hearing about the man. But now, as I once again stood before him, it seemed no longer possible. Look, a voice in my mind whispered, he is a man of flesh and blood, just as you are. He is about your age. The Son of God? No. Clearly he is a man. If you cut him, he will bleed. If he goes without food, he gets hungry; without water, he gets thirsty. He gets tired and lonely. He laughs and he cries. He even flew into a rage not long ago when he threw the moneychangers out of the Temple. God Almighty? Hardly.

"For judgment I have come into this world," he said, "that the blind may see, and that those who do see might be made blind."

"One of the ever-present Pharisees angrily spoke up, dimly sensing a rebuke lay somewhere in those words. "Are you implying that we are blind?"

Jesus' eyes never left mine as he answered the question. "If you were blind," he said, shaking his head sadly, "then you'd be guilty of nothing, but, since you have seen, yet act as if you were blind, you are in sin." So saying, he turned away, and I never before or since, felt lonelier in my life than I did at that moment.

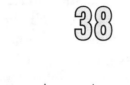

It's hard, so very hard, to describe the mental tumult, the frequency and intensity of the thoughts, doubts, suppositions, theories, and ideas that cascaded down and around, over and under the lobes of my brain every moment of every day in the weeks that followed. My confusion was total. On one hand, I *wanted* to believe but continued to be plagued by the unsettling thought that I had no absolute proof. Yes, I had personally witnessed phenomena that I could not explain in terms of natural causes. But just because *I* couldn't explain them, did that necessarily mean that the incidents were cases of supernatural intervention? No scientist, or layman either for that matter, worth his salt will assert that mankind knows all the secrets of the universe. In that regard, one thinks of the stereotypical scene of the early twentieth century explorer in darkest Africa flicking his cigarette lighter before an awed village assembly, explaining, "Me white god." *He* knows how a lighter works; *he* can explain it in natural terms. To the natives, however, the flame jumping to life in the strange man's hand is totally inexplicable in terms of the natural laws *they* know.

But, as I said, I so wanted to believe him. His words, his teachings, made good sense; they made more than good sense. In listening to him day after day and reflecting on his words, I came to feel then as I continue to feel now—that he was the world's only real hope. That his message is the most important message in all of human history. But Bertrand Russell, in his *The Impact of Science on Civilization*, says it much better than I ever could:

> The root of the matter is a very simple and old-fashioned thing, a thing so simple that I am almost ashamed to mention it, for fear of the derisive smile with which wise cynics will greet my words. The thing I mean—please forgive me for mentioning it—is love, Christian love, or compassion. If you feel this, you have a motive for existence, a guide for action, a reason for courage, an imperative necessity for intellectual honesty.

The more I tried to work things out, the more convinced I became that, in a very real sense, no one can ever *prove* anything beyond all doubt. Sure, you can prove to *your* own satisfaction that you exist, in some form or another. Otherwise, how could you be thinking about it at all? But once you try to go beyond your basic Descartes, you find yourself in deep philosophical waters indeed. Strictly speaking, you can't be sure that your friends, relatives, or even the features of your own body exist as you perceive them, if at all. They could all be figments of your imagination. Your life to date, complete with all your memories, may only be an elaborate and very long dream. Your home, your car, your town, may all be illusions. I may only be imagining that I'm sitting at a typewriter writing this book. By the way, how do you *know* that there is a major world city called Moscow? Have you ever *been* there? Even if you think you have perhaps you really haven't. Even if you have, care to try to prove it beyond all doubt to a determined skeptic?

Even in our judicial system, which we use to make some pretty serious decisions, such as whether or not to sentence people to life in prison, to free them, or to execute them, we don't demand proof beyond *all* doubt; we demand proof beyond any *reasonable* doubt.

Such was the tenor of my thoughts during those weeks. Nothing new or creative or original. Just the same thoughts that everyone mulls over somewhere between the cradle and the grave. Only my thoughts became an obsession. Looking back on it now, I can see that the problem was, to paraphrase St. Augustine, that I was trying to understand so that I could believe, instead of believing so that I could understand. Later I would realize just how apt Bartholomew's description of me had been; I was indeed blind.

So I drifted along, mechanically interviewing people, watching and listening to the Nazarene, and keeping records. Bartholomew remarked upon my turning inward, but respected my privacy. (Incidentally, when his self-appointed hitch of thirty days was up, he continued to stay with me as I followed Jesus. I said nothing about it, and neither did he.) I was so preoccupied those days that I often forgot to eat or even to sleep. On more than one occasion, Bartholomew found it necessary to shake me after I'd been sitting motionless for hours, staring unseeingly into the embers of our campfire. Then he'd tell me to get some sleep. But just as often, I wouldn't go to sleep. I'd just roll onto my back, stretch out, and continue staring and thinking. But then my gaze would be on the cold brilliant stars as they wheeled in the vastness of outer space.

I felt as if I was waiting for something but didn't know what. Then it happened.

We were on a hillside about three miles outside of Capernaum. It was early afternoon, and the sky was bright and sunny, a rich cobalt blue with rounded heaps of brilliant white puffy cumulus clouds. A cool and gentle breeze blew off the nearby Sea of Galilee. We and between 900 and 1000 others were reclining on the grassy slope in blissful coexistence with a few large herds of sheep which were grazing on it. Jesus was telling the story of the man who had prepared a great feast for his friends and sent out his servants to tell them that it was ready, at which point they all began to make excuses, saying that they had more immediate concerns that had to be attended to.

For no particular reason, I glanced back over my shoulder and saw a dazed man on the fringe of the crowd. His eyes firmly fixed on Jesus; he stumbled forward purposefully, with all the single-minded determination of a salmon swimming upstream during spawning season. He was totally oblivious to the people he was tripping over and bumping into. If he wasn't in a state of shock, he was close to it.

He was a very well dressed man, and I noticed that most of the crowd seemed to know him and respectfully made way so that he could get through the press.

"Who's that?" I asked Bartholomew.

"That's Jairus," he answered, "the head of the court of elders in the synagogue at Capernaum, a man much respected and loved. Something seems to be very wrong."

We watched him distractedly for a moment before it hit me. Thanks to the Bible reading sessions with Cindy, I knew exactly what was wrong! His daughter was dying! He was coming to ask Jesus to heal her, but, on the way back to his home, a servant would intercept them with the news that she had died. This was, quite literally, the chance of a lifetime.

"Bartholomew, do you know where Jairus lives?"

"Of course," he shrugged, "Capernaum is not exactly Rome, you know. Everybody knows where everybody else lives. Especially where a man of Jairus' station in the community lives."

"Bartholomew, I can't explain now. There's not enough time. But you've got to take me there just as fast as you're physically able to run. In fact, faster," I said, springing to my feet. He opened his mouth, but I cut him short with an impatient wave of my hand. "There's no time, Bartholomew! Trust me! This is vitally important!! Run like the Evil One himself is right at your heels and gaining!" As he rose, he saw the urgency in my eyes, and he heard it in my voice. He just nodded and took off in a lope, which, at my urgings as I ran one step behind, turned into a dead run.

Well, he wasn't in shape, and that's putting it charitably. The little innkeeper/philosopher was puffing like a steam engine before we'd run a mile. His short and bandy little legs pumped like pistons, but the cyclic rate began to slow drastically at about a mile and a half out.

"Faster, Bartholomew, faster! Don't let up now! Go! Go! Go!" I was now running alongside him, yelling these and similar encouragements into his right ear. With a visible effort, he picked up the pace again, his chest heaving like a blacksmith's bellows, and huge drops of sweat popping out on his forehead like transparent grapes. At two miles, the features on his face were twisted into a look of sheer torture.

"Come on, Bartholomew! Don't give up on me now! There's Capernaum right there! Just ahead! Just get me to Jairus' house! Go! Go! Go!"

The little guy's effort was a valiant one. Although his run was little more than a tenth the distance run by the original marathoner (who, as you'll recall, dropped dead after giving the Athenians the news), Bartholomew put in ten times the effort. Which is, I thought as I ran along beside him, yet another and better definition of courage. A man of courage is a man who gives it all he's got, regardless of how much that is, regardless of whether he wins or loses, and regardless of whether anyone ever takes notice of his effort.

Soon after we entered Capernaum, Bartholomew dropped like a sack of wet cement. There was such an air of finality about the way that he went down that I didn't even try to get him up. If he could just give me accurate directions, that would be enough. I knelt over him and grinned.

"Surprised even yourself, I'll bet! You're quite a guy. Bartholomew. You can just rest here until you're all right, then meet me at Jairus'. How do I get there from here?" Between gasps, he told me, then I was off and running.

A scant three minutes later I pounded into the courtyard of the house that I took to be Jairus' residence, and the moaning and wailing issuing from an open door confirmed it. I stopped and leaned against the wall for a moment to catch my breath and collect my thoughts. While I'd been running, I'd been trying to formulate a plan but had yet to come up with one. The only thing I knew for certain was that I had to confirm that the girl was really dead before Jesus arrived. Secondly, I wanted to be right there to see him raise her up.

My breathing began to slow, but still I had no plan. I looked over my shoulder. If Jesus came immediately and if he walked at a fairly quick pace over the terrain I had just run, I figured I had maybe forty minutes or so. There was no more time to think, to plan. I'd just have to play it by ear. I took a deep breath, tried to compose myself, and stepped across the threshold.

There were ten people in the dimly lit room. As my eyes adjusted to the gloom, I saw that three of the ten were professional mourners. Like the true leeches that they were, they had wasted no time in getting here, and they were all trying to outdo each other in terms of decibels. Two others I took to be servants, and the remaining five seemed to be friends or neighbors. It was one of the latter who approached me.

"Peace be to all in this house," I intoned, and he bowed in acknowledgement.

"Are you a friend of the family?" he asked in a voice that seemed to come up from a sepulcher.

"The girl's parents have sent for Jesus of Nazareth," I replied, neatly evading the question, "and I must see her immediately."

He looked me over from head to toe. "You then, are this Jesus of Nazareth, of whom we have heard so much?"

"Please," I said, ignoring this question as well, "I must see the girl now. Time is of the essence."

The man shrugged and spread his hands, palms up. "Time is no longer of any importance. The child died shortly after her father left here nearly two hours ago."

"Where is the child?" I said abruptly. The moaning and wailing from the three professionals was beginning to get on my nerves, as was this man's total lack of concern over time or whether I saw the little girl or not. Even as I asked the question, I knew that Jesus,

Jairus, Peter, James, and John were taking, long quick strides as they hastened on their way here. Again, the man examined me from head to toe.

"You are this Jesus of Nazareth?"

"No, I am not."

Another fatalistic shrug of the shoulders and spread of the hands.

"Then why . . ." That did it. I just could not afford to waste any more time like this. I clamped one hand on his shoulder in a vise-grip and pointed to the three mourners with the other hand as I looked him straight in the eye. My voice was even and steady as I spoke.

"Friend, those people have already got their next engagement booked for them if you don't take me straight to that child, and I mean now." Sometimes when I'm under intense pressure or am about to lose control, I'm told, my eyes tend to take on a wild look. That's how they must have looked then, because even in that darkened room, I saw the color drain from that man's face as if someone had pulled a plug. I released my grip and followed him through another door, down a short corridor, then through yet another door.

Unquestionably, the child lay in the stillness of death. I had been in the presence of death before and often enough to feel that it hung like an oppressive pall in this room. The mother knelt, sobbing uncontrollably, while an older woman held her heaving shoulders and tried to console her. An attempt doomed of course, to futility, but sometimes there's nothing we humans can think of to do except something futile. We stood behind them, and they hadn't heard us enter. With a curt nod, I dismissed my reluctant guide.

I was fully aware of each precious second as it ticked by. In my mind's eye, I kept seeing Jesus, Jairus, and the rest on the way, each step bringing them inexorably closer to this room. I cleared my throat loudly.

"Excuse me," I said authoritatively, "but I have come to examine the child." Well, it was the truth.

The older woman half-turned and simply replied, "leave us."

"But my good woman—" I harrumphed.

"The child is dead. The child has been dead for two hours now. Go." Her eyes were dry, if a bit red-rimmed, and the lines etched on her face told of a woman who was a tough customer indeed. She had it in her mind to protect the mother who was blinded by grief, and she appeared to be eminently suited for the task. I picked my words carefully.

"Jesus of Nazareth is on his way here."

"Jesus?" the older woman asked. And, at the mention of his name, the mother turned toward me for the first time. Then she looked at the older woman and nodded.

"Yes," she said, "Jairus went to find him, but . . . it's too late now." She looked like she was going to break down again, and that was the last thing I needed, so I tried to keep the ball rolling.

"Yes, Jesus is on his way and will be here momentarily. I have come on ahead of him. Will you permit me to examine the child?"

"But, sir . . . as my neighbor has just told you, she is dead."

"I come from a land far to the west, a land where our medical knowledge is far more advanced than even that of Rome's." Well, that was true too. "As you may know, there are some diseases which slow all the body's functions to such a point that a state which mimics death occurs. Perhaps that is the case here." I could see it in her eyes. She clutched at the straw of hope I held out. Her neighbor could see the effect of my words too and was having none of it. She sprang to her feet.

"How dare you! Who do you think you are, that you can hold out false hopes to a woman sick with bereavement! Swine!" she spat, advancing menacingly toward me, "I'll see you flogged!"

"Woman!" I thundered. "Listen to reason! You owe this woman and her daughter that much! If I am right, perhaps the child yet lives, and she can be healed. If you are right and the child is indeed dead, well, I can do no harm." I wasn't about to say that if the child were dead, then Jesus might be able to raise her anyway. That, I felt, would have been a bit too much to ask these two women to believe at that point. If the older woman was concerned about me hurting the mother by holding our false hopes that would have really had me thrown out of the house.

A long, long moment of absolute silence ticked by while the two women studied my face. Finally, the mother rose to her feet. "Very well, examine her then. You have my permission." She and her neighbor stood over me, virtually breathing down my neck, as I knelt to look at the little girl.

"Hand me that lamp," I said to neither of them in particular. The mother moved quickly and handed me the bronze lamp that had been sitting on top of a stand in the approximate center of the room. Like nearly all lamps of the time, it burned olive oil; the cost of any other type of oil was astronomical.

I had great difficulty in prying open the child's eyelids, a bad sign, since the first muscles to be affected by rigor mortis are the smallest—those of the eyelids. Considering the climate and the fact that the girl had supposedly died two hours before, this most likely was the onset of rigor. Having pried the eyelids open, I brought the lamp right up next to her eyes. The pupils were fixed and dilated. Bad.

Not that I really expected to hear anything, I nevertheless eased her bedclothes out of the way and put my ear on her tiny chest, right over her heart. I almost recoiled from shock when my ear touched her bare skin; it was so unnaturally cool. I listened for a full minute. Not the slightest flutter. Next I checked her throat for a carotid pulse. Nothing.

I plucked a long hair from my head, then held it first directly under one nostril, then under the other, then over her lips. A minute in each of the three places. Nothing. Had I had a mirror with me, I knew she wouldn't have fogged it. That did it. Or did it? I knelt there for a moment hesitating. Had I done everything? Jesus, Jairus, and the disciples would be here soon, and I was distinctly feeling the two sets of eyes of mother and neighbor boring through my back. Pressure. What else, what else?

Then I had it. Post-mortem lividity.

When the heart stops pumping, the blood, of course, stops flowing. And once it stops flowing, like any other liquid at rest, it will obey the law of gravity and settle to the lowest level it can. This is what causes post-mortem lividity. The settling is expedited by the dilation of blood vessels in death, and the result is purplish discoloration of the parts of the body nearest the surface on which the body is resting. The process begins as soon as the blood stops circulating, and the discolorations begin making their first visible appearance anywhere from thirty minutes to four hours after death, depending on a number of factors, like how much blood the person has lost, if any, the manner of death, and so on.

I gently turned the girl over on her stomach, and pulled and tugged the bedclothes out of the way. There it was. The purplish splotches on her buttocks, lumbar region, and the posterior parts of her arms, legs, and shoulders. That meant that she'd been dead for at least half an hour. I put my finger on a splotch on her shoulder and pressed. Her skin became white. When I took my finger away, the lividity reappeared. This meant she hadn't been dead for any longer than about five hours because after four or five hours, the blood clots, and pressure won't make it move. With a heavy sigh, I pulled the clothes back to their original position and again laid the girl on her back. The child was dead. At least by every sign I could see. I began to rise, then stopped. This was important. This was vitally important. Could I be wrong?

After all, I was no physician, and even twentieth century M.D.'s had been known to sign death certificates for people who were subsequently revived by alert ambulance drivers, nurses, boy scouts, or other physicians. There have even been a few cases when the "deceased" has spontaneously revived without any assistance from anyone. Such instances were rare, to be sure, but most embarrassing to any M.D. who'd pulled the sheet over the face of the person a few moments before and had uttered the solemn pronouncement. I must be certain. I reached out and touched her waxen cheek. Her facial muscles were stiffening as the rigor mortis spread. Well, you might say that if a person shows no vital signs, if rigor mortis has begun to set in, and if there's post-mortem lividity, then that person is dead. And normally, I'd be the first to agree with you. But this wasn't a normal moment.

As I knelt there, I felt the full weight of two thousand years of human history on my shoulders. I thought of the thousands who would die for the Nazarene, from the sands in the center of the Roman Colosseum in the first century to squalid prison cells in Red China in the twentieth century. I thought of the countless millions in my own time and those still further in the future, whose lives of quiet desperation and agonizing futility could be given meaning, dignity, hope, and joy if it could be proven that Jesus was indeed the Son of God. I thought of these things and more, not the least of which was finding peace for my own troubled soul. For this mission had changed me. In precisely what way, I didn't know. All I knew was that things would never again be the same for me.

I knew what I had to do. I would sever the carotid artery, an act that, if performed on any living human being, was guaranteed to render the subject unconscious in five seconds, and dead in twelve seconds, or so I was told by Riley, the CIA close combat instructor, during the training that Clarence had arranged for me. Time. Time. Time was running out. I had to act quickly.

In retrospect, my decision to do this seems irrational, even to me. In my own defense I can only say that I was "killing" someone who had been dead for two hours, and that I had to be certain about Jesus, not beyond any reasonable doubt, but beyond *all* doubt, else this whole project was pointless. In first century Palestine, as in twentieth century America, there were a number of people who could apparently foresee the future, perform seemingly miraculous healings, and who could speak quite impressively. Simon Magus was such a person in those times, (Acts 8:9-24) and the twentieth century versions write books and appear on radio and television.

But how many can raise someone from the dead? This kind of evidence was priceless. Time. Jesus would be here at any moment, and I had to get the two women out of the room. I made a show of cocking my ear to one side.

"I can hear him now," I announced. "Please go and greet him at the door, and show him in quickly," I ordered matter-of-factly. To my great surprise and relief, they readily obeyed. A moment. I only had a moment. I drew the British commando knife from the neck scabbard between my shoulder blades. Although its color was flat black, its surfaces being blued so it wouldn't reflect any light, its appearance was deceptive. It was made of the finest grade of surgical steel and designed precisely for what I was going to use it—instantly severing major arteries. Without hesitation, I brought the knife to her throat and did the job.

As I'd expected, there was no high-pressure pulsatile spurting of bright red arterial blood. Instead, there was only the seeping of dark deoxygenated blood. Yet another proof that she was dead. But more than that, it meant that even if her heart started beating again, either spontaneously or through some outside force, she'd be unable to live more than a few seconds, because the heart would simply pump the blood right out of the severed carotid. I watched transfixed, knife still in my hand, as the dark, dead, evil-looking blood continued to ooze out of the wound and trickle down the side of her neck, down onto the bedding, where it began to soak in.

I was struck with sudden horror. What had I done? What in the world had I done? Had I been handpicked and highly trained, had I traveled halfway across the world and two thousand years back in time to slit the throat of a poor little dead child? Was this the act of a rational man? Mesmerized by the blood on my knife, unable to take my eyes off it, I knelt frozen into total immobility while my mind shrieked inside my skull.

Move. I must move. Absently, I wiped my knife on my left sleeve and replaced it in its sheath. The blood continued to ooze slowly out of the wound and trickle down the side of her neck.

There was nothing for it but to cover it. I pulled the thin blanket all the way up to her chin, where I folded it over several times so there was an accordion-like fold of four or five layers over the wound. No sooner had I done that when I heard voices behind me.

I rose to my feet to face the group as it entered the room. Jairus' wife clung to him fiercely, weeping disconsolately. The disciples were crestfallen, mumbling dispiritedly among themselves about arriving too late, and that the child had been too young to die. If only the Master had been told of this sooner, then this tragedy surely could have been averted. Jesus said nothing but stood alone, apparently deep in thought. Pointing to me, the neighbor woman spoke to him, saying, "Sir, this man has given us to believe that he is one of your men. He barged in here and insisted on examining the child thoroughly, behaving most curiously. Do you know him?"

A faint smile was on his lips as he replied.

"I know my own, and my own know me . . . isn't that so?" he asked, his eyes gazing full into mine.

"Yes . . . that is so." Then it seemed that there was no one in the room, in the world, in the universe, except him and me. A most unnatural hush fell over the room.

"You have examined the little girl thoroughly," he said. It was a statement, not a question. Nevertheless, I nodded.

"And what then have you to say?"

"She is dead." That drew a heart-wrenching sob from the mother. We all watched spellbound and silent as he walked up to where the child lay and looked down. His words came like a thunderclap even though he spoke them softly.

"Why the wailing and weeping? She is not dead but only sleeps."

At that, the neighbor woman and a few others who had pressed through the doorway began to ridicule and laugh bitterly. He looked sadly at each of them and shook his head. "Leave us," he said, the softness still in his voice. In a moment, the room was cleared except for Jairus, his wife, Jesus, the disciples, Peter, James, and John, and me. The disciples had moved to escort me out of the room but Jesus had restrained them with a motion of his hand.

He knelt over the child, took her hand in his, and said, *"Talitha koum,"* Aramaic for "Little girl, I say to you, arise." I don't think I would be exaggerating when I say that all hearts stopped beating when the child rose to her feet, smiled happily, and walked over to hug her mother and father.

"Give her something to eat," Jesus instructed them, "and do not speak of this."

Astonished, although by all rights I shouldn't have been, I ran over to look at the child's neck. Not a scratch on it. I next checked the bed. No bloodstains anywhere. Not a drop.

I became aware that He was watching me, and I turned around to see a twinkle in His eye. I walked over to Him. Outside the room there was quite a commotion going on as the parents told all the mourners that there had been a mistake; the child wasn't dead but had only appeared to be.

"Master," I bumbled, "I must see you. I mean I must speak to you." He looked at me with affection tinged with amusement. I blundered on, aware of all the curious eyes upon us as people started to drift into the room. "In private. You see, I come . . . from a far land, and . . ." He nodded, as if to Himself, and held up a hand to silence me.

"My Father in heaven has revealed to me where and when you come from. Camp by the shore tonight, and I will come to you."

When you come from! He had said, "When you come from!" He knew! Dazed, I could only begin to make my way through the now joyous crowd to the courtyard.

artholomew, now fully recovered, was waiting for me in the courtyard. It was hard to tell whether the sun shone more or his face.

"Again He has raised a person from the dead, Lightfoot! Can there be any doubt remaining, even in your hard head?" I was still dazed as I answered him.

"He raised that girl from the dead. I saw it with my own eyes. No, Bartholomew, I no longer have any doubt." I felt limp and washed out. As if I had just stumbled out of the cockpit after a fierce touch-and-go dogfight with three hot MIGs. I felt dehydrated, and my legs were rubbery. I leaned up against the side of the house.

"What now, Bartholomew?" I said more to myself than to him. Bartholomew shrugged.

"We follow Him. What else *can* we do?"

"But we're back in Capernaum now. You've been gone well over the thirty days you gave yourself. Anna must be furious. We're just a few minutes' walk away from your house. You mean you're not going home?"

"I'm not going home. Are you?"

"I can't go home."

"Neither can I."

"You don't know what you're saying. All *you* have to do is take a short stroll, and you're back in your own home, with your wife, family, and friends. You've been gone only a relatively short period of time. Things don't move all that quickly in this age and in this country. In no time at all it will seem as though you've never been gone. Things will be as they were before."

"Friend Lightfoot," the little innkeeper smiled sadly, "don't you see? Things can never again be as they were. Not for you or for me or for anyone who has heard the words of Jesus of Nazareth."

"But what of Anna?"

"Anna doesn't need me. She never has. But besides that, I've found that this is bigger than family relationships. Don't you remember what the Master said only last week? 'No one who has left home or wife or brothers or parents or children for the sake of the Kingdom of God will fail to receive many times as much in this age and, in the age to come, eternal life.'"

"What about your business?"

"That is of even less consequence. You have heard His words just as I have, Lightfoot. Surely you know that."

"Yes . . . yes I do. It's just that . . . I don't know, but just now, in there . . . He really is the Son of God, Bartholomew . . . I'm afraid. If I could go home as easily as you could . . . I would think very seriously about it . . . I'm afraid." In reply, the little man, who only weeks before was a henpecked buffoon, a pompous, self-important zero, spoke with conviction, assurance, strength, and wisdom.

"Don't think of the past, my friend; therein lies death. Remember what Jesus said. 'Anyone who loves his father or mother more than me is not worthy of me; and anyone who does not take his cross and follow me is not worthy of me. Whoever finds his life will lose it, and whoever loses his life for my sake will find it.'"

"Bartholomew, I'd be honored if you'd continue to walk with me as we follow Him."

"Friend Lightfoot, I was about to speak the very same words to you."

40

Time was measured with great imprecision in those days, especially during the hours of darkness. But as nearly as I could estimate it was about 1:00 a.m., or the first hour of the third watch, as it was termed in those days. One of the customs the Romans brought with them into Palestine was that of dividing the night into four watches, a custom that had been rapidly picked up by the inhabitants. The night was still and quiet, the only audible sound the gentle, almost imperceptible lapping of the Sea of Galilee against the shore. The stars were so clear and bright that I might have been standing in a planetarium.

Bartholomew had gone to sleep long ago, and he was as sound a sleeper as I had ever run across. But I was too keyed up with nervous energy to even lie down. The Nazarene had told me that He would talk to me privately this very night. How could I or anyone else have possibly slept? The only reason Bartholomew was asleep was that I hadn't told him about the Visitor I expected. I had to talk to Jesus alone. I had traded the whole rest of my life for this moment to come, and I wasn't about to invite guests. I couldn't even if I had wanted to, for security reasons. All the cards were going to be laid on the table. We would speak of the twentieth century tonight. God willing.

The excitement was almost too much to bear. This meeting could literally alter all of human history. I thought of Clarence's explanation to me of long ago. He'd told me that the reason he'd thrown in with Ike rather than return to the classroom was that he wanted to help *make* history rather than teach it. This making of history was heady stuff, and my moment was fast approaching. I could feel it in my bones.

I'd been scanning the shore line, which is why when I first saw Him, it was out of the corner of my eye. At first, I got only the faint impression of a spot of phosphorescence out on the water, quite some distance off. I raised my eyes and watched transfixed. The luminous cloud ever so gradually became larger and larger. It was moving from where Peter and the others had dropped anchor a couple of miles out to escape the crowds and get a good night's rest, directly toward me. He was about 150 yards off when I recognized Him. Jesus was walking across the surface of the water. The hairs on the nape of my neck stood straight up, and my heart began to pound at about three times its normal rate. Even though I knew who it was, and that He meant me no harm, for a few wild moments I wanted to just turn and run away as fast as my legs could carry me. That ghostlike apparition, coming slowly, inexorably, ever closer to me, the concept, the idea of it, was so alien to my scientific mind, that I yearned with every fiber of my being to run, to run fast and far, and later, in the light of day, when I was once again calm and rational, to convince myself that I'd been dreaming or hallucinating. But, summoning up more strength than I'd ever imagined I had, I forced myself to remain rooted to the spot where I stood.

As His feet touched shore, the aura of luminosity disappeared, and He stood before me, apparently as solid and as real as I was. But, as though He sensed that I needed physical confirmation, He stretched out His arm and put His hand on my left shoulder. The moment had come, and I was speechless.

"As I have told you, my Father has revealed to me from where and from when you come. And now, in your own words, tell me why."

"I have come to ascertain whether or not you are the Christ, the Messiah, the Son of God. Upon ascertaining the truth, one way or the other, my instructions are to compile documented proof, incontestable evidence, so that the people of my time will know once and for all. Finally, if you were indeed the Christ, the leader of my nation asked me to ask you to give us guidance, because he isn't sure that we're following the right path."

An infinite, an ineffable sorrow filled his brown eyes, eyes only two feet from my own. He shook his head sadly. "Not long ago, I saw your face in the crowd when I told the story of Lazarus the beggar and the rich man. Do you recall it?"

"Yes, I do. When both died, Lazarus went to heaven and the rich man went to hell. Across the gulf that separates the Kingdom of God from Hell, the rich man saw Abraham and Lazarus. He begged Abraham to send Lazarus to him with but a drop of water to cool his tongue, but Abraham said that he could receive no comfort, because the gulf was impassable. Then the rich man asked Abraham to at least send Lazarus to warn his five brothers, so that when they died they wouldn't go to Hell too. Abraham refused, saying that if the brothers didn't pay any attention to Moses and the Prophets, then they wouldn't listen to Lazarus either. That even a man risen from the dead wouldn't be able to persuade them."

"Precisely. Proof . . ." He shook His head again. When He resumed speaking, rebuke was in His words. Rebuke and grief and heartrending disappointment. "Four of those men," He gestured toward the apostles' fishing boats, "will write accounts of my ministry. Have not their accounts and the rest of the Scriptures survived? Haven't you the Gospels? Are the Scriptures not freely available, particularly in your own country?" I could only swallow hard and nod. "And yet," He continued, His hands raised in angry frustration, "you and those who sent you seem to feel that a fifth gospel is necessary. Why not a sixth or a seventh or an eighth? What will it take?

"You are on a fool's errand, and I say that not unkindly because your intentions are good, and to do what you have done took great courage and commitment. But it is a fool's errand nonetheless. Don't you understand? Whatever evidence you amass will not change the mind of a single doubter. Those whose hearts are hardened will not respond to a fifth gospel anymore than they would to the four which preceded it. The writer was deluded, they will say, or he was imagining things, or he was purposely lying. He was tricked, they will say, or the writer himself never really existed, or he was exaggerating, or any number of things to give themselves excuses to turn away from what, they know in their hearts, is the truth. You cannot 'make' anyone believe in anything, Aloysius Lightfoot O'Brien. For faith must be freely given."

"*I* believe," I said, hoping to ease His distress, His sorrow. But it only seemed to hurt Him even more.

"You believe because you have seen. Anyone can do that. Can't you or your countrymen believe without seeing?"

"It is not our way," I answered lamely.

"You and your countrymen, I fear, are very much like Thomas. You will believe only in things you can see and touch, and sometimes not even in those. You have not life and will not obtain it until you can believe without seeing. You have not believed me even when I have spoken of earthly things. What then will your reaction be if I speak of heavenly things? You would do well to take a lesson from your friend sleeping over there." He nodded toward Bartholomew, then I spoke.

"He believed in your divinity even before we laid eyes on you. He was certain you were the Messiah the first time we heard you speak, before there was any kind of physical evidence that could be validated. His faith is childlike; it comes from his heart, not from his head."

"Precisely. Hear me, Aloysius Lightfoot O'Brien, and mark me well. You were made in the image and likeness of God, and God is more than a Cosmic Abacus or Ethereal Scale, counting and weighing and measuring rights and wrongs. Would such a dispassionate dullard of a Being send His only begotten Son to suffer and die so that those who sinned against Him would be forgiven and attain Eternal Life?

"Hear me, and if you understand nothing else, understand this: the God, whose image man was made in, has a heart. Else what am I doing here? The Lord your God shows mercy, compassion, and love because He has a heart. So you too, made in His image, were given the capacity for all these things. So you were given a . . . heart. Do not ignore it, my friend; use it. Listen to it." Jesus sighed a deep and sorrowful sigh and turned to gaze out over the Sea of Galilee, reflected brightly under the full moon. I longed to touch Him, to comfort Him, but could not. What could a man, as stupid as I had proven to be, possibly say to comfort God?

"You speak of evidence," He said. "Two millennia after my death you still are more interested in signs and wonders than you are in what I came to tell you, more excited by the changing of water into wine or the multiplication of loaves and fishes than by the fact that I loved you enough to die for you. Miracles must be performed before you will believe. Tell me, how many lepers must be cleansed? How many blind, deaf, diseased, and crippled must be cured before your people or the world is satisfied? Ten? Fifty? A hundred? A thousand? I came into this world, not to heal, but to die that you all might live. I came into the world to tell people how they might gain eternal life, but most seem to feel it more important that I heal the withered limbs of their temporal bodies, bodies that are here today, gone tomorrow." His voice was drenched in sorrow. "Of what use are healthy limbs if a person loses his immortal soul?

"You put great stock in my raising Jairus' daughter from the dead. I tell you, to raise one from the dead is an insignificant thing. I could with a few words from my lips, raise all who have ever died. It is easy. But for what purpose? For what end? I came to save the souls of all men from eternal death, and I cannot do that with words. To do that, I must die a horrible death." He shuddered at what He saw in the near future, and the entire world, I felt, held its breath for the next few moments. I dared not break the silence. He turned back at last to face me.

"Tell me Aloysius Lightfoot O'Brian, do you honestly think that a fifth gospel will make any difference?"

Now it was I who gazed out over the water, seeing more than the water. He was right. How stupid we'd all been! How arrogant and prideful! I'd had faint glimmerings of doubt at various stages in the project but had suppressed them. A fighter pilot who was also a Chiricahua Apache can be pretty good at suppressing things, and a man always has doubts about any big mission anyway. But now, it hit me with crystal clarity and with all the momentum of a speeding freight train. I looked into those eyes and admitted it, not only to Him, but for the first time, to myself.

"No. No, it won't make a bit of difference." I sighed heavily, suddenly feeling very old. "You're right. Most would say that a trip such as this is impossible, and that it was all just a hoax, no matter how much evidence was amassed. The handful who could understand and accept the trip as a genuine occurrence, would say that the report, the 'fifth gospel,' as you call it, was written by a man who was deranged or had his own theological ax to grind, or both. It was all so stupid, wasn't it? So very stupid. It was all for nothing."

His eyes softened, and He smiled a gentle, loving smile. "Any endeavor, any endeavor, that brings even just one more soul into the Kingdom of God is worth it." That smile and those spoken words brought me greater happiness than I'd ever known.

"Me?" I asked. He nodded. I felt as if my heart were going to burst.

"Perhaps," I said, feeling the beginning of a powerful revitalization, the birth of a new and boundless enthusiasm, "perhaps the 'fifth gospel' can bring a few more to you. And for their sakes, I will continue to stay by your side, and I will write it. Even though nearly all will reject it, why there's still those on the project team who know that this trip took place. Maybe they'll believe the words I've written. Once they open the canister . . ."

Jesus raised his hand to interrupt. "There is, for those on the project, for those very logical and scientific people, a more graphic way, a more powerful and forceful way to reach them."

"How?"

"Deliver the fifth gospel to them in person."

Outright shock was my initial reaction until I remembered that I was speaking to the Son of God. Then I paused and considered for a moment. My reply surprised even me.

"That would make quite an impression, and, if you'd have offered me the opportunity to return to my own time a few weeks, even a few days ago, I'd have jumped at the chance. But now . . . now, I'd prefer to stay with you."

"To write the Fifth Gospel?" For the first time, I noticed the crinkling laugh lines around His eyes.

"To be with you."

He shook His head. "My Father in heaven calls different people to do different things. There is a Plan. You are called upon to do several things in your lifetime, and one of them is to be a messenger. Go back and tell people the Good News, Lightfoot, but more than that, live the Good News. Some of the seeds will fall on fertile ground."

"I will do what you tell me to do. But before I go, there is another matter. The leader of my country has asked that you give us a message. Ours is a confusing time. We've come a long way very quickly. Some say too quickly. We want to do what's right, but sometimes we just don't know . . . that is, things just move too fast . . ."

There was a mild reproof in His voice. "But you already have the message. The message is the Good News. The message is that God so loved the world that He gave His only begotten son, that whosoever believes in Him should not perish, but have everlasting life. That is the message of the Fifth Gospel, as it is with the four gospels which precede it. Nothing has changed. And now," He said, raising His right hand in preparation.

"Wait! There is one more thing that . . ."

239

He nodded and smiled reassuringly. "Even now the child is being healed. I will do no less for her than I have just done for the daughter of Jairus. She is sleeping now, but will awake whole and healthy."

My eyesight began to fail. Things were fading. I felt lightheaded, as if I were going to pass out. As things began to go black, I kept my eyes on His face. He was regarding me with a sorrowful, an inexpressible love that I'll never forget. His eyes. I suddenly, in a rare flash of insight, realized what His eyes told me. What they told everyone who looked into them.

Then I slipped and was falling into a dark tunnel, but was unafraid. All I could think of was those eyes. They said to everyone who gazed into them, "I know exactly who you are and what you've done, but I love you anyway. I love you with a boundless, eternal love that you can't even begin to understand, and it causes me great pain to see you hurt yourself whenever you turn away from me. But always remember that even if you were the only human being who had ever existed, I'd still go through pain and suffering and death just for you and you alone. I love you."

The universe swam around me with dizzying speed, but I felt only peace. For the first time in my life, I felt true and total peace. Then all was darkness and as still as the grave.

41

For a moment, I couldn't believe that I was still on my feet. But I was. Still harder to believe was what I saw as my eyes refocused. No longer was I on the shores of the Sea of Galilee, but I now stood on the parking lot of the L-2 Facility in Oak Ridge. As I turned to take in my surroundings, I was astonished to see Clarence, head down, treading heavily toward me. He was carrying the B-4 bag he had used to bring me my first century clothes.

"Clarence!"

Look like he'd seen a ghost? He sure did. When he looked up to see me, he dropped the B-4 bag along with his jaw. He stood frozen like a rabbit caught in the middle of a flashlight beam. I thought his hair was going to turn white right on the spot. I ran up to him.

"Lightfoot! How . . . what . . . in God's name are you doing here?"

"He sent me back! Clarence, I saw Him, I spoke with Him! He's God, and He sent me back!"

Quickly recovering, Clarence summoned up something resembling composure, but he was still as wound up as a five-dollar watch.

"You mean it worked? You saw Him? You really spoke to

Him?" I could only keep nodding, my head bobbing up and down like a cork in a stormy sea. Then I burst.

"The mission was a success, Clarence! A complete success. We've got our documentation; all my notes are in the large inside pocket of the cloak I'm wearing. We've got ourselves a miracle and a healing, and I even got a message for our time, although I doubt it's the kind of message Ike had in mind!"

"A healing?" Clarence's tone was cautious, yet eager. I grinned and pointed to the B-4 bag at his feet.

"You've got the clothes I changed out of in there?" He nodded.

"But what about . . ." I had already hefted the bag up onto the hood of the nearest car, unzipped it, and was rummaging through it.

"I'm getting to that . . . here they are." I pulled out my twentieth century pants and fished the keys to my rental car, a '58 Ford, out of the right front pocket. "My car's over there," I said, tossing the keys to him. "You drive; I'm a bit tired and we've got a long way to go."

"Are we going where I think we're going?"

"Right. The Jones residence in College Park, Maryland."

"Cindy?" he asked excitedly. "We'll have to get on the phone right away to see if it really—"

"No, we don't," I cut him off. "He told me. That's enough." I was right and Clarence knew it. He looked properly chastened.

"Lightfoot," he said, thoughtfully looking down at the keys in his hand, as if they unlocked something far more valuable than an automobile, "I do believe that, as we say in Christian circles, you have come to know the Lord."

Clarence started the engine, put the car in gear, and then sank back in the seat for a moment in silence.

"You know, we really shouldn't be doing this. We should go right back in the facility and get on the horn to the Old Man." I was already in the process of changing back into my twentieth century clothes as I answered him.

"Aw, Clarence. Look, no matter where we are, the first step is a thorough debriefing, right?"

"Right."

"And who should be debriefing me?"

"Well, of course we had never expected that you would come back, so we never made any provisions for it. But I guess that Ike would probably want me to take care of the initial debriefing."

"So debrief me while we head north."

"Sounds reasonable to me," he smiled, as he let out the clutch and we began moving.

"How long have I been gone, Clarence?"

"I closed the cowling on you," he glanced at the luminous dial of his wristwatch, "twenty-two minutes ago." I whistled.

"How long were you there? Judging by the growth of your beard and hair, I'd guess about four months."

"Closer to five."

"Amazing. O.K, Lightfoot. Start at the very beginning, and don't leave anything out. Not a single detail. Day by day. Everything."

So I began. I talked for literally hours. I talked myself hoarse. We stopped for gas and coffee, and then I continued to talk. Clarence's concentration was absolute. I knew that remarkable memory of his was recording my every word and inflection, with all the fidelity of a tape recorder. He wouldn't forget or misplace a single syllable. Somehow I managed to stay awake long enough to finish the story. I had just finished telling Clarence Jesus' last words to me before I lost consciousness.

"Lightfoot! We're here! Come on, you can sleep all you want when we get you in bed!"

"Huh? Where are we Clarence?" I replied sleepily.

"My house, where else?"

That galvanized me. "Why didn't you say so?" I demanded unreasonably, springing out of the car.

243

I won't keep you in suspense, because we weren't kept in suspense. In fact, she was the one who opened the door for us. Not only did she look healthy, she looked robust, vibrant, radiant. The big Secret Service agent gathered her up in an enormous bear hug and began to weep.

Between Clarence, Cindy, Marge, Clarence Junior, the twins, and the dogs, all was pandemonium. And, being a wily Apache, I took advantage of the noisy confusion to make good my escape.

'd first heard his approach when he was still about 150 yards off. He might have been adept at stalking men in cities, but, out here on the desert, he was as clumsy as the day is long. Pebbles crunched beneath his boots, the nocturnal animals fell silent at his passage, and the change in his pocket jingled.

Lying on my side, I gazed into the campfire I'd built for the sole purpose of guiding him in, for I'd known he'd come before too many days had gone by. This was the sixth day I'd been out, and my camp was atop a rocky hill I shared with a family of coyotes and some other assorted denizens of the desert, animal, bird, and reptile. Aside from the man now laboring up the hill, the nearest human being was more than twenty miles away. The night breezes were cool, almost chilly.

Now he was no more than twenty yards away. I rolled onto my back, and my eyes drank in the cold and silent beauty of the velvet canopy of thousands of silvery stars. "'The heavens declare the glory of God; and the firmament showeth his handiwork,'" I said softly to myself.

"Lightfoot," he said, breathing heavily, "when you get a notion to be alone, you sure don't do things halfway." He shrugged off his backpack and sat down.

"It's good to see you, Clarence."

"It's good to see you, too. You left quite suddenly, quite suddenly indeed. The Old Man was hopping mad."

"I needed to be alone. I needed to think. The desert is the only place a man can think."

"You came real close to seeing how well a man can think in a federal penitentiary. Stealing that fighter plane was a bad move, Lightfoot. I had to do some fast talking to square that."

"I didn't steal it; I borrowed it," I said reasonably. "I'm still an officer in the United States Air Force. Since my temporary assignment was completed, I returned to my permanent duty station, using government transport."

"Yeah, and then as soon as the plane came to a stop, you checked out on thirty days of leave and were off in a cloud of dust."

"I had accrued the leave; in fact, I had forty-two days of leave accrued," I said, just as reasonably. Clarence just shook his head. "How's Cindy?" I asked.

"Perfect. Completely, totally healed. Happy. Very happy."

"The doctors?" I ventured. Clarence snorted and set his jaw.

"Since acute myeloblastic leukemia can't be cured, the doctors say that it obviously follows that they were wrong in their initial diagnosis. She must have had some strange disease, the symptoms of which are identical to those of acute myeloblastic leukemia, but a disease they know nothing about, except that one can apparently recover from it. Case closed."

"The canister?"

"The archeological team dug it up right where you buried it. Portions of the dating elements embedded on its exterior were sent to the laboratories of the Smithsonian, the British Museum, MIT, the National Museum of Natural History in Paris, the National Center of Scientific Research in Madrid, the Center of Forestry Research and Analysis in France, the Department of Prehistoric Studies at the University of Bordeaux, the Cairo Museum, and the National Scientific Academy of Japan. All tests were conducted independently, and, and except for Dr. Linstrom in the Smithsonian, none of the labs were told the origin of the samples of the dating elements. The dating elements, as you may recall, were primarily different types of wood. Wood, as you may recall Dr. Linstrom telling us, is what we're most successful in using to determine the age of an item. New techniques have already made Carbon 14 dating obsolete. The Smithsonian, along with the other institutions I've mentioned, have used four relatively new testing methods to date Tutankhamen's coffin, Egyptian canoes, and ancient wooden implements, with most impressive and extremely accurate results. I refer to measuring the degree of lignite formation, the gain in wood density, the degree of fossilization, and cell modification—"

"Clarence, you haven't changed a bit. What's the bottom line?"

"That canister has been in the ground for 1,950 years, plus or minus thirty years. Period."

"There can be no doubt?"

"No."

"What about Ike? What's he going to do?"

Clarence wore a pained expression as he began to pack his pipe with Cherry Blend. He didn't answer until he finished packing it, lit it, and had taken a few long draws.

"Well . . . he's not going to do anything, Lightfoot," he said softly. "He's not going to do anything at all." Clarence finally broke the long silence that followed with a heavy sigh. He went on. "As he sees it, there's nothing he *can* do. You see, your reports were not in the canister, and the whole point of the dating elements embedded in the canister was to establish exactly when the reports were written, or, to be more precise, when the reports were sealed in it. When the seal was broken, lo and behold, there would be your reports, or the fifth gospel as you referred to it in your debriefing. And we'd then be able to establish, to prove, that they were written in the first century.

"Instead, you brought the documents back with you, on your person. And neither your body nor your clothes can be proven to be two thousand years old. For all anyone knows or can prove, you could have written those reports last week in Newark."

"But the fact that the canister itself was in the ground for two thousand years . . ."

"Proves nothing. It's just another anomaly of space and time, like the Piri Reis map, the Salzburg Cube, and certain pre-Incan artifacts."

"What?"

"Piri Reis, also known as Ahmet Muhiddin, was a famous naval officer in the Ottoman fleet of Suleiman the Magnificent. He was, by avocation, also a map maker. His most famous map was drawn in or before the year 1513, but the fun didn't begin until three years ago, in 1956, when a visiting Turkish naval officer gave a copy of it to the U.S. Navy Hydrographic Office. Surprise. Even though the existence of Antarctica wasn't verified until 1819, the map accurately showed its coastline, including islands and bays underneath the ice sheet, that we've only recently begun to chart using seismic echo soundings.

"In 1957, after the Western Observatory of Boston College had examined the map, they announced that so great was the detail that it showed an Antarctic mountain range that wasn't discovered in modern times until 1952. There are other quite remarkable features of the map, but you get the general idea.

"The Salzburg Cube. Not a true cube, but an object composed of a steel and nickel alloy, measuring 2.64 by 2.64 by 1.85 inches, weighing 1.73 pounds, and having a specific gravity of 7.75. Found in 1885, when a block of coal dating from the Tertiary period was broken open."

"What's the Tertiary period?"

"It's comprised of the Paleocene to Pliocene epochs."

"That helps."

"Sorry. That means that it would appear that the machined metal cube had been around for anywhere from two to sixty million years ago."

"That's impossible."

"Sure it is. But you explain it."

"You also said something about pre-Incan artifacts?"

"Yes. There are a lot of curious ones, but one of my favorite is something that the government of Columbia sent as part of a collection on tour to six of the major museums in the United States. This was in 1954. This particular item is at least a thousand years old, made of solid gold, about two inches long, and worn as a pendant on a chain around the neck. It bears an uncanny resemblance to a modern jet aircraft. Others have been uncovered since, not only in Columbia, but in Costa Rica, Venezuela, and Peru."

"That's impossible."

"With your recent experiences, it seems to me that you'd be the last person to dismiss anything as impossible. At any rate, the point is, that without your reports sealed inside it, that canister is merely a very unusual and very interesting, very curious hunk of junk. The world is full of strange artifacts that we know nothing about, things which we can't even begin to explain. Theories abound: lost civilizations of Atlantis, Mu, and Lemuria, prehistoric practical jokers, people from outer space, time travel, you name it. What I'm trying to tell you, Lightfoot, is that the mission was a failure. As least from where the Project Council sits. Some very strange things happened, sure, but there is no concrete proof that you traveled back in time. And because of all the time, money, and resources devoted to it, it has become nothing more than a potentially profoundly embarrassing incident. The lid is on."

"But the scientists and the technicians at the L-2 Facility . . ."

"Are sworn to secrecy. And even if they weren't, none except Dr. Jankor would dare jeopardize his career by telling such a fantastic yarn. No one would believe it. No one would believe Dr. Jankor either, of course, and that's never stopped him from discussing projects before, but he's holed up in the New Jersey Pine Barrens working on a new project—an ion propulsion drive for spacecraft. As far as he's concerned, this project is past history."

"But my notes . . ."

"I told you, there's no way that they can be authenticated. Even if there were, you brought us back nothing new, Lightfoot. The major events and the teachings of Jesus that you recount, well, it's all been told before."

"In the other four Gospels," I said woodenly, experiencing a sinking feeling in the pit of my stomach. For a time, we both stared moodily into the flickering campfire. "Well, there's nothing to stop *me* from telling the whole story," I said with a flare of defiance.

"There are two things. First, you knowingly and willingly signed that oath when I first met you back in Nellis Air Force Base. It swears you to secrecy until such time as the project is officially declassified by the President of the United States. Second, if you tell this story, you'll wind up in a rubber room. You know it and I know it."

"What about Cindy being healed?"

"What about it?" Clarence shrugged. "They don't see any connection."

I nodded resignedly. "Well, I guess that's about it then. I can't talk about the trip. But there's nothing to keep me from spreading the Good News."

"That's about it," Clarence affirmed, rising to his feet and shrugging back into the straps of his backpack.

"Hey! Where are you going?"

"Back home. I've got a lot of things to attend to if I'm going to start teaching this coming semester."

"You're resigning from the Secret Service?"

"Yes, I am. What are you going to do? After the Old Man calmed down, he told me you could have your choice—an Honorable Discharge or a promotion to Major."

"A discharge sounds good. Thank him for me."

"Sure. By the way," he said, carefully extracting a piece of folded fabric from his jacket pocket, "I thought you might want this. I cut it from your first century tunic." He handed it to me. "Your left sleeve. Is that stain what I think it is?"

I could only stare at the spot and nod. Finally, I found my

voice. "That's right, blood. It's where I wiped the blade of my knife after cutting through her carotid artery. It's the blood of Jairus' daughter."

The moon was full and incredibly large and bright. A couple of my pals, the coyotes, began to howl at it, in that low, crooning kind of howl, the one they seldom use, the one that does funny things to the hairs on the back of your neck.

Epilogue

★ ★ ★ ★ ★

More than twenty years have passed since that night in the desert. Clarence returned to College Park, where he has been teaching history at the University of Maryland ever since. All of his students say that he has the ability to really make history come alive. They don't know the half of it. He has a thousand anecdotes about the great and the near great from his days with Ike, both in the Army and in the Secret Service, but he'll never tell them. Because Clarence David Jones is that kind of man. Neither will they ever hear (at least from him) the story of a curious experiment that took place in the L-2 Facility at Oak Ridge in the summer of 1959.

Cindy is happily married. She is a beautiful woman with a loving husband, two sons, and a daughter. They live in Alaska, where he is a pipeline engineer.

1st Lt. Clarence Jones, Jr. U.S.A.F., was shot down over North Vietnam on his 24th birthday. To this day, he remains unaccounted for.

The twins went their separate ways. Mark became a statistician and now lives in Chicago, where he works for a major insurance company. Ann got married just recently, and she and her husband run a dairy farm in Wisconsin.

And then there's my erstwhile companion, Bartholomew. Did he continue to follow Jesus? Clarence did some research and told me that Eusebius, the early fourth century historian and bishop of Caesarea, records that an Alexandrian traveler in India discovered a "Gospel of Matthew," written in Hebrew and left behind by "Bartholomew, one of the apostles." According to tradition, Bartholomew was flayed alive in Armenia. It is said that his last words were that there are worse things than death; that he would rather die than betray what he believed in. My friend, I salute you across twenty centuries. Rest in Peace, Bartholomew the Bold, for you went on the biggest adventure of them all.

After being honorably discharged and drifting for about a year, I became a police officer. When I was discharged, I knew I wanted to follow Christ, and, at the time, I thought that meant becoming a minister or a missionary or something like that. It took me a while to realize that each of us has his or her own unique way in which we can best serve our God. It doesn't really matter how you do it, as long as you use the talents that God gave you, and resolve to do the very best you can. So, after much thought and reading and soul-searching, I returned to the way of the warrior, for those are the talents which He gave me. I have used those talents for twenty years now to protect the lives and property of the men and women in my community.

That community is Pacific Grove, California, located on Monterey Bay, just about a hundred miles south of San Francisco. And the breathtaking beauty of the peninsula and the gentle waves that ceaselessly wash up against its shores are matched only by the beauty and gentle spirit of the girl I met here and married eighteen years ago. Irene is of Polish extraction, and Poles are far more practical and sensible people than either the Chiricahua Apaches or the Irish, if not as spontaneous or quixotic. So we balance each other out, as I've found man and wife are meant to do.

Among her many other accomplishments, my wife also does excellent needlepoint. So there are a number of beautifully stitched things in our home. But my favorite hangs framed in my den. It is a course and dirty piece of white woolen fabric with a large bloodstain in its center. Around the borders, Irene has sewn the words, "I am the Resurrection and the Life; he that believeth in me, though he were dead, yet shall he live."

You couldn't get me to part with it for a million dollars.

Every Christmas, we all gather at Clarence's home in Maryland. Irene and I, Cindy and her family, Mark, Ann, and until he was shot down, Clarence Junior. It's a very special time for all of us, but especially for Clarence and me. And for Cindy, because even though Clarence and I never told his kids about the project, the look in her eyes when she finishes reading the Christmas story aloud from the book of Luke, is unmistakable. She knows.

But then, she knew the Truth all along.

ABOUT THE AUTHOR

William Roskey's published articles have appeared in *Military History, Parameters, Military Technical Journal, Soldier of Fortune, Gung-Ho,* and other publications. His novel *Muffled Shots* received accolades from such nationally known military writers as W. E. B. Griffin and J. C. Pollock. During Roskey's active duty with the US Army, he served as a translator and analyst with both US Army Intelligence and the National Security Agency. Roskey currently lives in Arizona.